OF GRAVE & GLORY

TENEBRIS: AN OCCULT ROMANCE, BOOK THREE

KATHRYN ANN KINGSLEY

Copyright © 2022 by Kathryn Ann Kingsley

ASIN: B0B5PMMZ7D

Paperback ISBN: 9798845846549

All rights reserved.

No part of this book may be reproduced in any form or by any electronic or mechanical means, including information storage and retrieval systems, without written permission from the author, except for the use of brief quotations in a book review.

This is a work of fiction. Names, characters, places, and incidents either are the product of the author's imagination or are used fictitiously, and any resemblance to locales, events, business establishments, or actual persons—living or dead—is entirely coincidental.

A WARNING

This story contains content that may be upsetting to some readers, including torture in the form of LGBTQIA+ conversion "therapy," murder, madness, and consensual relations with monsters that involves the enjoyment of fear.

For those with an extreme aversion to medical horror, I might recommend skipping chapters three through six, or going straight to chapter seven. I apologize for whatever might not make sense if you do.

CHAPTER ONE

"This is easily the stupidest thing I've ever done."

"If the rumors are true, that's a high bar."

Emma turned and shot a glare at Robert, the "helpful" vagabond. She was glad for the distraction he provided, if she were being honest with herself. Anything to keep her from focusing too much on the building that was looming up ahead of them.

But it'd take a lot more than one smirking, cocky, entirely-untrustworthy ruffian to keep her from looking back up at Arnsmouth Asylum. It'd probably take several explosions and maybe a few clowns. Because if she wasn't mistaken...the asylum was *staring* at her.

The windows of the multi-story institution were black against the morning light, looking like so many empty holes into the abyss. Like sockets in a skull.

It was a bleak, gray morning. The sky was that kind of bland and uninteresting gray that hadn't even had the decency to have any kind of texture to it. But it made a perfect backdrop for the cutting angles and sharp spires of the asylum.

The bricks were damp from the rain the night before.

Buildings like that were built to intimidate. Built to impress. They wanted everyone who walked up to it to know they were somewhere *important* work was done. That neither the building nor its poor inhabitants were going to go anywhere anytime soon.

Other than that, she supposed it was perfectly fine.

Shaking her head, she turned back toward the street. "I can't do this."

"Hey." Robert caught her upper arm. "Don't chicken out now."

"Chicken out?" She huffed a laugh. "There's a difference between chickening out and going in *there*." She pointed at the building with the fire poker she was still carrying around. She had a gun, and while the firearm was ostensibly more useful, something about holding the wrought iron thing in her hand made her feel better.

"Look, I know you and Kirkbride haven't gotten off on the best foot, what with Gigi and all, but—"

"I should go get the Bishop." Pulling her arm out of his grasp, she took a step away from him. "Or at least ask for his help. This is"—she couldn't help but snicker—"insanity."

Robert stared at her flatly. "Not funny."

"Pretty funny, actually."

He sighed. "You won't be saving her, you'll be killing her. If the Bishop goes in there, people are going to get black-bagged and dragged off to wherever he takes his so-called prisoners. You know, the ones who don't come back?"

"And why do I care?" She couldn't look away from the asylum. It gave her the willies, but she felt like if she turned her back on it for too long it was going to *do* something.

"Fine. Getting the Bishop will start a war, Emma. If he goes in there to 'save' Gigi, then the Blade is officially in league with the Church, and all the other societies will come to stomp her out anyway."

Letting out a long sigh, she had to admit there was sense in that. She didn't know if Gigi and Patrick were really working together, but she couldn't imagine the other cults would take kindly to it. "If I walk in there, I'm walking into a trap."

"No. Kirkbride's a man of his word. And if he said you're free to come and go, then you're free to come and go." Robert tucked his hands into the pockets of his threadbare trousers. "He's a lot of things. But Thaddeus isn't a liar. And he keeps his promises."

"Right. And I can trust what you say exactly how?" She arched an eyebrow at him.

"Because I—would you stop gesturing with that thing?" He pointed at the fire poker. "It makes me nervous. Why do you still have it, anyway?"

"I like it." She lowered the iron implement to her side. "It's effective."

He shook his head. "You can trust me because…well…" He hesitated before huffing out a single laugh.

"See?"

"Well, let's fix that, then. Let's make a deal. I'm a man of my word."

"You're asking me to take you—a mercenary at best—at *your* word to trust that a deranged cultist is a man of *his* word."

Robert paused. "Yes."

She shot him a flat glare.

"But when I make a deal with someone, I never break it." He cracked a lopsided smile at the notion, clearly excited by the concept. "I'll give you my word that I'll have your back in this, no betrayals—that you're now my employer, and nobody else."

"You work for Kirkbride."

"No, he hired me to come get you. That's all. What happens after that wasn't ever discussed." He kept that shit-eating grin on his face, as though this were all working out just delightfully for him.

Emma narrowed her eyes. She hated mercenaries. They were all alike. "And what'll it cost me?"

"A future favor."

"Oh, no. No, no." She laughed. "I know how that nonsense goes. I owe you a 'favor,' and in six months you call me up asking me to murder somebody. And if I don't, you'll come after me. No. I'm not falling for that."

"I don't need you to murder anybody. I can do that just fine on my own, thank you *very* much." He actually looked vaguely offended. "But fine. You want stipulations? Here. It'll be a medium-sized favor. No murder, larceny, or federal offenses."

"You've had to stipulate this before, haven't you?" She chuckled again before wiping a hand down her face. "What've I gotten myself into?"

"An enormous mess."

Looking back over at the asylum, she went quiet for a long moment. What were her options? She had to try to help Gigi. She had to. The woman had tried her best to look out for Emma, even if it had been in her own unique way and… hadn't really quite worked out.

To be fair, that had been Emma's fault, not Gigi's.

She wouldn't go so far as to call them friends—she knew next to nothing about the beautiful blonde. But it just felt wrong to leave her trapped at the asylum.

Walking away was out of the question.

She'd bashed Rafe's head in with her new favorite weapon, so…he wasn't going to help. Or "they." Or whatever he was now.

The Bishop wasn't an option.

Yuriel had disappeared. Again.

"What do you know about Kirkbride?" She gestured aimlessly. "Besides the obvious public stuff. Founded the asylum, rich, well-connected. What's the dirt?"

Robert tilted his head to the side slightly. "Well, rumor has it he might *not really* be the leader of the Candle."

"Oh?" She raised an eyebrow. "Who is?"

"Nobody knows. Kirkbride's happy enough to pretend he's the head of the society. He's certainly power-hungry enough." Robert shrugged. "He won't confirm or deny if he takes orders from anybody."

"Great. That's all I need." Shaking her head, she looked back up at the building. The Mirror wouldn't help her. The Blade was a prisoner. The Idol was out of the question, and the Candle was the problem. Without the Bishop, her options were nil. "What does the Key think about all this?"

"Who? Oh. Them? They're recluses. As far as I can tell, they don't actually exist." Robert shrugged casually. "I've tried to find them before, but never got anywhere. It might be a dead society—no members, meaning. Not actually dead. That's…" He gestured at the building. "His job."

"Excuse me?" That dragged her attention back to her pseudo-companion. "What's that supposed to mean?"

"The Candle, well—" He grimaced in disgust. "All right, how much do you know about the different societies?"

"That they exist and there's five of them."

"Right, but." He sighed. "This one's a freebie."

"I don't understand what's happening right now, but thanks?"

He smirked for a moment before joining her at staring up at the asylum. "Each society has power over a part of the human condition."

"Oh. I think Yuriel said that. But he never explained what that meant."

"'Course not. Shifty bastard." He snorted. "Never did pay me for getting you those things."

"Sorry?"

"Not your fault." He chuckled. "Just happens sometimes in business."

Talking to Robert felt like walking in circles. "So…the societies."

"The Mirror has power over knowledge. Things that are known and not known. The Blade has power over the flesh—over the body itself. Want to be big and buff? Want to change your skin? Wish you were pretty? Wish you were ugly? That's what the Blade does."

"Seems like a weird thing to be obsessed about to the point of black magic."

"That's because you're spoiled and pretty." He glanced at her, his expression thin. "You've never been beaten up for having dark skin and an accent like *some* of us."

That was fair. Her shoulders fell. "Point taken."

He smirked at his victory before continuing. "The Idol deals in the soul. What makes you, you." That explained Yuriel and what had happened to Elliot. "The Candle deals in…well…life. Being alive or not. Or…being not, then being alive again." He cringed. "Some of the people in there have died a long time ago but just haven't figured it out yet."

That was disgusting. And terrifying. She shivered only partially because of the damp air. "You're really making me want to go in there, Robert."

"I'm telling you, *you'll* be fine." He snickered. "Gigi, however?"

"I know, I know." Shutting her eyes, she let out a long breath. She had no choice. She wasn't going to go in there without any backup at all, and Robert—shifty as he was—was her only option for help. "So, the deal is—you watch my back. You make sure this isn't a trap, that I get back out of there in one piece. That I don't wind up in a padded room in a straitjacket or cuffed and handed over to the Idol. And you'll do this in exchange for a 'medium sized favor of undetermined purpose but isn't a federal offense.' Have I summed that up?"

"Yep."

She shot him a look. "I don't trust you as far as I can throw you. And I throw like a little girl."

He laughed. "Then you're not a complete idiot. But you'll see. You'll be fine. And before you ask—no. I can't make any promises for Gigi. Some things I can't fix. And that's one of them."

"Fair enough." She struck her hand out to him. "Deal."

"Deal." He shook her hand, grinning like an idiot, and she was left wondering how deep of a grave she had just dug herself. But honestly, Robert was probably the least of her concerns. If the Idol didn't get her, Rafe—and all the rest of the Things in his head—were probably *very* mad at her right about now.

Heading up the path toward the front door, she tightened her grip on her fire poker. No, she wasn't going to leave it behind. It made for a strange safety blanket, but it was the only one she had at the moment. "What about the Key? You never said what they did."

"I honestly don't know. Never seen them do enough work to figure it out. As far as I can tell, they just put doors in weird places. I don't even know if they call themselves the Key. That's just what we dubbed them."

"Huh." She froze in her tracks so quickly Robert almost slammed into her. "Wait." She turned to him. "Doors?"

"Yeah. You saw the one leading to the tunnels under the city, right? Yuriel took you there."

"I did, but…" She felt the warmth drain from her face. There had been another door where it hadn't belonged. Right after she had gotten her memories back from the mirror in Rafe's basement, she had climbed the tiny little staircase in the dark.

And there had been a doorknob there. Stuck to the bricks. She hadn't felt a door or anything like that. Nor should there have been one there—it'd been impossible. She had even had an entire one-sided conversation with the doorknob.

"What?" He walked around in front of her, dark eyes flicking between hers, as if trying to pry her secrets out of her by that method alone. "What've you seen? What do you know?"

"Nothing. Just nothing. It's fine." Another shiver ran down her spine. What did the Key want with her? Why was *everybody* after her for one reason or another? "I want to go home," she murmured. And for once in her life, she actually rather meant it.

"What did you see, Emma?" Robert put his hand on her arm. "Tell me."

"No, unless you're using your favor." She smirked through the dread. "In which case, sure."

He whined, pacing away a step and turning his back to her as he thought it through. "No. No, I'll figure it out eventually."

"Darn." She snapped her fingers in sarcastic disappointment.

"Are you messing with me?" He eyed her narrowly. "I think you're messing with me."

"Turnabout, fair play, etcetera." She resumed her climb up the stone steps to the entrance of the building. She tried to ignore the wrought-iron bars over the windows of the first floor. Each one was hammered out in perfect decorative filigree and twisting acanthus leaves. They were *fancy* bars.

Something about the attention paid to them made their existence all the more offensive.

The large, wooden double doors opened as they approached, and she once more stopped in her tracks just at the base of the stairs that led into the building.

A man walked out to meet them, relying heavily on a cane, and she couldn't tell if he just looked so damn tall because he was three steps above her, or if he really was that imposing. His incredibly thin frame didn't help matters at all, she figured.

He had graying hair that was swept back from his face, and sharp features that reminded her of a hawk. His gray eyes were so pale they almost looked white. The lower half of his face was covered by a surgical mask.

The man was dressed better than the two orderlies who stood behind him, flanking him as though she were some kind of threat, though he did still have a long white doctor's coat on.

Instantly, she decided he was terrifying. And not to be trusted, under any circumstances. "Dr. Kirkbride, I assume?"

"Indeed. A pleasure to finally meet you, Miss Mather." He placed his cane in front of him, resting both his hands on it. "And it is good to see you again, Robert."

"Sure." The vagabond sniffed dismissively. There was no warmth in his tone. "Here she is, as promised. My job is done."

"As we agreed. You may go."

"Can't. New deal." He jerked his head at Emma.

"Of course." Kirkbride turned his nearly-white gaze back to her. "I would expect no less from such an enterprising young woman. Come in, Miss Mather. Let's talk."

She cringed. She didn't like being the center of attention. Not like this, at any rate. "I'm here to get Gigi. That's all."

He tilted his head slightly to the side. "I believe Gage is the least of your concerns. Or have you fallen victim to all the nonsense surrounding the Idol and your brother?"

"Elliot's gone." She had to loosen her grip a little on the fire poker. Her fingers were going numb from squeezing it so hard.

"He is not gone. He is simply unwell. They tortured your brother. Drugged him. Convinced him he had some sort of…*spiritual* issue." Kirkbride's sneer was audible, even hidden as it was behind his mask. "No, Miss Mather. There is science behind his ailment. Not *magic*. Such things do not exist."

Robert muttered something about torture and drugs, but she didn't quite catch it.

"I would have been inclined to believe you if I hadn't lived through the last few months." She shook her head. "And I can't blame any of that on my own…eh…issues."

"Nor was I insinuating that you should. No, Miss Mather. Your disease is benign enough that I do not think it is worth either of our time to explore treatment for it. Your brother was not so lucky, I'm afraid. Nor am I insinuating that what you have witnessed in Arnsmouth is not to be believed. The darkness you have witnessed is very real. I am merely insinuating that there is science behind all of it. Some of which is just not yet understood, like cavemen fearing a storm and thinking they had angered their primitive gods."

Sadly, that made sense. She frowned and looked away, not enjoying the way the doctor seemed to be able to stare straight through her. "You're telling me there's still hope for Elliot? I don't believe that. I've seen…I've met what's there now."

"Perhaps he is too far gone. Perhaps he is not. Please, Miss

Mather. It's a cold and ugly morning, and I would prefer to have this conversation in my office."

"I don't like the idea of walking in there. I don't trust you."

"Your fire poker made that quite clear." Kirkbride chuckled. He glanced down at the makeshift weapon in her hand. "Why do you have that, by the by?"

"It's useful for hitting things. And people." She glowered back at him. "Ask the professor."

After a pause, he replied. "I suppose it would be, yes." He shrugged. "Keep it as you wish. And I understand your hesitation for trusting me. You believe I have senselessly kidnapped one of your allies. I am merely asking for the opportunity to explain. You are not my prisoner or my patient, and that will not change if you enter my institution, I give you my word. And my word is my bond."

"Right. Sure." But she had no choice. None at all. She had to *try* to help Gigi. Or at least to go see her.

"Otherwise, I suppose that's what the fire poker is for." Kirkbride chuckled again. "Although I will admit to you, I am terrible in a fight. You wouldn't need it."

"Who says I'd need it for you?" She gestured at his orderlies. With the fire poker.

"Ah. Yes. Forgive them. I didn't know if you were coming alone. I have heard tell that the professor has…changed." The wrinkles at the edges of his eyes creased further, and a line between his brows appeared as he considered the notion. "Which is concerning."

"No. I'm here alone."

"Hey!" Robert threw up his hands. "What'm I?"

"Deeply problematic," she retorted with a glare.

"As charming as this conversation is, I would much rather have it in the warmth of my office with coffee." Kirkbride turned to head back inside, waving a hand at his orderlies to dismiss them. The two men walked off into the corridors of the asylum. "Come or not as you see fit, Miss Mather."

Who was she kidding?

She knew what she had to do.

With a groan, she climbed the stairs. "C'mon, Problematic."

"Yeah, yeah." Robert followed her.

The sound of the double doors closing behind her felt like the slamming of a tomb.

Only time would tell whether that was true. But something told her at least she wouldn't have to wait very long to find out.

CHAPTER TWO

Rafe whistled as he walked.

As they walked?

He wasn't quite sure anymore. But to be honest, he was not inclined to care. It was a unique experience sharing one's mind with an unknowable sea of millions of other voices. But now that he had learned to swim in the ocean, he found he much preferred life amongst the waves to that on the shore, afraid of what would happen when the tide took him out.

So many years of his life...*wasted* because he was too afraid to swim. Too afraid of what those dark waters might hold for him. Afraid he would be consumed by the monsters that lurked in the depths. He wasn't consumed—he wasn't reduced. He was simply now part of a bigger whole. Rafe was not gone—he was simply no longer alone.

And he had one person to thank for it.

Emma *fucking* Mather.

Twice now, she'd killed him. Twice. Which was precisely two times too many for most people. But that was all right. Both times, he couldn't say as he blamed her. He had been so afraid of the darkness as well, so terrified to realize that what he was being offered was a gift, not oblivion. And that was truly what it was. A gift of power, of freedom, of taking a look at his small, pointless, human life and realizing how *little* he had been.

He wasn't little anymore.

The Dean had learned that the hard way. Now there was no trace left of that smug, insignificant arse who had been such a thorn in Rafe's side for so very long. He had made the man suffer before death, of course. It had been such a joy to hear him scream. Such a pleasure to listen to his joints dislocate, the bones popping from their sockets as easily as a chicken wing. The memory of the wet, juicy *crunch* sent a shiver of pleasure down his spine.

He smiled. And he whistled as he walked.

The morning was oppressively gray, making the world around him look stained and dirty. No one else at that time in the morning looked nearly so pleased with their life, and many glanced at him as though he were a lunatic.

Several times now he had glanced down at himself to ensure he wasn't, in fact, covered in blood. No, they were simply concerned by his chipper attitude. He didn't blame them. Little mortal humans, going about their little mortal lives…and they had no clue what kind of fun Rafe was about to walk into.

Murder. Mayhem. Death.

He was going to slaughter every member of the Candle and devour their flesh. Those frustrating upstarts would be wiped from the face of the city by lunchtime. He would start there—but he wouldn't end there. The Bishop. Gage.

Now he was laughing to himself, chuckling in excitement for what was about to happen. This was freedom! True power. And there was nothing in his way of seeing his plans through. Nothing at all. He had to stop himself from skipping like a child—that might be pushing it a little too far.

Soon, so very soon, every Dark Society would fall before him…including his own. The Mirror would try to stop him, if they knew what he had become. So there was only one path forward for him now.

The total ruination of Arnsmouth.

Well…total ruination except for *one* other individual.

Emma *fucking* Mather.

"IF YOU WOULD LIKE to put your fire poker in my umbrella stand, you are welcome to."

Emma glanced down at the weapon in her hand and then to the wrought-iron, antique umbrella holder that sat by the door. It seemed like it'd be the polite thing to do—and kind of funny. A cane, two umbrellas, and a murder weapon.

"No, I think I'd like to hold on to it, if it's all the same to you." She looked back to Kirkbride. The man's office was opulent, and she didn't expect anything different. The floors and walls were elegant and elaborate pieces of woodwork stained to a dark mahogany. Three of the walls were dominated with bookshelves, floor to ceiling, and stuffed full with volumes she suspected were more than just decorative. The last wall was stately windows that despite their size did little to let in any light. The brick walls were so thick, and the woodwork so dark, that the light only served to cut the doctor out as a sharp silhouette against the pale gray sky behind him.

"Suit yourself." He gestured to the chair across from him. She was struck by how long and narrow his fingers were. But everything about the man was that way. "Sit, please."

Robert had been asked to wait out in the hallway. It was a

decision she hadn't wanted to go along with at the moment, and now she was even less certain of it. With a long exhale, she shook her head. This was the only way forward. She *had* to help Gigi. Or at least do all she could to try.

And something told her Kirkbride had answers to things she really probably should know. Walking to the chair as if it might explode on her at any moment, she carefully sat down, placing the fire poker on her lap. "I'd like you to let Gigi go."

"Gage is safe within my care, I promise you. Treatment has only just begun, and interrupting it at this point would be dangerous." He picked up a pen from a metal holder and, dipping it into a small pot of ink, began to write on a crisp sheet of white paper in front of him.

"You broke into her club, murdered half her staff, and kidnapped her."

He paused in his writing and glanced up at her thoughtfully. With a slight lift of his shoulders, he went back to his paper. "I suppose you could think about it that way."

"Tell me the way you think about it. I want to know how big of a bag of nuts I'm dealing with up front."

He chuckled. "You have a way with words, Miss Mather." He set his pen back into the holder and sat back in his wood and leather rolling chair. "You have found yourself caught up in very dangerous business. And unfortunately, dictated by its nature, dangerous business is not without cost."

"I know that. I'm not a child." If there was one thing in the world she hated more than anything, it was being belittled.

"Forgive me. I meant no insult. I am used to being a…" He waved his hand in the air lazily as he searched for the right word. "Source of authority, I suppose. But you, Miss Mather, have no need for someone such as me. If the rumors are true, you are quite capable of handling your own affairs." His eyes squinted a little as he smiled beneath the surgical mask he had yet to take off. "I am sure the professor would have much to say about that."

"I am sure he would." She smirked. "He's lying in a puddle of blood in the middle of his kitchen floor right now, if I'm lucky. If I'm not, he's probably on his way here to kill everyone in this damned place." She paused. "Maybe including me. I'm assuming he's angry."

"Hence the fire poker?"

"Hence the fire poker."

Kirkbride laughed quietly and rubbed a hand over his forehead. "I can see why you've made such waves in town. Do you realize what you've done?"

"I get the gist of it. He's…" She cringed. "He's not all right."

"Well. I can assure you that the asylum is well prepared for an entity such as him. He will not have such an easy time breaking through these walls. You are safe here."

That was a truly horrifying concept. "I won't be staying."

"You'd rather take your chances with your hideously angry and now *entirely* inhuman paramour who, by your own admission, is on a murderous rampage, than to take shelter in my institution?" He arched a thin, salt-and-pepper eyebrow.

She snorted a laugh. "Yeah. Yeah, I would."

The doctor let out a long sigh. "There are deep misconceptions you have about this place and my work that I would like to do my best to set right. I will start at the top. Whatever you believe I have done to Gage, I assure you my treatment methods are of the most humane variety. Regular social exposure, walks in the gardens when the weather is right. Reading material, music, whatever my patients wish to have to make their stay here more pleasant and to aid the healing process, they have it."

"And what if they don't want to be here? What if they don't think they need to be healed?"

"That depends entirely on the nature of their disease. Let us examine your case, for example."

She went rigid and slowly grasped the handle of the fire poker.

"Now now, please." He lifted a hand to calm her. "I gave you my word."

"Right. And how do I know your word is worth anything? I'm sure the kid in the hallway would love to sell me a rock that repels tigers."

That made the doctor laugh. It was a real laugh, and there was shockingly little sinister about it. Although she guessed that even if he was wearing a pink paisley dress and carrying a lace parasol, he'd still manage to be unnerving. "Touché, Miss Mather. Touché. I know you have no justification for trusting me. In fact, you have a litany of evidence to provide to the contrary. And that is a stigma my profession carries with it far outside your more…personal reasons. Allow me to explain."

"As a side note? Before we go too far? I also have a gun." She narrowed her eyes at him again.

He chuckled again. "I am sure you do. And I hope you have no reason to use it."

She gestured for him to continue. "You were saying? How you handle 'cases' like mine?"

"Yes. Well. You, for example, are fully cognizant. You are not prone to fits, seizures, missing time, hysterics…at least, from what I know of you." He picked up a manilla folder on the desk beside him and, opening it, began to leaf through various pieces of paper and newspaper articles.

He had a file on her. That gave her goosebumps in the worst possible way, though she shouldn't have been surprised. It wouldn't take much for a man of his connections to procure her medical files.

"Emma Mather seems fully cognizant that her delusions

are a symptom of her disease. She is not violent to herself or others and is not deemed a risk," he read from the file. He paused to glance up at her without lifting his head. "The professor notwithstanding."

"He's a special situation."

"Indeed. I will not argue with that." He returned to the file. "Your illness, as far as I can gather, is as benign as something like psychosis can be. You have learned, for lack of a better word, to cope with your illness in a functional way." He closed the file and sat back to watch her again. "I see no reason you would need to be restrained and treated against your will."

"I guess that's a relief."

"Tell me, how does your illness manifest? I am deeply curious." There was an exacting, imperial look in his gray eyes that made her think of Rafe. Something that made her feel as though she were under a lens. Although Kirkbride's gaze lacked the fire of the professor.

In many ways, he resembled his building. That underneath, he was as bleak and unwelcoming as the bricks of his institute.

It wasn't a comforting thought.

But she needed something from him. She needed to get Gigi out of here. So, she'd play nice for now. And talking about her condition wasn't anything she was really ashamed of, besides. Nor was it an enormous secret.

Shrugging, she turned her attention to his bookshelves as she talked, taking in the crisp covers of rows and rows of encyclopedias. "Mostly, I experience memories like they're real. Either in the voices of people playing as if they're standing next to me, or in sensations. Like if I think about it too hard, I can smell the desert or the markets of Marrakech. I can taste my favorite childhood dinner. Hear my mother's voice. Hear Poppa scolding me for doing something foolish.

Things like that. But I can focus my way through it. Or at worst, ignore it."

"Fascinating. Please go on."

"I had shadows growing up. I still do from time to time. People who aren't people, lurking in corners, or…whispering from other rooms. They aren't there, but they are at the same time." She cringed. "They're my least favorite."

"And how do you manage those?"

"I name them." She chuckled. "Usually something stupid. Like Jim." She smiled at the memory of the giant, terrifying monster the Idol had sent her that she had mistaken for part of her insanity. "It humanizes them. Makes them less frightening."

"Who taught you to do this?"

"My mother."

"And what of your brother's illness? Twins suffering from the same disease is…a fascinating data point. But that it seemed to evolve differently is also deeply interesting to me."

"And why should I tell you anything?"

"Because I mean you no harm, Miss Mather. In fact, though it may be impossible to believe, I wish to *help* you. And Gage."

"Can I see her?"

"After we speak."

The message was clear. With a sigh, she shook her head. Again, none of what he was asking her was hidden knowledge. It seemed like half the town knew about the details of Elliot's problems. She shouldn't be talking to him. But she needed him to let Gigi go. Or at least to agree to let her see her friend. "Elliot's voices were…not nearly so kind. They were vicious, derisive. They mocked him, tore him down, told him he was worthless." She shut her eyes, trying not to tear up at the memory of her brother and his suffering.

"Emmie, I'm scared…"

And as if on cue, there were the voices from her memory. Or maybe it was the Idol still using her brother's voice to torment her. It didn't really matter either way.

"Come play with me, Emmie!"

She forced herself to keep talking. "The voices were always there, scaring Elliot. They were incessant, and no matter how hard I tried to help him, to teach him what I'd learned, it never seemed to help him. He couldn't sleep. He couldn't eat. He turned to drugs to quiet them, but it never worked for long."

"And when the drugs and alcohol ceased to ease his pain, he turned to even darker sources of comfort." Kirkbride clicked his tongue. "I tried to help him. I sought him out and offered my assistance. I was going to treat him forcefully if need be."

She opened her mouth to shout at him, but he raised his hand and interrupted her.

"But he ran to the Idol to stay away from me. And all things considered, I do believe you would agree that was the far more destructive option." The doctor put his hand back down on his desk. "Think of me what you will, Miss Mather. But I am not a murderer. I do not force delusions upon people—I seek to cure them. I can cure your brother."

"His eyes have *changed*, Kirkbride." She shook her head. "One is gold and the other is silver. He's not human anymore. He isn't Elliot. He's—his soul is gone."

The doctor sighed tiredly. "Metaphysics is still simply that —physics. There is science behind all of what we are capable of."

"You're honestly telling me you don't believe in magic? There's a very angry professor on his way here with a lot of squiggly friends who want to prove otherwise." She wiggled her fingers at him.

He chuckled. "I believe there is an entity, a creature that

exists outside our dimension of understanding, who has infested this city like ants might invade a home. Simply because we do not currently comprehend its nature does not mean it is *magic*. Saltonstall is infected, not cursed. The Idol drugged your brother, tortured him, and used the power of the Great Beast to force your brother into a hallucination."

"But where do you draw the line? You don't think it can replace souls?"

"I do not believe in souls. Our personalities that seem to be unique are only the product of our cellular functions. A billion tiny variables that have arranged themselves to create what appears to be an individual."

"Ah." That'd explain it. "So, ghosts?"

"I would not put it past the entity—the so-called Great Beast—to be able to replicate such patterns of human behavior and mimic them using what I believe to be electromagnetic fields."

"Ghosts exist outside of Arnsmouth."

"And I am sure there are other creatures like ours in many other places around the world. Or echoes of their existence travel out in waves." He shook his head. "Sadly, I am not a physicist, I am a psychiatrist."

Turning her attention to the books on his shelves, she pondered his words for a long moment. He was trying to kindle some kind of hope in her. Hope that she had tried so very hard to kill since coming to Arnsmouth. Elliot was gone. She had looked in those mismatched eyes of Yuriel and seen only a stranger. "There's no bringing Elliot back, no matter what you're promising."

"I dislike making promises. The mind is…tricky. Each one operates upon its own systems and structures. Curing one is nothing like curing the next. But I believe I can try, Miss Mather. And I believe I can succeed."

Part of her wanted to cling to that hope. Part of her

wanted to believe him. She would give anything to have her brother back.

But Elliot was gone. She had to keep repeating that to herself. And more importantly…Elliot *wanted* to be gone. Who was to say he would come back resembling the man he used to be? And what kind of torment would she be subjecting him to? He had ended his life—thrown himself into the void, begging for silence from the voices and the incessant whispers—and who was she to drag him back into it?

Her brother was a man. Not a boy. Not the twin she had held in her arms as he wept in the early morning hours. He was a man who could make his own choices. And this was what he had picked.

But it didn't matter. "I don't know where Yuriel is. I can't help you. And unless you plan on using me as bait, you're not exactly going to talk him into walking through those doors."

"And you likely wouldn't tell me, even if you did. That is fine. I have my own means of locating him." Kirkbride picked up his pen once more and began writing. "I simply wanted to make you aware of the fact that your brother may not be as dead and gone as all the others would have liked you to believe."

Emma wasn't sure what to say to that, so she said nothing at all. She watched him take notes—or do whatever it was that he was doing—for a moment. "I need you to release Gigi."

"No."

"Why not? She's not insane."

He laughed. He laughed as though she were the most adorable and petulant child in the world who had just asserted that cows could, indeed, write operas. "You know absolutely nothing about your so-called 'friend,' Miss Mather. As the leader of the Blade, Gage has been responsible for the death and mutilation of hundreds." Reaching into his desk, he produced another file and placed it down on the desk in front of her.

Cautiously picking it up, she began to leaf through it. But two pages in, she had to look away to breathe for a moment before she got sick. It wasn't that dead bodies bothered her—she'd seen her fair share—but these were…as he said, mutilated.

Cut to pieces. Or pieces cut *off*. Skimming through the rest of the images, she saw they were all of the same thing. She shut the folder. "I don't understand."

"They call themselves the Blade, my dear." Now he sounded darkly amused, though nothing showed on that thin and hawkish face of his. "We take our names quite seriously."

The Mirror did own a big fucking mirror, so she supposed that made sense. She rubbed a hand over her face. "So, the Blade…cuts people up?"

"Cuts themselves up, most of the time. They sacrifice their own bodies to remake themselves into whatever they wish. Power like that is not given for free. The 'Great Beast' demands its…well, pound of flesh. If it works. As you can see, its failure rate is quite high. Most of those who are given the opportunity to do such things to themselves are not deemed worthy." He sat back in his chair again. "Gage thrives on blind devotion—on *fans* and *sycophants* mutilating their bodies out of hopeless love."

There was no way she could argue. There was nothing she knew that could refute any of what he was saying or otherwise. And honestly…she believed it. With a sigh, she glanced out the window. "It's not like anybody else in this damn city is any better. You have literal corpses walking around, as far as I've been told."

"A matter for another conversation."

Eyeing him narrowly, she chuckled. "Right."

"There is another matter you must understand about your 'friend.' Another reason why it is important that Gage remains in my care. Gage is deeply ill, and it is dangerous for such a person to be allowed loose in this city." He produced another folder and placed it down on the desk in front of her.

Blinking, she picked it up. The name on it was confusing. Gregory Gage.

A brother? Was that why Gigi cared so much about Elliot? Or maybe a father? Opening it, she furrowed her brow at what she saw. A young man, thin-boned, and extremely pretty. He reminded her a little of Elliot, being almost too beautiful for their own good.

There were pages and pages of notes, but she didn't take the time to read them. "So, she has a brother. And?"

"No, Miss Mather. With all that you now know about the Blade and how it manifests…Gigi Gage is a delusion of the man you see before you."

Emma touched the photograph, as though that might help her connect with what she saw. It was the eyes. It was always in the eyes. For the same reason she knew Elliot was gone, she knew what Kirkbride was telling her was true.

Because the eyes were the same. But in this photo, they were marked with a deep sadness. That despite the smile on the young man's face, there was no joy in his soul.

Shutting her eyes, Emma let out a breath. She had to fight down the anger that suddenly welled in her. The need to pick up the fire poker and *bash Kirkbride's brains out all over the walls.* Maybe she'd get the chance to do that.

But it wasn't her right to do it, either. That belonged to somebody else.

Once she could breathe through the rage, she put the folder back down on the table and stood. Fire poker in hand. "I'd like to see her, if you please, Dr. Kirkbride."

The doctor watched her in silence for a moment, then nodded. "Of course. You may visit as often as you like. A friendly face will do wonders for Gage's progression." Pushing away from the desk, he picked up his cane and began to head toward the door. "Unless your visits become disruptive, naturally."

She glared at his back. "Naturally."

Walking down the sterile walls painted sickening shades of green and blue, with white tiles beneath, she glanced at Robert, who fell in step beside her.

He nodded once, answering her silent question, his expression grim.

He knew. Probably for the best.

Emma gave him a look she hoped conveyed exactly how she was feeling. And judging by the widening of his eyes, it did.

I'm going to burn this fucking place to the ground.
I'm getting Gigi out of here.

CHAPTER THREE

"I am going to warn you that he has shown violent tendencies, as you might expect." Kirkbride gestured aimlessly with his free hand as he walked, the other leaning heavily on the cane.

Emma glared at his back but tried to keep it to a minimum. He had orderlies everywhere, standing in every hallway.

Some looked a little paler than others.

She tried not to stare too hard at one of them as they passed, as she was convinced—entirely convinced—that the man standing guard at the corner was not of the living. Without meaning to, she stopped. His skin was gray, save for the hollows beneath his eyes that almost looked bruised.

But it was his hands.

His hands were *purple.*

She had seen that once before. She had been little, and with her Poppa on a trip to the depths of the jungles of South America. Another adventurer, someone they luckily hadn't known, had been killed by a local tribe who had likely not taken too kindly to them. They had been speared to a tree, left there as a warning to others.

Emma wondered if she had even been older than eight.

"Why are his hands like that?"

Something about her young brain had skipped over all the violence and the death. Of the vacant, empty stare in the man's eyes. The blood. No, her mind had latched on to the dead man's hands.

Because they, too, had been a shade of dark purple that was nearly black. Emma could smell the jungle. She could feel the heat and the oppressive humidity, even in the chill hallway of the asylum.

She opted not to tell Kirkbride that another memory had come to visit.

"Well, I taught you all about the heart, and how it moves blood around the body, yes?"

"Yeah."

"What do you think happens when the heart stops working?"

"The blood stops."

"And you remember your lesson about gravity, don't you?"

Emma nodded, just as she had done as a child. Blood pooled downhill in corpses. And the man she was gaping at… was just that. A corpse. Never mind the fact that he was standing, staring at the wall across from him, his eyes just as devoid of life, but open.

But there was something else that kept her gawking at the man. It was the nature of his skin. Something about it seemed…off. Almost fake. And she couldn't explain why.

"Do not mind them." Kirkbride's voice dragged her out of her thoughts. He had stopped and was now turned to watch her. "They are simply patients who were too far gone. Too far beyond treatment. This man suffered psychotic episodes where he would become extremely violent. He murdered his youngest son. Broke his wife's arm so badly she lost all use of it. He was resistant to treatment."

"You killed him?"

"He is not dead, as you can see. He simply is not of the living as you would imagine it. But he is no longer a drain upon our public systems. And, furthermore, he is of use." He tilted his head to the side slightly. "Would you not say that was an improvement?"

"No." She took a step away from the standing corpse. "No, I would not."

"Then you do not sit in as many city council meetings as I do. Once you see past the surface horror of it, you will see it is a mercy. That it is a boon to both the troubled man you see before you and society at large. Would you rather have this man here"—he gestured at another one of his orderlies, who was just as vacant as the first—"continue his pattern of violent rapes? He confessed to brutalizing over two dozen women in a ten-year span. Can you imagine that?"

"I…" She hesitated.

"Several of the women did not survive their attacks or took their own lives from the resulting trauma. Others shall never recover emotionally, even if their bodies heal and the scars fade." Kirkbride shook his head. "Would you have him loose in the world?"

"N—no."

"Then would you have him instead rotting in a prison cell, draining public resources away from hospitals and schools? Do you have any idea how costly it is to keep someone imprisoned?"

Cringing, she had to look away. "Can't say that I do." She hated feeling like she was being lectured by a teacher. She hated feeling so very small.

"I have successfully treated and returned to society hundreds of individuals who are now happy and functioning.

This is merely what happens to those who cannot heal. Those who are too far gone." He shrugged. "I am doing a service in the name of the greater good, Miss Mather. Even if you feel disgusted at my methods."

"And is that what you'll do to Gigi, if you can't cure her?"

He sighed, likely at her refusal to accept that Gigi had once been a man. "He inspires others to do great harm in his name. Perhaps if he were harmless in his errancy, like you, I would not mind."

"And this has nothing to do with the fact that she's been trying to stop the Idol?" Emma tried not to let knowledge of how close she was to joining Gigi bother her. "Or help me?"

Kirkbride shut his eyes for a moment. "Yes, perhaps it does. Namely because the former and latter subjects are inherently tied in this instance." Those nearly-white eyes of his focused on her again. "He was about to begin a war between the Societies, Miss Mather. All in the name of protecting you, Gage was willing to cavort with the Bishop. In partnering with the Church of the Benevolent God, he would have put all the rest of us at risk. The other Societies would not stand for such a flagrant disregard for our safety. I stepped in to do what was necessary."

Gage and the Bishop were working together? She looked at Robert with her silent confusion.

He nodded. And with a cheeky grin, created an O with one of his hands and stuck a finger through it with the other hand.

She rolled her eyes. "You're a child," she mouthed at him silently.

The urchin snickered but didn't deny it.

Shaking her head, she looked back to Kirkbride. "So, this is political, not medical."

"The two are not mutually exclusive." He turned to continue down the hallway. "You must think about the larger issues at play, Miss Mather. I understand it can be difficult when one is in the thick of things." He stopped at a door by the end of the hallway and fished a ring of keys from his pocket. "But you must understand what is truly at stake here."

"I want to talk to Gigi in private." She stepped closer to the door, though she was careful to keep her distance from Kirkbride. "Without you, or any orderlies, or Robert, or anything."

"What the fuck did I do?" Robert huffed.

Kirkbride eyed her thoughtfully for a moment, before lifting his thin shoulders in a shrug. "As you wish. I see no harm in it." He opened the door and gestured for her to go in. "You will have fifteen minutes."

"Thirty." Crossing her arms across her chest, she did her best to sound authoritative. Judging by the slight crease in his eyes as Kirkbride must have smiled under his mask, it was about as successful as she would have suspected.

"Twenty. Final offer." He chuckled.

Jaw twitching, she glowered. "Fine."

He gestured once more to the open door. "Gage is drugged and may be lethargic."

Stepping inside, she heard the door click shut behind her. She didn't know what to expect. But what she saw…broke her heart.

It wasn't the padded room that bothered her. It wasn't the sickening green of the tiles. It wasn't the cot by the wall. It was who sat atop it.

Gigi.

Or whatever was left after what they had done. The beautiful woman was hunched in the corner, her knees up to her chest. Dressed in a hospital gown, her head was down against her arms that were folded on her legs. There were bruises on her arms that looked suspiciously like handprints, and several circular imprints from a needle being forcefully jabbed into a vein.

And her head was shaved. The cuts on her scalp were raw, the job having likely been hastily done with electric sheers.

Emma's stomach twisted, and she fought the urge to be sick. "Oh, god…what've they done?"

Gigi didn't react. She didn't even move. And somehow that made it all so much worse. Approaching carefully, Emma sat down on the edge of the cot and gently reached out to touch the other woman's arm. "Hey…"

Gigi flinched, recoiling from her.

Frowning, Emma scooted to put her back against the wall, sitting beside the jazz singer. "I'm going to get you out of here. I don't know how, but I'm going to. Even if it means I have to burn this whole fucking place down."

Silence.

Emma pulled her legs up onto the cot as well, bunching her skirt up a bit to fold her legs in front of herself, knee-to-ankle. "Because you would have done the same thing for me." She smiled weakly. "Not like I understand *why.* We couldn't be more different, you and I. Except…I guess for one thing. Neither of us really felt like we belonged, did we?"

Looking down at her hands, Emma fiddled with the hem of her coat. "I grew up feeling like my brother and I should have switched bodies. That I must have been meant to be him, and he was meant to be me. He was the delicate, feminine one. I was the one off climbing trees and hunting buffalo with my Poppa." She smirked. "All the men at Poppa's club used to tell me how they wished their sons were more like me. It…I hated being the exception, not the rule."

Still, Gigi didn't move.

"Kirkbride told me." She leaned her head against the other woman's shoulder. "And no wonder you turned to magic to fix things. I…can't even imagine what it must have been like, feeling *wrong* all those years." Shutting her eyes, she let out a breath. "I know how this world treats people who are different. I saw what it did to Elliot. Having to hide the fact he loved men instead of women was nearly as damaging to him as it was to be insane. But I suppose to people like Kirkbride, it's the same thing."

Anger flared in Emma again, and she bit it back down. "I just don't know why people have to *care* so damn much. What does it bother them if a man loves a man? What does it bother them if someone feels more like something other than what was assigned to them? What do they care if I wear pants and climb a tree? Why fight to keep people miserable?" She sighed. "Maybe the Idol is right. Maybe the world should end, if this is how it's going to be."

Gigi's shoulders shook. Lifting her head, Emma turned to her and reached out her arms. Without a word, Gigi leaned into Emma's embrace and began to weep.

Kissing the top of her head, she rested her cheek against the woman's shaved scalp. "I'm so sorry…"

Maybe Rafe would tear the place to pieces to get to her. Maybe she could convince the Bishop now that she knew what they were doing to Gigi. Maybe.

Maybe, maybe, maybe.

No. She couldn't rely on anyone else. She couldn't count on them. They were all after their own ends. Holding Gigi tight, she shut her eyes. "I'm getting you out of here. Because we women have to stick together."

The rest of the twenty minutes passed with Gigi quietly weeping in her arms without a word. At some point, Emma joined her.

Rafe walked up the steps to the Arnsmouth Asylum and looked up at the dreary building. He tilted his head thoughtfully as he considered how best to dismantle it, brick by brick. He would turn it into a hole in the ground. A pile of rubble.

He would murder every single thing inside.

Smiling, he tucked the bouquet of flowers he had purchased on the walk under his arm. He would present them to Emma as a bit of a thank you, and a bit of an apology, for all of what he was and all of what he was about to do.

The beautiful girl would be the only one to survive the slaughter that was about to unfold. He hummed cheerfully to himself as he walked up the steps toward the front door. It was about twenty feet away that he heard it. A strange kind of buzzing.

Pulling up his steps, he paused. What could that b—

Click.

Floodlights attached to the building turned on, the bright electric lights blinding him. It seared him as if he were touching a hot stove, and he had to stagger back, his arm over his eyes.

We probably should have warned you. Sorry about that.

"Warn me about what?"

Light hurts us. You know that. You've been using that damned lantern to keep us at bay for years. Well...guess what, friend?

Rafe had to retreat another good thirty feet before the light was dim enough that it didn't feel like he was on fire. Snarling in rage, he watched as the door to the asylum opened, and a tall, painfully thin man stepped out, his weight resting on the cane at his side.

"Hello, professor." Kirkbride greeted him dryly.

"Doctor." Rafe clenched his fist at his side. The lamps circled the building, posted every fifteen feet around the structure. "Your electric bill is going to be ridiculous this month, I fear."

"Yes, I suppose it shall be. Your paramour is inside, as I am sure you know." Kirkbride placed his cane in front of him and folded both his hands atop it.

He sneered. "That would be why I'm here, yes. Please let me in, doctor."

"I fear I cannot. And you are quite well aware as to why."

"Then send her out, and we'll be on our way."

"We? Interesting." The doctor looked off for a second. "It seems Robert's information was correct. You are bound for Sainthood, if I am not mistaken."

"But not yet."

"No, I suppose not. I do believe I might beat you to the finish line, for better or worse, when I finish my treatment of Gage." Kirkbride chuckled. "I believe he will be my finest work."

"Is that what you're after? Sainthood?" Rafe shook his head. "Come, now. You know what happens to those who ascend to power. They conveniently go missing shortly after."

"Yes. But I do not think even the Bishop will be able to stop me once I light the final candle."

"You would sacrifice another leader of a Society?" Rafe straightened his back, looking at the other man in surprise. "You know that means war."

"No, dear boy. Not when she is in league with the Church. Then, I think the others shall look upon this as a necessary sacrifice, don't you?"

Rafe cringed. Yes. Yes, they likely would. His tenuous truce with the Bishop was one thing. But working together was another altogether. "I don't care what you do with Gage. If you want to sacrifice her to the Candle on some foolish crusade for power, so be it. But Emma is *ours.* And you *will not* harm her."

"When have I said anything to the contrary? Please, professor, you needn't be so melodramatic. Although I am certain your newfound company"—he tapped his temple with a long, thin finger—"is clouding your judgment. You know, I could likely rid you of this disease. I can help you, Saltonstall."

Rafe laughed, low and cruel, grinning at the foolish notion. It was as much of an answer as the doctor needed.

"Suit yourself." Kirkbride shrugged. "Miss Mather is free to come and go as she wishes. Although I will have to alert her to your presence here, though it is not unexpected. I do think you have rather frightened the girl."

"She can handle herself." He winced at the memory of waking up with a splitting headache. "Trust me."

"I gathered as much."

"I will find a way to end you, Kirkbride. You and everyone else in this city." Rafe smiled. "I look forward to seeing if your ascension to Sainthood will be enough to stop me."

"As do I. Have a lovely morning, professor. I am sorry that your flowers will go undelivered."

"We shall see." Rafe turned to leave, his thoughts already whirling through his options.

He would not go far. Darkness had a way of finding itself inside of places. Despite the setbacks, Rafe knew he would have Kirkbride's head on a pike for lunch. Today, he would murder everyone. Today, he would make sure Emma never escaped again.

Today was going to be a *good* day.

CHAPTER FOUR

Emma kissed Gigi's forehead as she had to let the poor woman go. Finally, the jazz singer looked up at her, and although Emma had been certain her heart couldn't break any further, it seemed she was wrong.

The shadows under Gigi's eyes were reflected in them. The joy and life was missing. Instead, all Emma saw was fear…and pain. Cradling Gigi's cheek in her hand, Emma kissed her other one. "I'll save you…I promise."

She just had no idea *how.*

Gigi didn't respond. Simply crumpled to the sheets and curled into a ball, hiding her face beneath her hands as Kirkbride entered the room with an orderly.

"I know, time's up." Emma picked up her fire poker. Hesitating, she looked back at the poor, broken thing on the cot. "Let her go, doctor. Let her leave here with me."

"You know I cannot do that, Miss Mather." Kirkbride watched her with all the expression of a stone.

Emma was at a loss. She shook her head. "But…"

He let out a sigh, and softness eased his expression, just a little, at the edges. "I know you believe I am some kind of monster. What I am doing is not cruel."

"Can I ask you something?" She fidgeted with the fire poker, twisting it in her fingers. She was eager to use it on the doctor. But he wasn't alone. "Do you honestly think you're going to 'heal' her?"

His gray eyes flicked to Gigi then back to Emma. "Come. Let us speak outside." He retreated into the hallway, and she was left with nothing to do but follow him. Robert was leaning against the nearby wall, one leg bent with his foot flat against the plaster. He had that knife out and was flicking it around his fingers in boredom.

Kirkbride shut and locked the door before slipping the keys back in his pocket. "I did not wish to frighten Gage. This is normally information I would reserve for the next of kin. But since he has none—and his compatriots are likely lurking in the shadows, hiding from all of this—I suppose you shall do. In short, no. I do not believe I can cure Gage." He paused, considering her thoughtfully again. "But that does not mean I intend to release him, either." There was no pride in the doctor's voice. No gloating. No threatening. Merely a promise.

He is going to turn her into one of his mindless, lifeless things. Going rigid, she felt the cold chill of fear run down her back. "No. No. You wouldn't."

"It is not death. It is not murder. In fact, he will serve a greater good in his sacrifice." Only then did an inkling of pride enter the doctor's tone.

Robert groaned but said nothing.

Glancing at the urchin briefly, Emma knew she was missing something. "What? What're you talking about? What's going to happen?"

Robert sighed. "He's going to try to ascend into Sainthood."

"I don't understand." She looked back to the doctor. "I thought you didn't believe in magic."

"That remains true. I may not yet understand the science behind the more arcane workings of the universe, but that does not mean I do not use them to my advantage." He chuckled as though she were an adorable child. "Cavemen wielded fire before they grasped the workings of it, did they not?"

Emma didn't know what to do. Her thoughts reeled, racing between options. She needed to find a way to save Gigi, but time had run out. Rafe was trying to break in to kill them all, possibly including her.

Something told her that if Gigi had to die…she'd pick the professor over what the doctor was going to do to her.

Stall for time. That was what she had to do. Steeling herself, she grabbed the first thing in her head that made even a lick of sense and let it rush out her mouth. "Show me."

"Hm?" Kirkbride arched an eyebrow.

"I would like to see how you do your magic-science… whatever." She straightened her shoulders and raised her head, trying to do her best to pretend she wasn't nearly as frightened as she was. "If I can't save her, I want to at least understand what's happened to her. And—"

He raised a hand to stop her. "No need to expound. Yes, what I do is a fascinating part of our universe." He paused. "I see no harm in showing you. You may never have the chance to see anything like it again." His attention turned to Robert. "But not him."

Robert threw up his hands. "Fine by me. I don't like the idea of dying. Have fun, Emma. This doesn't apply to our deal—you're walking into this mess."

"That's fine. It's not like you have anything better to do." She smiled at him, trying to impart some sense of meaning in her expression. Some kind of hint. "Especially with Rafe on his way…who knows what might happen if he got inside."

Robert's expression narrowed just a tick.

"Ah. On that note." Kirkbride raised a finger to add on another thought. "Your professor is outside and in quite a mood. I don't think it's precisely safe for you to leave at the moment. You can sit in the lounge if you like, or I can put you up with a room. Unlocked, of course."

Damn it! She tried to keep her expression even as she regarded the doctor. "How are you keeping him out? Magic?"

"Science, Miss Mather. His infestation has made him extremely weak to light. The easiest solution is often the correct one, remember that. The electric lamps on the outside of the building are doing wonders." He chuckled. "I do rather suppose you have nowhere else to go. Another reason to show you what will become of Mr. Gage. Perhaps that will bring you some peace, and you will accept that you are safe here."

"Safe. Sure." She suppressed a shudder. Safe until Kirkbride did to her exactly what he planned to do to Gage. She looked at Robert. "Go wait in the lobby. Find something to do."

Robert's dark eyes flicked between hers, searching for understanding.

She had to give him one more hint. "At least the lights will keep Rafe out."

There it was. Robert's expression turned from one of confusion to one of anger. Anger, directly at her, because she was asking him to put them all in extreme danger. And probably turn himself into a snack for Rafe.

But the urchin was clever and dangerous. He was the least of her concerns. And hopefully, he didn't want Kirkbride to ascend, even if he didn't give a lick about Gigi.

"Yeah. The *lobby.*" Robert bit at her. "Because it's *safe* in the *lobby.*" He sighed, frustrated, and turned to walk away. "Sure! Fine. That's fine by me."

Once he was gone, she turned to Kirkbride.

"Odd fellow, isn't he?" The doctor shrugged. "I hope this time he does not nick several of my valuables on the way out." Turning on his heel, he led her deeper into the asylum. "Come, Miss Mather."

I am following a deranged doctor into the bowels of his insane asylum, to go learn about precisely how he turns people into terrible shambling corpses. All in the hopes it'll buy my equally-deranged man-eating boyfriend and his "friends" enough time to figure out how to come in here and rip this place apart.

Yeah, Robert. This is the dumbest thing I've ever done in my life.

And of course, wherever Kirkbride was leading her was in the basement. Creepy things were always in the basement. He said nothing as they walked, merely turning down corridors and stairs, deep into the ground, before he reached one large metal door down a dimly lit brick hallway.

Finally, he stopped and regarded her. "I ask you not to touch anything you see." Producing the keys from his pocket, he unlocked the large metal door and walked in first. At least he didn't ask her to go ahead of him.

It was only around then that she realized her hands were shaking. No, all of her was shaking. She was trembling, her heart pounding, her breathing feeling shallow. Clutching her fire poker tightly in her hand, she slowly crept into the room.

The first thing she noticed were the candles. They lined the room, each one burning bright. There must have been hundreds of them. They cast so much amber illumination the overhead lights were left off.

She supposed candles were the Society's namesake, after

all. She shouldn't be surprised. But it was the strange combination of dancing shadows and all the rest of the medical equipment in the room that made her skin crawl.

Metal tables on wheels dotted the huge space, in rows of two, leading to one larger workspace at the front. Almost set up as though he were teaching a lecture. Or…preaching at a church.

Strange machines that looked like soup vats lined the walls. Large, cylindrical tubes with gas burners underneath them. Not soup vats—a distillery. The setup resembled how she had seen some people making bootleg alcohol.

Slowly walking up to one, she peered at it, trying to understand what she was looking at. Some of the vats were clear with glass slides that looked cloudy and smeared from some kind of substance on the inside. It looked like…candle wax?

"It is not without a sense of irony that I tell you the Candle and the Blade are very similar in our dealings, if… very different in our results." Kirkbride walked up to the main metal table by the back wall. It was lined with medical implements. Not the kind she would expect a surgeon to use —but a mortician. He picked up what looked like a bone saw. "Everything in life requires sacrifice, Miss Mather. Everything comes at a cost."

"And what do you sacrifice?"

"The Blade sacrifices flesh for its power. I…sacrifice life in order to wield it anew. The method is arcane, and I have attempted to sterilize the process as much as possible." He placed the saw back down on the table with a clink. "To modernize it. But it still remains…far more akin to the trappings of 'dark magic' than I would like."

He stepped to the side of the table and gestured for her to come closer. It was then that she saw what Kirkbride had been blocking. At the very end of the room, arranged amongst the candles...was a hand.

A severed hand, placed on a platter. Fingers splayed wide, the palm facing her. And from the tips of the fingers were *wicks.* All the fingers were lit, save for one—the pointer finger.

It sat in a puddle of hot wax, though it looked like it had not melted low. The wax that streamed from the fingers was thick, viscous, and looked like the color of mud in the amber light. The wax was flowing from the plate into a divot that let the substance ooze down into a large medical beaker.

Picking it up, Kirkbride replaced it with an empty one. He walked up to her, holding the half-filled glass container out for her to see it. "This is a powerful drug, Miss Mather. It slowly euthanizes the subject over the course of several doses, turning their flesh to wax."

Emma's heart almost stopped in her chest. That was what had been so strange about the man she had seen in the hallway. *Wax.*

"Once the process is complete, the patient is docile. Peaceful. Cured of their ills."

"And entirely at your command," she whispered.

"Well, of course." He chuckled, the edges of his eyes creasing with a smile. She had never seen him remove his surgical mask. "Who else?"

"And Gigi..."

"Is a source of life large enough to illuminate the final candle, I believe." He turned to the severed hand. "A fascinating thing, it is. A few hundred years old, as far as I can track. The candles light and extinguish on their own, determined by the power of those who wield it."

"Who...did it belong to?" It was a stupid question, but she was trying to stall for time, wasn't she? And besides, the doctor seemed to like to talk. Men with egos always loved to talk.

"One of the original leaders of the Dark Societies of Arnsmouth. One of the ones who had been hanged by the Church of the Benevolent God for their so-called crime. A crime that was merely seeking to understand the world around them." He huffed indignantly. "Fools, the lot of them. One of his ardent students retrieved his corpse, severed his hand, and… here we have it."

Emma wanted to be sick. "What will you do when you become a Saint?"

"Unravel the Church. Their closed mindsets, their inability to adapt to new beliefs—their desire to ignore science at all turns—it must be stopped. They breed ignorance and incuriosity. They lull their followers into a false sense of security, whispering to them that all will be well, if only they just *believe*." Kirkbride turned to her, the hawkish angles of his face looking even sharper in the flickering shadows of the candles. "Think on it—a world where science was praised above belief. Where ignorance was no longer sheltered. Where zealots and idealogues held no power."

She wavered, uncertain, taking a step back from him.

"Would you prefer how we have it now? Where the Church tells people that women cannot vote? That they are lesser creatures? Where the color of one's skin or personal beliefs makes you more or less of a human being?" He shook his head. "No. I reject that the world must be as it is. And I have the power to reshape it to how I like."

"But—" She wouldn't bother arguing. There was no point in explaining to Kirkbride that he was just as blind as the people he fought against.

It seemed she showed too much of her opinion. "I understand." Placing the beaker in a wooden rack, he let his fingers trace over several other steel implements on the table. "And I will be the first to admit that science is still crude. It will always be unfinished. There will always be facts we do not yet know, or observations we hold true that later come to be false. Perhaps Gregory Gage is correct in believing he was born in the wrong gender. Perhaps he is not. All I have to rely on is what I, and my medical community, have observed. Certainly, you cannot fault us for that."

"It's…it's evil, what you're doing." *Way to make friends out of the scary doctor, Emma.*

"The process is painless. My subjects are slowly eased into another state of being, into peace, without knowing it is happening. I am not condemning them to be hanged, or stoned, or burned at the stake." He sighed. "And you fail to remember the blood that Gage has on his hands. Or the death and suffering that he has caused. He is a villain, through and through, Miss Mather. Do not forget that, simply because he wept in your arms and you believe him to be a friend. If you were in his way, he would cut you down."

Wincing, she looked away. She knew he was right about that last bit. Gigi was her friend…up to a point. She was also the dangerous and notorious leader of a Dark Society. She was hardly benign.

"You are an intelligent young woman, Miss Mather. Fiery, passionate, and most of all, loyal. I do not credit you lightly with that last honor, for loyalty in this world is a rare and wonderful blessing. I implore you not to waste it on the likes of Gage." He headed toward the exit of the room. "Come. Let me have one of my orderlies fetch you breakfast, and—" He froze in his tracks. "The lights are out. *Why are the lights out?*"

Sure enough, the hallway beyond was pitch black. It was a void of darkness and silence, illuminated only by the candlelight of the room that spilled out through the door.

Emma instantly decided the only thing more frightening than Kirkbride…

Was a frightened Kirkbride.

Robert had killed the power.

And now Rafe was going to kill everything else.

It didn't take long before the screams began.

CHAPTER FIVE

It was a funny thing, chaos.

Patrick had grown up with eight siblings. *Eight.* All right, three of them had been cousins, but it was all the same when everybody was living in the same tiny apartment. There was a certain kind of noise created when eight children and three adults were all shouting and bustling about at once.

That was a little of what it sounded like when he stormed up to the doors of Arnsmouth Asylum.

He had paced his office long enough. He had tried to ignore his conscience long enough. Damn it if there weren't *right* things and *good* things. He wasn't sure if his decision to come save Gigi was either of those things, but he knew it was going to just eat him alive if he chose to let her rot.

The front door was ajar when he approached. The sound from inside told him that something had gone awry in the madhouse. Glancing over his shoulder at the three teams of Investigators he brought, he jerked his head toward the building. "Get it under control."

The white-robed, white-masked men and women went

quickly to work. There was more shouting and screaming as the Investigators streamed into the building around him. More people might get hurt because of their presence, but he wasn't stupid enough to go charging into Dark Society nonsense without backup.

Pulling his revolver from the holster he wore at his side, he walked in and surveyed the situation. The lobby was empty, save for a few roving patients who must have escaped their keepers. It looked like the power had gone out, with nothing lighting the room but the gray glow of the early morning streaming in from the overcast sky outside.

His people fanned out into the building. They would not hesitate to cuff everyone in their way. When given a task, they followed it to the letter, for better or worse. Many of the arrested would probably be innocent. But he'd rather sort through innocents handcuffed and sitting on a sidewalk than through a pile of guilty corpses. Or no corpses at all, if Saltonstall was at work.

"Penny short and a day late," he murmured to himself as he walked down the main corridor. Whatever was going on here had started long before he arrived. And the screaming told him it wasn't simply chaos of the human variety.

An orderly ran down the hallway past him, and he snatched the panicked man by the arm, reeling him around.

"Let me go!" The man's eyes were wide. There was a bloody slash on his arm. "Please, oh—oh *fuck*, please—"

"What's happening?" Patrick glared down at him, using his size once more to intimidate. "Calm down and tell me, and maybe I can help you."

"M—monsters." The man stared down the hallway in the direction he'd come, entirely uninterested in how big and scary Patrick was trying to be. "Monsters in the shadows!"

Patrick let the man go, not caring if he escaped or if his

Investigators grabbed him. He let out a long, heavy sigh. *"Saltonstall."*

Now things were about to get complicated.

EMMA WATCHED as Kirkbride snatched a candle from the wall and used it to peer down the darkness of the basement corridor. He abandoned his cane, instead deciding to use his other hand to produce a gun from his side. With a heavy sigh, he turned to look at her. "You are to blame for this. Or more specifically, that little rat of yours is the one who chewed through the cords."

"Look, I hired him, same as you." She very much didn't like the fact that he was blocking the exit. Or the fact that he had a gun. She had a pistol as well, but the odds of her being able to draw it in time before he popped her one were slim to zero. "Don't be bitter because it worked."

"I am not bitter. Merely disappointed. But I suppose you are, as I said, loyal above all else. I should hardly be surprised." He drew back the hammer of his revolver with a click. She wondered if he was going to shoot her, here and now. He pondered the weapon as if he was considering the same thing.

"Killing me won't stop him. It'll just piss him off. Either because he'll be angry you stole his kill, or because you killed his girlfriend. One of the two." She hoped he was a logical man. He was a doctor—doctors were supposed to be reasonable, even if they were insane.

"Quite true." He released the hammer of the gun and put it back in his holster before scooping up his cane. She let out a breath of relief that didn't last long. "You should serve a purpose." He turned to the large, thick metal door of the strange candle-lit room and closed it. Turning the huge lock, it clunked into place.

Now she had time to draw her pistol.

When he turned to her, he saw the weapon and chuckled. "Oh, Miss Mather. Go ahead. You'll find I'm not so easily put down." He walked toward her slowly, clearly in no rush.

Emma backed away. "Please don't make me try anyway. Because I'm about to try anyway."

"Allow me to explain to you what is about to happen, Miss Mather. Because I know that in your infinite curiosity, you might find peace in the knowledge. I am going to restrain you. I am going to insert a catheter into the major artery in your throat and drain your blood. At the same time, I shall replace it with my serum. The process will be faster and far more painful than if I had my way, but here we are." He took a step toward her.

Emma retreated again, far faster than he was advancing. But unfortunately, she had nowhere to go. Her back hit the metal surgical table in front of the disgusting altar with the hand. Exactly where he wanted her to be. "No—no, please—"

"This was not my intention. But if Gage cannot be the sacrifice to light the last candle of my ascension…then you will have to make do." He hummed thoughtfully. "Although I think the Great Beast will find you more than suitable. Don't you?"

"Don't take another step closer, I swear to *fuck*—" She tightened her grasp on the pistol. "I'll shoot you until you're down and then keep smashing your head up with my fire poker until someone comes and saves me."

"That might work." He reached up and, with one hand, unhooked the surgical mask from his ears. "Or it might not." He pulled the mask down. And smiled at her. "Shall we find out?"

Emma screamed.

And pulled the trigger.

Rafe whistled a cheerful tune as he walked through the darkness of the asylum. Anyone who came too close to him was quickly dealt with. The voices in his mind were reveling in the slaughter, and to be honest, so was he.

There was freedom in accepting what he had become. What he had always been meant to become. This was his fate—his destiny. Chosen for him by the Great Beast. Rafe was meant to wallow in the endless void that was so empty and yet so very full. But at least he would have *her*.

"Emma," he called. "Oh, *Emmmaaa...*" Laughing, he grinned as he felt the darkness beneath him coil and writhe at the sound of her name. "Where are you, Emma?"

The lifeless, shambling things Kirkbride commanded were like chaff to him. Easily broken. Though it seemed the fouled meat was of no interest to the hungry shadows. That was fine. Leaving the crumpled corpses in his wake was just as acceptable as leaving none at all. The screaming, living, terrified orderlies were plenty of food for his friends.

One of the orderlies stood before him, blocking his path. The unliving man had skin the shade of ash in his fireplace, and the shadows beneath his eyes were as dark as the soot. And just like the log in question, he was clearly spent.

Spent but still standing. Rafe sighed and tucked his hands into his pockets. "Go away."

The thing simply stared.

He shrugged. "Very well." With that, the tendrils of his shadows snaked along the walls, trailing around the meager sunbeams drifting in from the open rooms. The overcast day was wonderfully serendipitous. He wouldn't complain.

The tendrils took hold of the man and without a sound

from their victim, broke him into a crumpled mess. The snapping of bones and rending of tendons was like music to his ears. With a *crunch,* the tendrils snapped the man's neck back at a ninety-degree angle, tearing the weak flesh that more split than it did rip, as if it were slightly viscous.

As if it were made of wax.

Rafe grimaced in disgust. Kirkbride's shambling monsters were vile. But they were nothing compared to the power Rafe wielded. To the power he was now a part of. Stepping over the crumpled body, he went on his way, resuming his whistling, until something caught his attention.

The sound of movement.

Turning, he furrowed his brow. His surprise lasted only a moment before he began to laugh. Yes, he supposed that made sense.

It was hardly going to be that simple, now, was it?

The man was getting back up, each bone in his body slowly popping back into place, the injuries done to him healing in reverse order. But it seemed the neck injury was a bit tricky to resolve, as the shambling corpse managed to get back to his feet with his head still cocked back at an unnatural angle.

He wasn't alone.

There behind him, following Rafe's path through the asylum, was a small horde of the waxy, unliving victims of Dr. Kirkbride.

"Well." Rafe adjusted his tie and straightened his clothing. "I suppose that is what I get for not paying enough attention." Addressing the things in his mind, he complained. "You could have warned me."

This was more fun to watch.

Fixing his cufflinks, he shook his head. "Children."

No. Just extremely bored.

"Well, this will certainly prove to be entertaining." Rafe

felt their silent agreement as he took a step back, letting Them take control. He heard his own laugh as They went to work, hurling bodies and tearing them in two.

Couldn't very well heal from that, now, could they?

He sheared a head from the neck of the man he had crumpled, popping it off like the top of a dandelion, and sent it skittering into the corner of the hallway with a wet *thump*.

Yes, today was going to be a very good day, indeed.

Patrick rounded a corner and slammed into a much smaller man. The impact sent the stranger to the ground with a pained grunt. It took Patrick a second to recognize him. With a blink, he reached down to offer him a hand up. "Robert? What the fuck are you doing here?"

"Hired by Kirkbride then by Emma." Robert accepted the offer of assistance, though quickly brushed himself off and took several steps back. "What the fuck are *you* doing here? This is—" His face smoothed in realization. "Oh. *Oooh*."

"Yeah. Don't look so smug, you little piece of shit," Patrick grumbled as he pushed past the street urchin. "Get out of here before you get bagged by one of my men. I won't hesitate stringing you up for abetting."

"Can't. Made a deal with the girl. Said I'd do what I could to get her out safely. Although—" Robert paused as screams echoed down the hall from somewhere deeper in the asylum. "Letting the professor loose in Arnsmouth Asylum wasn't *exactly* where I figured this was going to go."

"So, leave."

"I always uphold my end of the bargain."

Patrick rolled his eyes. "Honor amongst thieves. Fantastic. Well, enjoy yourself. Where is she, anyway?"

"That's the problem, I don't know. She was stalling for

time and asked Kirkbride to show her exactly *what* he does to people. Which means she's probably halfway to becoming one of his wax freaks by now." Robert made a *pleh* noise. "They creep me out."

"And Gigi?"

"Locked behind a steel door. So, unless you plan on kicking it in, you'll need the keys."

"Keys that Kirkbride has." Patrick rubbed his hand over his face. "Fuck."

"Yeah." Robert grunted. "I think they went to the basement."

"Of course, they did." He threw up his hands. "All right. Take me there."

"I don't work for—*gah!*"

Patrick grabbed Robert by the front of the shirt and lifted him until his feet were off the ground. Easy enough to do with one arm, with how scrawny he was. "You work for me until I tell you otherwise. Unless you really enjoy hanging from the neck, of course." He shook the young man once for good measure.

Robert grabbed Patrick's arm, desperately trying to support some of his own weight or break free. It did zero good. "Okay, okay! I work for you. I'll take you down to the basement."

"Good boy." Patrick dropped the young man with a smirk. "Lead on."

Robert was busy cussing under his breath as he walked away, straightening his shirt. Patrick couldn't help but laugh. It wasn't the time to laugh. People were dying. Emma might already be dead. Who knew what had happened to Gigi.

But damn it if he didn't enjoy how extremely put out the conniving little thief was at being manhandled. He had to hold onto humor, even in the darkest times, or else there wasn't a point in living.

Robert reached a door and opened it. The stairs that led downward were almost instantly consumed in darkness. "Are *you* going down there without a torch? Because I'm not."

Patrick smiled thinly. "Oh, ye of little faith." He lifted a hand out in front of him. Shutting his eyes, he whispered a prayer in the tongue of the Benevolent God. He felt the energy rush through him as his savior answered his words.

"Well, *fuck.*"

Patrick nearly lost focus but managed to keep his laugh until after the prayer was completed. There, hovering just above his fingers, was a small, glowing orb. It flitted down the stairwell, casting odd, almost golden light.

"Come on, kid." He walked down the stairs after the orb. "Time to go be a good guy for once."

"I'm plenty good!" Robert trailed after him.

"Uh-huh. Good that you've done for hire doesn't count."

"Does too."

"I'm the Bishop. You don't get to argue with me about these things." He lifted his gun as he walked, not wanting to be caught off guard. "You don't get to argue with the Church."

"That's entirely why I don't like you people. That and the white masks. What are they, anyway?"

"Saved souls who wish to do the same for others."

"Great. Brainwashed zealots fighting undead monsters fighting shadow tentacles. What could possibly go wrong?" Robert threw up his hands in exasperation.

Patrick couldn't help but agree with the sentiment. "Seems like a normal Thursday to me."

EMMA'S HEAD was still reeling from having been bounced off a metal table. Her vision was swimming, and she wondered idly if she had a concussion. Maybe that explained the man who was looming over her, his face a contorted mass from the nose to the chin. She marveled at how he could speak with his lips nearly missing, his skin bubbling and oozing as if it were melted wax.

"N…no, please—" She tried to sit up. But straps held her down. Kirkbride had wasted no time in restraining her. Nor did he waste any time wheeling over a contraption with two glass canisters and thin rubber hoses with angry-looking needles attached to them.

One of the canisters was already full with that muddy, oozing, wax-like liquid that was forever dripping from the grotesque hand.

The other was empty.

For now.

"This will hurt, Miss Mather. For that, I apologize. I do not have any supplies of opium down here, or else I would do what I could to dull the pain for you." A section of Kirkbride's cheek oozed away, revealing his teeth and jawbone by his molars, before sealing back shut a moment later.

Emma wanted to retch. "Please…"

"I know. But if I am to stand a chance stopping the professor from disassembling my institution brick by brick, I must ascend to Sainthood. And to do that…I need a meaningful sacrifice." He grabbed her head and forced her to look away from him, pinning her cheek to the cold steel. "Hold still."

She did nothing of the sort. Kicking and thrashing as hard as she could, it did nothing to stop the pinch of the needle as he fed it into her throat. Her stomach churned, and she screamed. Screamed as loud as she could, until a leather strap was crammed into her mouth and fastened behind her head.

"That is enough of that."

She wailed against the gag, tears flowing from her eyes

and drifting along her cheek into her hair. *No, no, no! This can't be happening. This can't be!*

Help! Anyone, please, help!

Kirkbride sighed and gently stroked away her tears. "Shush, dear girl. It will be over soon." He picked up the other needle that led to the vat of muddy liquid. He pressed the needle into the vein of her opposite arm. "Just be still. I promise I will make it as fast as possible."

No, no, no!

He walked to the machine and took hold of a crank attached to the side of it. It was a simple wheel, meant to create suction.

It was a transfusion machine.

Dr. Kirkbride began to spin the wheel.

And Emma felt herself begin to die.

CHAPTER SIX

Rafe felt it.

He didn't know how. He didn't *care* how. But he felt it. Emma was suffering somewhere—and she was going to die. Snarling in rage, he felt a strange kind of panic well up within him. The woman he loved was in pain, and he needed to put a stop to it.

He needed to put a stop to it *now*. Never mind the shambling creatures that were trying to overwhelm him. There was a more important priority now.

"Where is she?" He shut his eyes, trying to listen to the power within him.

Down below.

"Take me there."

He didn't know if he could do anything of the sort—travel through the emptiness—but he willed it to be true. He stepped into the darkness of the hallway and felt himself move. A moment later, he stepped out into a different corridor. This one didn't make him squint against the dim sunlight. Here, there was no light at all. It was such a relief to not be troubled by the light.

If he weren't so frightened for Emma, he would have wallowed in the relief of the shadows. No. He had work to do. Turning, he ran toward the source of the pain he felt eating away at him. She wasn't far.

Hold on, Emma.
Hold on, my love.
We will save you.

"Is it just me, or did the darkness just get—uh—darker?"

The kid had a point. Patrick only grunted in reply. The orb's light wasn't reaching nearly as far as it had been a moment prior. Something—and he could guess what—had joined them in the recesses of the asylum.

"If the doctor's done something to Emma, I really don't want to get between him and the professor." Robert was almost stepping on Patrick's heels, trying to stay within the dim circle of light. It made the basement of the asylum feel claustrophobic and too close.

Patrick bit back the fear that was seething in his chest from it. He hated small spaces. *Hated* them. He focused on the task at hand—stop the doctor. Save the ladies. Get on with his goddamn day and clean up the mess.

If he was lucky, he could tangle with the professor another day. Dealing with both Kirkbride and Raphael at once was a recipe for failure. "Can't help but agree with you."

"I say we let them sort it out." Robert accidentally bumped into Patrick and muttered an apology but didn't walk any less on his steps. "Monster to monster."

When they arrived at an intersection, Patrick stopped. Robert bumped into his back, but it didn't budge him a step. He narrowed his eyes, considering his options. Forward, left, or right. He had no clue which way to go. "Any ideas?"

"None. Never been down here before. Okay, that's a lie, I came down here to turn off the power. But I wasn't *here,* here." Robert smiled nervously. "How about we retreat?"

Patrick rolled his eyes. "I—"

The sound of steel tearing in half was particular. There really wasn't anything quite like it. He had unfortunately born witness to a bridge collapsing, the metal bending and *ripping* in two as the poorly designed thing gave out under a streetcar.

Somewhere in the darkness, metal was being torn to pieces. Somewhere to the right.

"Well, at least we know what direction to go."

"No, that sounds exactly like the direction we *shouldn't* go." Robert couldn't sound any less enthused. "But great. Why not. What could go wrong?"

Patrick once more shared the sentiment.

Emma was dying.

She could feel it.

Life was being sucked out of her body with every rotation of the crank. The muddy, terrible substance was being pushed into her veins. Each time the wheel reached the bottom of its track, she felt the poison ooze into her, thick and viscous.

"It is much like the process of embalming." Kirkbride smiled thinly. It seemed he wouldn't give up on the opportunity to teach her something. "In fact, it's what inspired my work."

She was being embalmed.

Alive.

Tears flowed unchecked from her eyes. The terrible ichor was warm, and she could feel it creeping into her. She couldn't tell if her vision was swimming because of her head injury or if it was because of the awful poison.

She supposed it didn't matter.

She was dying.

Please...

Not like this...

RAGE FILLED him in a way Rafe had never known before. It fueled him. Drove him forward. Nothing would stop him. Nothing would get in his way.

She was dying, and he could feel it.

She is ours! Ours to keep, ours to devour. Not his. Not anyone's. Ours.

There was a door in his way. Built thick like a bank vault or an ice room, it only gave him a moment's pause before They took hold of it. Locks did no good if the door itself was pulled to pieces.

The steel buckled and folded, letting out a deafening sound as They tore the metal in two and tossed the pieces aside. The discarded barrier crashed and thudded to the ground in the darkness. It didn't matter. He stepped into the room that smelled of burning candles, melting wax, and foul, dead flesh.

Kirkbride stood beside a transfusion machine. One container was slowly filling with crimson liquid while the other was emptying of what looked like pond sludge. But he knew better. They knew better.

There, strapped to the metal table, was their Emma. Their poor, suffering Emma.

"I am going to tear you apart for this..." Rafe stepped into the room, his shadows reaching out through every flickering scrap of darkness in the candlelit room. "And I am going to make it *hurt*."

Kirkbride stopped the crank, moving to stand between Rafe and Emma. He lifted a gun and pointed it at Rafe.

He laughed. *They* laughed, a thousand voices all at once exiting him. There was a time once that he would be horrified by it—fight against it, rail to maintain his solitude. But he embraced Them now. For They were freedom, and They would save Emma together.

"You think that will stop me? Please, doctor, have some sense." He took another step into the room. Tendrils reached out toward Kirkbride, flickering just the same as the shadows cast by the candles. He was weaker here, in the light, but it was dim. Dim enough to be overpowered. He commanded Them to snuff the candles.

One by one, they obeyed. One by one, each candle was slowly wrapped in darkness until the fire burned no more.

Kirkbride pulled back the hammer on his revolver. "Leave. Now. If the Mirror declares war upon the Candle, all the Societies will riot. If you wish to avoid chaos in Arnsmouth, you will retreat."

"The Candle won't *exist* before the day is out." Rafe grinned. "We will kill you all one by one. We will fill the smoldering crater left behind by this building with your disgusting corpses that are too perverted to even be considered food."

Kirkbride fired his weapon. The bullet embedded into Rafe's shoulder, but he felt nothing. He was long past that point.

Candle by candle, the room grew darker.

Another bullet.

Rafe reached out his arms and embraced what he was meant to become.

Another bullet.

Rafe laughed.

No. *They* laughed together.

Welcome home, Saltonstall.

Now...let's get to work.

Patrick's steps hitched. He felt it. He could taste it in the air like the ozone before a thunderstorm. Thick and bitter.

A Saint had risen.

There was only one question left—who had it been?

Saltonstall or Kirkbride?

With a growl, he doubled his stride, leaving Robert jogging behind him. Patrick wasn't certain which he wanted it to be. Which one would be worse? Kirkbride was exceptionally connected in the city of Arnsmouth. His death would not go unnoticed. The vacuum left behind by the man's disappearance would let the cockroaches rush forward to fill the slot. The head of the Candle could not simply be severed without sending ripples out into the city.

And if it was the professor, the city was in danger from a far more present and immediate danger. Who was to say what the man had been twisted into? What kind of demon was now going to be stalking the streets of Arnsmouth, destroying everything and everyone in his path?

Everyone except one person, he suspected.

Emma *fuckin'* Mather.

Even the darkness could find love. And there was something deeply redeeming in that, even if it was extremely problematic. Perhaps that was the one glimmering shard of hope Patrick could hold on to—that if Rafe truly loved Emma, he might choose peace.

Patrick slowed his steps as he approached the end of one hallway. A large metal door had been ripped into two pieces and was now lying against the wall. That had clearly been the source of the noise.

Something came flying out the open door, hitting the wall with a wet *splat* before flopping to the ground.

"Is that…a leg?" Robert groaned. "I'm gonna be sick."

Gritting his teeth, Patrick put away his pistol.

"What're you doing?" Robert shoved his arm. "Are you insane?"

"It won't do any good." He took a step toward the gaping doorway. "It's too late for that now."

A figure stepped from the room, a silhouette cast in the amber glow of candlelight from within the room. It was the figure of a man, cradling a young woman in his arms. The darkness around him writhed as though it were made of a pit of worms, wriggling and tangling around each other.

Patrick had his answer.

Professor Raphael Saltonstall had risen to Sainthood.

Damn it.

Damn it all to the hells.

"Good morning, Bishop." Rafe—or the things inside him—greeted him with a smile. Patrick's little glowing orb did almost nothing to illuminate the hallway, but Patrick suspected the professor's eyes would be nothing but empty darkness. "Fancy meeting you here."

Patrick glanced at the woman in his arms. Emma was unconscious, her skin unnaturally pale. Patrick knew precisely how the doctor did his work and could only hope it wasn't too late for her. "Is she alive?"

"Barely." Rafe's expression twisted in rage for a moment before smoothing again. "We're going to take her home."

Patrick wasn't equipped to take on a Saint. Especially not one who had a very important prize to keep safe. He let out a breath. "I will have to come for you, Saltonstall."

"We know." Rafe shrugged. "You'll try to stop us. And you

will fail. But for now, I think we should continue our little truce, hm?"

Patrick listened to the man jog between referring to himself in the singular and plural and knew it was likely just as confusing to the professor as it was to the rest of them. He almost felt pity for the man. Almost.

"If you're here to save Gigi, you'll find the keys in Kirkbride's lab coat." Rafe turned toward the room and narrowed his eyes thoughtfully. "We think his torso is in the corner there. Sorry if you have to dig for it. I rather enjoyed peeling his ribs out of his chest."

Robert whined. "Gonna be sick..."

Rafe headed toward them down the hallway. Patrick held his ground and refused to retreat as the professor approached.

As Rafe was about to pass him, the professor paused. Patrick's theory about the man's eyes was confirmed. They were pure black from lid to lid. "We love her, Bishop. And we will do whatever it takes to keep her. Any attempts to save her from us will end in the ruination of this entire damnable city. Do you understand that?"

"Yes."

"Good. Now go save your jazz singer. We do think she's likely quite a mess." Rafe smiled halfheartedly. "It seems we shall both be playing nursemaids to the women we love."

"I don't..." Patrick sighed. It wasn't worth arguing about. Especially not with the unknowable multitude of monsters that now possessed Saltonstall. He might as well argue with a swarm of bees for the good it'd do. "Go. Leave. Try not to kill my Investigators on the way out."

"We'll do our best." He grinned. "But no promises." Rafe turned his attention to Robert. "Ah. Yes. It makes sense *you* would be here."

"Made a deal with her to keep her safe."

"You did an absolutely *wonderful* job." Rafe sneered, laying the sarcasm on thick. "We commend your brilliant performance."

"Yeah, well." Robert took a step away from Rafe, putting Patrick in between him and the Mirrored Saint. A wise move, all things considered. "Win some, lose some."

"Indeed." Rafe resumed walking away from them, heading into the darkness without any need for illumination. "Have a wonderful rest of the day, gentlemen." Patrick could no longer see him as the man spoke from the darkness. "Oh, and Bishop?"

"Yes?" He hated not being able to see the professor. But he knew that he likely no longer resembled a human man when he was outside the reach of illumination. It was something he did not need to see.

"Burn this place to the ground for me, will you?" Rafe chuckled. "Call it a favor between *friends.*"

Patrick clenched his fists at his sides hard enough that he wondered if he didn't break the skin with his nails. He said nothing. And it was only when the darkness was silent for several seconds that he felt confident enough that the professor was gone to turn his back on the hallway.

"I hate this. I hate this. I hate this." Robert was holding his knife tight in his hand. It wouldn't do shit against a monster like Saltonstall, but Patrick couldn't blame the kid for wanting to hold on to something.

The room Rafe had come from was nearly destroyed. There were a dozen or so candles lit around the room, several of them burning from the floor where they had been tossed. Metal tables were broken and bent, discarded wherever they landed from being hurled about.

One candle caught Patrick's attention. A candle with four wicks that were smoldering, smoke slowly curling up from the extinguished flames. A candle he recognized and dreaded.

"Is that a fucking *hand?*" Robert finally had enough. He walked to the corner of the room and emptied the contents of his stomach.

All the medical equipment in the room was smashed to smithereens. And scattered about, bit by bit, piece by piece, was Dr. Kirkbride.

A leg here. A piece of an arm there. And all of it slowly melting like ice cream in the sun.

Or like wax on a hot summer day.

It took Patrick a second to find the man's torso. As Rafe had said, most of it was in one corner, the white fabric stained a milky red by whatever was oozing from Kirkbride's corpse. He fished the keys out of the pocket, glad to find they weren't covered in the same disgusting substance.

"Let's go." Patrick paused as he went to leave the room, however. He stared at the waxy hand upon a ceremonial plate by the wall, four of the wicks still smoking. He could take it with him, but he knew firsthand what kind of misery it caused to contain such a cursed totem.

It couldn't be destroyed. He knew that from experience as well.

Bury it under rubble. Burn this place down like Saltonstall said. It was a fitting way to end this reign of the Candle—through soot and ash, smoke and flames. Disgusted, he turned from the scene and went back into the darkness, his little orb obediently staying close.

Save Gigi.

Burn this place down.

Then promptly get trashed on communion wine.

Maybe Robert could get him some whiskey.

I hate Thursdays.

Gigi felt someone touch her head. She flinched, curling away from whoever it was. She moaned. It was the only sound she could make. Her tongue didn't work right anymore. It felt too thick, too immobile in her mouth. They had done this to her. They were trying to take her away from herself.

Arms picked her up, and she whined, weakly struggling against the orderly.

"Hey, now…it's me, Gigi. It's me."

The voice cut through the fog in her mind like a knife through butter. She blinked, blearily trying to focus through the haze that had overtaken her. Someone was holding her in their arms, cradling her gently against a broad and warm chest.

She knew the smell of him, before she even placed the voice. Before she even saw his face, she knew him.

She forced the word from her mouth, disobedient tongue be damned. "Priest…?"

"Yeah…priest." Lips touched her forehead. "You're safe now."

Safe.

Safe.

Safe.

Gigi shut her eyes.

CHAPTER SEVEN

Patrick's heart was broken. Shattered in two. And he knew why. He just didn't want to accept it. Accepting why he was silently crying as he carried Gigi out from that damnable asylum was a dangerous road to travel.

The woman in his arms was limp, her head resting against his chest. He wondered if she was unconscious. He rather hoped she was sleeping. Her skin was a shade of ghastly grayish-yellow that made him think of old paper from an attic, water-stained and forgotten.

Forgotten.

He leaned down and kissed the top of her head. Her hair was gone, her scalp shaved raw and ragged by the carelessness of an orderly, he was certain. It was torture, was what it was. Her arms looked thin when they were so sallow. It only accentuated the dark purple bruises on her upper arms left there by hands.

Patrick was going to burn this place to the ground.

Robert was still dogging his heels, staying close to him and glancing nervously at every shadow.

"The professor is gone." Patrick sighed. *I suppose we will both be playing nursemaid, won't we? The Bishop and the Saint, crying over the women we...* He couldn't finish the thought in his own mind. He wouldn't let himself. Instead, he focused on the matter at hand. He would take Gigi to the Church, and he would help her get back on her feet.

Then, he would have to contend with the professor. He gritted his teeth. The Bishop and the Saint indeed.

Two halves of the same coin.

He never mourned what it was he had to do to the foolish cultists who ascended to Sainthood to keep the peace in Arnsmouth. It was their own fault. They chose the path they walked on, and they suffered the consequences.

Saltonstall knew this was the inevitable consequence of his work.

But it wasn't the professor he mourned for. It was Emma. She would be once again left suffering in the absence of someone she loved. First Elliot and now Rafe. But it had to be done. It *had* to be. Because otherwise, a hundred thousand lives would be lost with a hundred thousand tragedies.

One love lost was not enough to put the whole city at stake.

"Uh…Bishop?" Robert tugged on his sleeve.

They were standing in the lobby of the asylum, the double doors thrust open and left that way by the fleeing employees. Or whoever was left that hadn't been devoured by Saltonstall.

"What?" He turned and froze as he saw the source of Robert's concern. "Ah."

It was not a man that was shambling after them in the darkness. It was what remained of one.

Dr. Thaddeus Kirkbride had been his name. But now, he was barely recognizable. He was dragging one leg behind him as he moved. With one arm he leaned heavily on the wall. And with the other, he carried a waxy hand that was not his own. It was a candle with five fingers illuminated.

All five.

Patrick let out an annoyed grunt.

Fantastic.

Now he had *two* Saints to deal with.

He really hated Thursdays.

The remains of Kirkbride laughed, a sound that came out wet and gooey. His face peeled apart as he spoke, like the wax that he had become. "I did not need to sacrifice Gage...I merely needed to sacrifice myself. Look—look..." He held up the waxy burning hand. "I have been given true power..."

"I suppose you have." Patrick walked over to a chair by the wall. He carefully put Gigi down in the seat and shrugged out of his cassock and wrapped it around the much smaller woman. He could almost hear her teasing him for the gesture, and oh, how he wished she would. But instead, she simply stared ahead, eyes glassy and empty.

She wasn't too far gone. Yet. But she had been very, very close.

Pulling his gun from his holster, he placed it on her lap. "I know you'd ask me for this if you could. I'll be right back."

"Uh—Bishop? Pat? Patrick?" Robert's voice scaled up in pitch as he backed away from the Saint of the Candle.

"Go, Robert." Patrick cracked his neck from one side to the other. "Get out of here. Your contracts are completed for the day." Rolling his shoulders, he felt the knots in his muscles grind. No matter. His knuckles were next, popping audibly as he readied himself for what was about to come.

"Don't need to tell me twice." And with that, the street urchin turned and bolted from the building, running into the meager sunlight and away from the asylum.

It was for the best. Patrick hated witnesses. And normally, he hated when he had to resort to this kind of thing.

But today?

Today he was going to *enjoy* this.

And he honestly hoped Gigi was watching. Because as much as this was for him…this was also for *her.*

"You cannot stop me." Kirkbride stepped free of the hallway. He straightened, his limbs bending in strange and unnatural directions, as though he had no joints. As though he had no bones. Saltonstall probably broke them all, and now that Kirkbride was a true Saint of the Candle, they were more of a *suggestion* than a *rule.* "I control life itself. I am unstoppable! I am immortal!"

"Yeah. We'll see." Patrick walked toward the doctor, balling up his fist.

Maybe he could end today on a better note than it started.

Emma felt so very strange.

It was as though everything was just slightly out of sync, or out of reach. The world was a hazy mess around her. She felt numb and removed and floating just a little to the left of where she should be. Or maybe it was the right. Or maybe it didn't matter at all.

A hand stroked her hair, and all at once she felt as though her soul had been dragged into her body. She could feel it all again, and she really wished she couldn't. Because *fuck* did everything *hurt.*

All she could manage was a broken-sounding whine.

"Shh…it's all right." Lips pressed to her temple.

She couldn't see. Wherever she was, it was dark. She was lying down on something soft. She assumed it was a bed, but she honestly couldn't tell. But she did know the sound of the voice and the feeling of the lips against her.

Rafe.

Rafe was there.

Was she dead? Or had he saved her in time?

She really hoped it was the latter, as she *really* hoped death didn't hurt as bad as it hurt right now. She tried to speak, but nothing came out.

"You're safe. I wish I had opium to give you, but sadly, that isn't my particular vice." An arm draped over her, and she felt him pull her close to his chest. He was lying beside her.

She could barely move, but she tucked her head against him, wanting the comforting warmth of his body. She shut her eyes, hating how the room swam when she tried to focus on things. It was like being drunk without the fun bits.

"I fear I've risen to the level of Saint. In saving you, I… may have opened doors I cannot now close. But we realize that we were approaching this all wrong, Emma. We didn't mean to scare you." He stroked her hair gently again, combing through the strands. "We will do everything in our power to protect you. I promise."

He was bouncing back and forth so quickly between Rafe and the rest of Them, he barely skipped a beat between his words.

Because they were one and the same now. She knew it. They were woven together like a tapestry, and there would be no untangling them anymore. Oddly, it didn't scare her, though she knew it should. She reached out, her limbs feeling heavy and hard to move. But slowly, surely, she managed to grasp the front of his shirt and weakly clutch to him.

Rafe was still there. He just was one thread in a larger cloth.

And Benevolent God or Great Beast, it didn't matter—she loved him. She would have cried if she could have found the strength. Because she loved him, and she knew what was coming next.

The darkness in his voice was thick as he made a vow to her that was as much a promise as it was a threat. "We're going to make sure there is no one left to hurt you. You and I will always be safe. Even if it means we have to devour all of Arnsmouth to do it."

Safe. She knew it was a lie. She was safe for the moment—he had saved her from Kirkbride.

Now that she was here, she had only one question left.

Who would save her—who would save the city—from *him?*

PATRICK WALKED down the stairs of Arnsmouth Asylum, Gigi once more in his arms, wrapped in the black fabric of his cassock. He had taken his gun back, however.

His hands were stained with blood that was the color of the mud of the Thomas River. He paused as the leader of his Investigators walked up to him. The eyes of the white mask were blackened out with fabric. And since they were forever mute, there was nothing to read from the man's posture or demeanor, but Patrick knew what he was asking all the same.

"Burn it down. Burn it all down."

Patrick walked away without another word, heading for the automobile that would take them back to the Church. He climbed into the back seat, still holding Gigi in his lap. The driver shut the door and climbed into the front, and they were off.

The day was as grim as he felt.

Silently, he simply held Gigi against his chest as they drove. It wasn't until halfway across the city that she finally moved. Her hand, thin and weak, slipped from within the folds of the dark fabric and pressed against his chest.

Placing his hand over the back of hers, he held it. He

didn't know what to say to the poor, shattered woman. She was his enemy, yes. She was the leader of a dangerous, deadly cult.

But torture was torture.

And what they had done to her was *wrong*.

"Thank..." Her voice was barely audible over the engine of the automobile. She couldn't even get the second half out.

"Ssh." He kissed the top of her head. "Rest."

Her hand went limp in his. And Patrick fought the urge to cry.

THROUGH THE HAZE and the pain, Gigi had watched Patrick beat a man to death.

Or rather, she had watched him beat the walking remains of a man back into the grave. It shouldn't have been possible. Kirkbride was right in his assertions of immortality—or at least he should have been.

Nobody should have been able to kill him. But when the priest had walked away with his hands covered in what the doctor had for blood, the pile of wax and bones that lay crumpled on the floor didn't move.

Gigi had always suspected the Bishop was dangerous. How else could he have simply *vanished* so many of her fellow compatriots in the Dark Societies? She could count on two hands the number of practitioners that had gone missing at the hands of the Church of the Benevolent God.

She had known why they had been taken.

Now she knew how. It wasn't simply the Investigators in their sheer numbers who could overpower those with gifts given from the Great Beast.

It seemed the priest himself had his own powers. It made perfect sense. Little by little, the pieces were falling into place. Her mind was still clouded, skipping from one thought to the next, but it somehow made her see the truth all the more clearly. Bishop Patrick Caner wasn't just a priest. Nor was he just a Bishop. No, he was something far more dangerous. And the implications of it…it would upend all the Dark Societies if word got out. Arnsmouth would be pitched into chaos.

For some reason, it made her smile. She would have laughed if she could. *The only thing in this world that has the power to kill a Saint...* She managed to chuckle, or maybe it was only in her head. Maybe she was asleep. Maybe it didn't matter at all.

It wasn't the Investigators. It wasn't guns, or drugs, or anything else that subdued those who went too far down the dark paths of power.

It was him. It was always only him.

Bishop Patrick Caner is a Saint...

But a saint of what?

CHAPTER EIGHT

It was very strange to be nursed back to health by a terrifying eldritch monster. That was the thought that ran through Emma's mind as she clutched the toilet, her body covered in a cold sweat as she emptied the contents of her stomach into the porcelain bowl.

The room was in utter darkness. She couldn't see any of what was around her. But that was probably for the best, as she knew what was coming out of her body wasn't pleasant to behold. It felt thick and viscous, like gravy left to thicken for too long on the stove.

It was that terrible, bloody, wax-like substance that Kirkbride had put into her body. It tasted as foul as she expected it to.

And all the while, tendrils supported her weight. They held her up by the arms, curled at her back as if trying to comfort her…and held back her hair.

Creatures from the darkest corners of the unknowable void were *holding back her hair* while she retched as if she was merely mending from some terrible night of drinking.

It would have been extremely funny if it weren't also so

miserable. When all the sludge in her stomach seemed to have been forced out of her body, she sat on the tiled floor and pressed her cheek to the wall.

The sink ran, then stopped. She felt a damp, cool hand towel press to her forehead, mopping away some of the sweat. At least it was a hand that was driving it. She hadn't heard Rafe enter the room.

He had drawn all the curtains and turned off all the lights, even with it being the middle of the night. Now that his home was in darkness, it seemed he could move around the shadows as he pleased.

"Do you think you can hold down some soup?" He sounded entirely normal, which made the entire thing all the more surreal. It felt as though she were dreaming.

"Y...yeah." Her voice was hoarse from all the vomiting. Taking the damp cloth from him, she wiped at her face with it. "I think so..."

"Good." He lifted her from the ground, carefully holding her in his arms. It was a lot more pleasant than being carried by the tendrils. "We're so happy to see you on the mend."

We.

It still sent a shiver down her spine. What was she supposed to do? She knew *she* was safe. But what about the rest of Arnsmouth? What about the rest of the damn world? "Rafe?"

"Hmm?" He brought her to what she expected was the kitchen, though it was hard to tell.

"What happens next?"

He sat her down on a stool, kissed her temple, and then walked away from her. At least she could hear his shoes on the floor now. It meant he had feet. That was some small comfort. "Well. First, we get you back on your feet."

"But after that."

"We are going to murder everyone." Rafe chuckled. Or perhaps it wasn't Rafe in the driver's seat at the moment.

Cringing, she lowered her head and shut her eyes. Though she didn't know why she bothered—she couldn't see shit, anyway. "Rafe, no. Please. You can't kill everyone."

"I will keep you safe. And to do so, we will need to dismantle every single one of the Dark Societies. Their web of corruption runs wide and deep, and like the roots of ivy, it's crawled through every crack and crevice in this forsaken city." She heard him tap a spoon on a pot. She should be able to see the gas flame from the stove, but…he wasn't letting any light exist around them at the moment.

He was talking about mass murder.

While making her soup.

She was too tired to laugh. Putting her head down on her arms, she sighed. "There has to be another way."

"We could eat Yuriel. That might stop the Idol. But what about the others? Gigi plays the friend *now,* but politics can change. And someone else will take up the Candle if they haven't already." He walked up to her, placing what must be a bowl on the surface of the kitchen island next to her. "Besides…you are overlooking one critical problem. I have ascended to Sainthood, dear."

"I know."

"The Bishop will be coming for us."

She winced again. "I know." She felt so weak. So utterly useless. Her world was crashing down around her, she had nearly died, and without even a second to breathe, she was going to be thrust back into the thick of it. She'd never felt this tired in her life, and here she was. Exhausted. Mentally, physically, emotionally. "Isn't there another way? What if you just—I don't know—"

"Promise to be a good boy? Boys?" He hummed thoughtfully. "To be truthful, I'm not sure as we entirely have gender.

Not really." He sat down next to her, gently running a hand up and down her back. "You know our word would mean nothing to him."

She repeated herself again. "I know."

"Eat your soup, dear."

Picking up her head, she glared halfheartedly in his general direction. "I can't *see* it."

He laughed and, wrapping his arm around her, hugged her to his side. Slowly, the world came dimly into focus. It was then that she realized he hadn't drawn the curtains—there were no curtains in his kitchen.

He was simply blotting out the light altogether. Like a veil, it began to lift. The lights in the kitchen had been on the entire time. He released the darkness enough that she could see, but barely. He smiled at her. "Is that better?"

His eyes were as dark as the world had been around her. Empty voids of nothing from lid to lid. She nodded hesitantly. He nudged the bowl closer to her. Chicken noodle soup. She should have known from the smell. Where he got it, she didn't know. She knew it wasn't in his pantry. She really didn't want to ask from where an interdimensional nightmare monster fetched soup.

Rafe should have terrified her. He looked, well, inhuman. Darkness curled from him in waves like smoke from a candle. But somehow, the way he was smiling at her, with all the concern and tenderness a creature could have for another…she didn't know. Evened out the scales, somehow.

Reaching up, she carefully placed her palm to his cheek. He felt real. Felt human. Felt like the man she knew. He leaned into her touch, those void-like eyes slipping shut as his smile softened even further.

She loved him. She really, truly did. But what part of him did she love? Rafe? The creatures within him? Or even more problematic, was the answer *both?* And if that was true, what did that make of her? Of her morals?

Would she let him—*them*—destroy the city in her name?

Could she even stop them if she tried?

I don't even know where to start. Stroking her thumb along his cheekbone, she let out a long, heavy breath. "Thank you for saving me."

"You don't sound terribly enthusiastic. What's wrong?" He arched a dark brow as he turned his attention up to watch her.

"I don't like the idea of murdering the entire city, is all."

He nudged her bowl again, urging her to eat. She picked up the spoon and went to it. Her hands were shaking as she did. They sat in silence for a moment before he replied. "It won't be the *entire* city."

The look she shot him made him laugh, even though that was far from the point.

He was smiling as he leaned in to kiss her cheek. "I know. But you will adjust. And once the Bishop and the Societies have been dealt with, we will live here in peace. Together. Because..." He paused.

"Because, what?" She frowned.

"Nothing you don't already know." He kissed her cheek again. "Eat. I need to go feed Hector as well."

An interdimensional nightmare monster with a cat. And a girlfriend. "If I asked you not to, would you listen?"

He blinked. "Not feed my cat? That's—"

"No, no." She smiled at his offended expression. "I meant if I asked you not to kill the Bishop and the Societies."

"Oh." He chuckled. "I was going to say." Leaning an arm against the table, he reached forward with his other hand and combed it through her hair, tucking one of her curls behind her ear. "It is us or them, Emma. All this has set in motion a series of events that cannot be stopped. Either we die, or they do. There is no middle ground. There is no peace to be had. It is simply about the collateral damage."

"Is this all my fault?"

Rafe pondered the question thoughtfully. "Yes."

With a grunt, she slapped him on the arm. Not like it must have felt like anything, she was a trembling leaf on a branch in the wind at this point.

Laughing, he tilted her head to him and kissed her for a long moment before pushing up from the stool to leave the room. "Eat, dear. I will handle everything."

That was precisely what she was afraid of.

The soup was good, she had to admit. That likely meant that Rafe didn't make it. Charming man in his own right, but a terrible cook. She hadn't found a single bottle of spices or seasoning in any of his cabinets, save some salt and a barely-used container of pepper.

Part of her wondered if he would like sushi, then promptly remembered he couldn't leave Arnsmouth. He wouldn't have been able to cross the city lines before, and now…now he was a Saint of the Great Beast.

There had to be another way. There *had* to be. She had to go find the Bishop and talk to him—to see if there was some kind of truce they could call. The other option was so much worse.

She didn't care what happened to herself anymore. Let her be consumed by Rafe and his *Things* if it meant the city was safe. There were too many other lives at stake.

Poking at the little squares of chicken, she made sure to finish the bowl. She'd need her strength for what she had to do. There would be no guns or fire pokers this time. There was no killing Rafe anymore.

No, she had to escape.

She just had no idea *how.*

Patrick carefully lifted the spoon of soup to Gigi's lips, frowning as the woman struggled to drink the broth down. It was barely anything more than a bowl of warm water, with how thin he had to make it so that she could keep from retching it up.

It had only been a night, he had to remind himself. It would take time to come back from the damage she had suffered.

She was half-lying, half-sitting in bed, propped up on pillows. He had brought her to the Church. And despite her mutterings, she did *not* burst into flames once she crossed the threshold. He had brought her to his quarters. She had taken the bed, of course, and he was sleeping on a mat on the ground with a few pillows.

"We could share," she murmured.

"Hm?"

She gestured weakly to his spot on the ground. Even through her broken state, the look of "you're being a fool" on her face was no less poignant than before.

When he tried to ignore her statement to feed her another spoon of soup, she touched his hand to stop him. "Patrick," she insisted. "We've fucked."

Clearing his throat, he fought the warmth that crept into his cheeks. "Yes, I—um. I remember. It just…I don't want to hurt you, if I roll over, and—the bed is small. Barely enough for me. I would crush you."

She smiled, just the barest twist of blue-gray lips. "I suppose."

He went back to quietly feeding her. She accepted his help without complaint, though he knew better. "I should have come sooner."

"Why?"

"Because—I knew...I knew what Kirkbride was capable of, I knew what he does to his problematic patients. But he wasn't *enough* of a threat, so I let it continue. And when he took you, I thought—let the Societies sort out their own issues."

"Precisely." She smirked. "So, why?"

The way she was watching him, with those beautiful blue eyes that were dull and hazy, still cut him to the core. It was as though she could see through him. With a ragged sigh, he felt his shoulders slump. "I should have come sooner."

A hand touched his cheek. "You came...when I needed you."

He could not hold back his tears.

CHAPTER NINE

It took several days before Emma could walk around the house on her own. It took several days after that before Rafe and his *Things* were not lurking nearby at all times, watching her like a hawk to ensure she didn't fall down the stairs and break her neck.

It was comforting and terrifying at the same time. The mix made for a rather anxious week and a half.

But she did have to chuckle as one of the shadowy appendages lifted her left shoe from the ground and handed it to her. "Thanks." Her smile widened as it curled a little as if relishing her praise. "That was nice of you." She reached out and touched it. And like a squid, it reacted to her presence and took hold of her fingers.

They were gentle, all things considered.

Gentle, murderous, tender, evil, caring, eldritch horrors.

My life is complicated.

The tendril released her before disappearing back into the darkness from whence it came. Putting on her other shoe, she stood from the bed and did her best to look as though she was all right. Physically, she was nearly better, though she did still feel weak. Occasionally, she would still cough up something that looked like mud and tasted like… she didn't want to know what.

But her healing was only a ticking clock. With every step she took toward mending from what Kirkbride had done to her, they took another step toward total war. Rafe was only biding his time because she wasn't well. The moment he felt confident enough to leave her alone, that was it.

More than once she debated throwing herself down the stairs in hopes of breaking her arm or ankle. At least then she'd stall for time. But she knew the inky darkness that filled his home would never let her hit the ground.

Heading into Rafe's study, she peered around the corner. He was sitting in his chair at his desk. He wasn't writing, nor was he moving. He was simply sitting there, palms flat on his desk, his eyes shut. His head was tilted to the side slightly, as though he were listening to something.

And she knew what.

Them.

How it hadn't driven him mad yet, she didn't know. *Maybe it has.* And she knew that someday, she too would be "lucky" enough to hear them when they decided to do to her what they had done to Rafe. Consume him.

She shuddered at the idea.

Walking up to him slowly, she felt like she was approaching a rabid animal. Maybe it'd lunge at her and rip her arm off. Maybe it'd nuzzle into her and lick her face. It was a roll of the dice. Walking behind his desk, she carefully put her hand on his shoulder.

He let out a hum, blinking as if waking from a dream. He smiled up at her and placed his palm over the back of her hand and squeezed it. "Hello, dear."

"I was hoping to go to the market and pick up something for dinner. I want to make some steak and panzanella." She smiled back and moved to stand behind his chair to slip her arms over his shoulders and rest her chin atop his head. "And you have absolutely shit for groceries in the house."

Leaning back into her embrace, he took a moment to ponder his answer. "We suppose it would be good for you to get some exercise."

Hope welled in her heart. Escape! Yes!

"We can go together." He chuckled. "Though I may need an umbrella if the sun is out."

Damn it! "I think it's evening. It's hard to tell since you're blotting out all the windows. You know, I don't think a human being can survive without sunlight forever. You might need to at least let me out into the courtyard on my own."

"I suppose. For now." He kissed her arm. "But if you're good enough to walk to the store, then I can begin my work."

"Must you?" She frowned, holding him a little tighter. "Rafe…"

Standing from his chair, he turned to face her and took her into his arms. Pulling her against him, he smiled mournfully. "I will not enjoy what will come next." He cringed. "Although *They* will."

That was exactly what she expected. Resting her head against his chest, she shut her eyes and tried to pretend that everything was normal. They were a normal couple—as normal as they were capable of, anyway.

Something wrapped around her ankle, thin and strong, and reminded her that they were anything but. The darkness within him was kind to her. Sweet, even. But she couldn't stand by and watch them murder who-knew-how-many people in the name of keeping her safe.

But out was out. And out meant she might be able to make a break for it.

"Or…We could bend you over this desk." His hand drifted

lower, grabbing her ass and squeezing it. "That was a great deal of fun."

"After"—she broke off as he squeezed harder, the sting of it sending thrills through her body—"after dinner. I need steak."

"Hm. We do appreciate how useful protein is to the body. Very well." He kissed the top of her head as he released his grip. His voice lowered, turning dark and sinful. "We haven't yet appreciated you fully, you know."

By the hells, that shouldn't set her on fire the way it did. Her stomach twisted into knots, and she couldn't even imagine what he was referencing. But that time she really, really did want to know.

Damn it all.

"After dinner." She smiled up at him.

"And after dinner, you'll be our dessert." He grinned. Before she could react, he fisted her hair and tilted her head back. When she gasped, he took the opportunity to steal her lips in a kiss, growling as he did.

Emma melted against him, the tension leaving her limbs as his tongue tangled with hers. The tendril around her ankle tightened, squeezing her possessively. She couldn't help it. She loved it. Combing her fingers through his hair, she pulled him tighter against her, seeking more of the passion.

His snarl turned to a moan. Pulling away from the kiss, he caught his breath. "Are you sure? We could have dessert before dinner. We're adults, aren't we? We can do what we want."

He almost sounded innocent in his insistence. She wasn't surprised to see that his eyes had not simply gone dark with lust, but turned entirely black. She traced her fingers over his —no, their—cheek, and watched as they leaned into her touch. "What am I supposed to call you, when you're like this?"

"Hm?" The question clearly confused him for a moment before he chuckled. "Oh, Emma. There is no name for us. Although your attempt to give us several was adorable."

"You remember that?"

"No one had ever thought to do it on an individual basis before. We fear you would run out long before you were done, however." They looked off for a moment, one eye narrowed in thought. "Although we can see why you might want one. We are in an unusual state of being for a small mortal such as yourself. You can still call us Rafe. It's technically true, if not the entire picture."

"I'm not small!"

"You're positively tiny." They grinned. "Don't make us prove it to you. We can show you the glorious expanse of the writhing void. We just don't think you'd like it."

Glaring up at him only made them laugh. She let out a disgruntled puff of air and rested her cheek against his chest. "Fine."

"Now. Let's go along to the store, buy some…human food, eat the human food, and then we will show you precisely what we are capable of doing to your *tiny mortal* body. Does that sound like a plan?"

They said it so casually that it was almost funny, if it wasn't for the way they were now smiling down at her. It was so wolfish and devious that it sent a shiver down her spine that was very different from those they usually caused.

"Y—yeah."

"Good!" He patted her on the ass as he let her go, before strolling out of the room. "We'll go get changed."

"You might want to let Rafe drive. I'm not sure the rest of the *tiny* mortal populace will take kindly to your eyes."

"Eyes?" They stopped to peer into the hallway mirror. "Oh. Well. Huh. Shit. No wonder you panic a little every time we come out."

Listening to an eldritch horror swear was too much for her. She sat down on the edge of the desk and laughed. "Yeah. That would be why."

"Charming." They wrinkled their nose. "Very well. We'll let Rafe 'drive,' as you say." He paused. "Oh. Can we drive a car now? I think we'd like to try."

"No."

"Why not?" They grinned. "It's not like we'll die from a crash."

"Fine, but I'm not getting in with you." She put her hand over her face. "I'm not having this argument. Go. Shoo. Get changed. Literally and metaphysically."

They walked away with a cackle. "That's a good one."

In their absence, she felt the anxiety and fear creep over her once again. When Rafe was near, even when he was possessed, it felt…right. She felt safe. She loved the stern professor, and she was quickly falling for the shockingly humorous monsters within him. Which made her an *absolute* lunatic. Even more than usual.

"You really must stop befriending your shadows," Poppa said through a laugh. *"Or else they'll decide they're your friends and they'll stay around."*

"But they are my friends, Poppa." She heard her own voice play through the memory beside her, the high-pitched tone of a child. *"If I'm nice to them, they're nice to me."*

"That is a very good way to go through life, I suppose. All right. I rescind my advice—befriend them all you like."

"Thanks, Poppa!"

Planting her hand over her eyes, she let out another long, ragged sigh. "I really do have problems."

ROBERT WHISTLED as he dug through the rubble of Arnsmouth Asylum. He had help, but there was still a long way to go. He had a lot of bricks to throw aside before he got what was rightfully his.

"Debt paid, kid," he muttered to himself as he tossed more of the charred bits and pieces of the building aside. "Though I'm not sure you'll ever get a chance to know it." Emma had purchased a favor from him—to protect her in exchange for a debt he would collect at some point in the future.

But the scales were even now. She had done him a huge boon without ever realizing it. And, hey, he always loved the chance to dance around like a total idiot. It was a fun change of pace. Mother always said he made a brilliant actor.

Normally, he would pretend she hadn't done a damn thing for him. That way, he could get an extra bonus favor out of it. But something told him Emma would be useless to him very quickly. Fuck, the whole world might be useless to him.

But he was going to stay the hells out of the three-way war that was about to break out, even if it meant the world ended.

The Idol. The Bishop. The Mirror.

The Blade was off the board, not that Robert figured Gigi would be stupid enough to throw her lot back in with the rest. That was if she survived what Kirkbride had done to her. Maybe she'd fight with Emma, but most of the Blade was dead, so Robert figured that would be fairly useless.

And usually Robert would always count out the Mirror in any kind of brawl. They were nerdy, reclusive types. More likely to huff indignantly and stare down their nose at you, not rip a man to shreds.

But Saltonstall...

Robert wasn't sure what it was like to be pulled apart at the joints by monstrous tentacles from the void, but judging by the looks etched on the faces of the corpses he had seen in the halls of the asylum before it burned? It wasn't fun.

So he was going to just take his quiet win and go lurk in the shadows until the dust settled. Speaking of dust, he coughed as he lifted a wooden door that was now more charcoal than anything else and tossed it aside. It kicked up all sorts of debris he was sure would do wonders for his lungs.

"Ahh, there we are." He grinned. Fantastic. He was worried he'd have to dig all day! Reaching into the crevice he had uncovered with the door, he grunted as he strained at the end of his reach. He could just barely—maybe—just a little farther—and—"Ah-hah!"

From out of the darkness, he wrenched a waxy object. The hand of a martyr, preserved and rendered into a candle. The wicks were unlit. But that was fine by him.

Kirkbride had been such a *pain in his ass.* He never listened to Robert, no matter how often he warned him. Sitting down on a chunk of roofing, he blew some of the dust and bits of burnt something that had coated the sacred object of the Dark Society of the Candle.

"I told that stupid bastard that ascension was suicide. And look where that got him." Robert turned the candle over. It wasn't damaged, nor did he suspect it would be. Nothing ever damaged the candle. Nor would it ever, ever burn low. "But Thaddeus was never the type to listen to his superiors, was he?"

Robert chuckled as he kicked his legs out in front of him, groaning from the exhaustion of digging through the remains of the asylum. "I told him the Candle needed to stay in the shadows, where we belonged. Not front and center. But some fools just can't be talked off their cliffs, can they?" He peered down at the candle. It didn't talk back, but that never stopped him from talking to *it.* Robert was fine with that. He'd heard rumors of the mirror's artifact being a bit *chatty,* and he wanted none of that bullshit.

"I figured the moment Emma stepped in those doors, Kirkbride was as good as dead, and I wasn't wrong. But I gotta admit." He turned his head to observe the level of carnage. "I didn't expect this. Lost a lot of good men and women in there. Eh." He shrugged. "We'll just raise them back up, won't we?"

Hefting up from the ground, he grunted. He was going to be sore in the morning. "C'mon, boys, let's go back to the docks." He started off down the path. "Where we belong."

"Yeah, boss," one of the nearby men said. It felt good to be called that again. Real good.

Debt paid, Emma Mather.
Not like you'll live long enough to know it.

CHAPTER TEN

"Troublesome. Troublesome, but not impossible." Tudor Gardner smiled gently at his follower as he placed his hands on their shoulders. "You must believe, my friend. It is in that faith that you will find the strength to overcome."

The man nodded. He straightened his back, his expression turning to one of grim determination. Good. He would need that determination. Because many of them had already been lost to the creature that was once Saltonstall. And many more would go that way before the night was through.

"The chosen will come to us, though she does not know it. They always come to us, don't they? Oh, they might scream and fuss, but that is only the surface fear." Tudor balled up a fist and placed it over his own heart. "Deep down inside, they feel the call within them that drew every single one of us here. The call to a greater power. The call to *belong*. The call to right all the injustices in this world."

"She is protected." His follower frowned.

"She is. For now. But she will allow herself to become vulnerable, my friend. Mark my words. She wishes to be free

—free of the monster. Free of the cage of flesh that was made for her. Free of the shadows in her mind." Tudor smiled reassuringly again. "Give her the option to run from his side, and she will flee. We simply need to engineer such a moment."

The man bowed and left, leaving Tudor alone in his small chapel. The candles in the old crypt flickered against the brick walls that arched overhead. He had repurposed the space for his use, for sadly they must worship their god in the shadows. But he didn't begrudge the populace their fear. The same as he didn't begrudge Emma hers.

It was normal to be afraid of the unknown. It was normal to fear "death" when one was uncertain of what was to come.

But Tudor knew what was coming.

As he turned to the altar behind him, he smiled. There, upon the dais, was a glowing green crystal, clasped in the claw of a creature not of this world. It pulsed, low and rhythmic, like the breathing of a living thing.

"What of the wayward Host?"

Tudor glanced over at the young woman who had spoken. Her short, dark hair barely reached her ears. She was one of his newer acolytes, though she showed no less promise than many of his elder members.

"He will come home." He turned back to the crystal. Reaching out his hand, he gently hovered it over the stone. He could feel the warmth against his palm, though he knew no heat truly radiated from it. "When she is here, he will come back to us. Our god has spoken, and our god has never led us astray. Now, go, all of you, and leave me to my prayer. I must prepare for what is to come. And you must all prepare for the task ahead."

He heard the rest of his acolytes leave, exiting the crypt and heading up the stairs to the defunct church they used as their current home. Not even the Church of the Benevolent God had all the money in the world, and it had been easy enough to purchase the land out from under them and force the structure to close.

The Bishop and the Cardinals had squacked and moaned, but there was little they could do. Their resources might not be unlimited—but Tudor's were. Or at least, it was as close as anyone could reasonably ask.

There were benefits of being the golden son of a golden family, and practicing law was always a lucrative business.

But he didn't care a lick for any of it. Not a damn dollar of it meant a thing to him. All that mattered was *this*—this higher purpose.

Soon, the crystal would shatter, and the end of the world would come. He would rip open the gate to the aether and pull all the lost angels and demons home.

Perhaps he would create hell.

Perhaps he would create heaven.

Either way, it would be *glorious*.

Kneeling at the altar, he bowed his head and began to pray.

Emma walked arm-in-arm with Rafe as they headed up the street toward the corner market. He was humming to himself, something she wasn't certain she'd ever heard him do before. She couldn't help but glance up at him with a smile.

"What?" He arched an eyebrow over his thin framed glasses. "Am I not allowed to hum?"

"You are." She chuckled. "I just wish your happiness wasn't because you're planning on destroying half the city."

"Not nearly half. Likely no more than a quarter, though I can't say for certain. And that is not why I'm content, Emma."

He lifted her hand to his lips and placed a kiss to the backs of her knuckles. "It is because you're here."

"Oh, don't get sappy." She playfully smacked his arm. "It's unnatural for you."

"I see. I am not allowed to be happy, nor am I allowed to express my appreciation for you?" He rolled his eyes. "So, you would have me brooding at my desk at all hours, then? Ignoring you?"

"I mean…" When he grumbled under his breath, she laughed. "I'm teasing, you fool."

"I am a fool now? Are you always so abusive to those you're with?" He tried to keep a straight face, but the flicker of a smile betrayed him.

"Always." Hugging his arm, she grinned. "And I wouldn't climb on your high horse, seeing as you're a mass murderer."

"I am not a—" He paused. "Fine. I suppose. But that is hardly the topic of conversation and has nothing to do with it. You're conflating morals—oh, don't look at me like that."

Now she was giggling. She shouldn't be. Nothing about her situation was funny. But it was. She was always the type to find humor in the bleakest of moments.

I need to find a way to esc—

"I know you're planning to escape."

She froze in her tracks. He stopped as well and turned to smile at her slyly. "Come, now. I'm not a fool. You are likely intending to 'make a break for it' and tearing off to the Church to see the Bishop, aren't you?" He narrowed his eyes slightly, stepping up close to her, using his height to his advantage.

"I—uh—" Her face went hot. "Um. Well."

"It would be what I would do, given the situation." He cupped her chin with his hand, his expression still wry. "To go to see if you can broker a truce. Aren't you?"

"I…um…" She gave in and sighed, her shoulders slumping in defeat. "Yeah."

"Good."

"What?" She blinked.

"Good," he repeated. "You've learned not to bother lying to me." Resting his thumb against the hollow of her chin, he leaned down to graze his lips against hers. "All right."

"Wh—what?" She pulled back, staring at him in shock. "Did you hit your head?"

"No. I've merely learned the futility of trying to stop you when you're set on something." He poked her in the forehead. "You are *infuriatingly* stubborn. And reckless to the point of borderline suicidal. But I suppose that is why we enjoy you so much."

She wanted to argue. She really did. But he was, as usual, correct. "So…what does this mean?"

"Well, we have two options." He straightened his back, rolling his shoulders. They audibly popped. "We can tie you up in our basement and keep you as our prisoner. Which, truthfully, has immense appeal on many levels." Voice dropping, his tone oozed sin and depravity. There wasn't any question as to what he meant.

Her cheeks went warm again, though not for the same reason as before.

"And I don't think you would mind it nearly as much as you'd like to pretend you would. That is option one. Which isn't out of the question, mind you." He smirked. "Option two is that I escort you there and allow you to have your conversations with the Bishop under my supervision."

"Isn't that dangerous?"

"Immensely. He has dealt with many, many Saints in his years in Arnsmouth." The playfully devious tone left him, his features smoothing into a far more serious expression. "He is far more likely to 'black bag' me than have a conversation with you. There is a good chance I would lose, and he would drag me off to dispose of me by whatever method he uses. I don't know what would become of me, but you would never see me again, Emma."

The thought of it broke her heart. Frowning, she hugged him around the waist, pressing her cheek to his chest. "No. I won't let that happen."

Gently, he wrapped his arms around her and returned the embrace. "If anyone could will the world into a different shape, it is you, Emma. But in this instance, you have to understand the risks involved."

"I could go alone."

"You know how stupid that is. The Idol would have you within ten feet of the house." He held her just a little tighter. "We will not allow it."

"I can't simply accept that you have to kill half—"

"Quarter."

Growling, she glared at him and found him smiling. "Quarter. I can't just let you do something that terrible."

"There is very little that you could ask of me that I wouldn't give you, Emma. But I'm sorry. You have no say in this. If the Idol takes you, they could end the world as we know it. Let alone what they would do to you."

Having her soul ripped out of her body and replaced with somebody else didn't seem like a great way to go, she had to admit. She held him tighter and sighed. "I don't know what to do."

"I say we pick up a nice dinner. We will enjoy our evening. And in the morning, you and I will phone the Bishop and see what can be done."

That...almost sounded reasonable. With a weak nod, she pushed away from him, though she decided to take hold of his hand. They resumed their walk toward the shop. Was she really going to pick out a steak and some ingredients, maybe even a fruit tart, knowing what was going to happen?

Did she have a choice?

Probably not.

She could trip him. Then what? He'd scrape his knee, complain about the damage to his suit, and then tie her up in his basement to torment her.

And no, that didn't sound nearly as bad as it should.

But—

Several things happened at once.

There was a roar of a car engine. A screech.

"Emma!" Rafe grabbed her by the shoulders and threw her. Literally *threw* her. Her feet left the ground as she went some ten feet before hitting the pavement.

The world spun around her as everything went up, down, up, down, up, down. Sky, pavement, sky, pavement, pain, sky, pavement.

She knocked her head on something. It might have been a lamppost. She wasn't quite sure. But suddenly the reeling world was also blurry. She tried to get to her feet, and while she was suddenly upright, it wasn't her doing.

Someone had grabbed her by the arms. And it wasn't Rafe. Because he—

"Rafe! No, R—" Her scream was cut off by a hand over her mouth. Not just a hand—but a rag. And the rag smelled strange, like chemicals. But it didn't matter. She struggled, trying to free herself.

Rafe was pinned to the building by the wreck of a car. The front windshield was shattered, and there was blood everywhere. The driver was slumped over the wheel, head busted open. They were clearly dead.

Rafe was draped over the crumpled hood that was now smoking. He was limp. Maybe dead. *Again.* And she—

Her eyes rolled into the back of her head as the world went dim around her.

WAKE UP, idiot.

Wake the fuck up, you useless sack of flesh!

Rafe came to with a jolt. He could smell burning meat. Oh. It wasn't meat, it was flesh. And some of it was the dead driver in the vehicle that had him pinned to a brick wall. The rest of it was his own burning skin.

Oddly, it didn't hurt. He watched it turn black and begin to flake like a steak left on a grill for too long. *How bizarre.*

Focus, you utter shit for brains.

Lifting his head, he let out a grunt. His hips were shattered. His legs were shattered. No matter—they'd heal. He let the darkness within him take control. The car was hurled away from him by the mass of black tendrils that took over the street, fading daylight be damned. The light was the only thing that hurt him.

But he had to save Emma.

His Emma.

Unfortunately, it seemed he was just a few seconds too late. It took him a moment to find her—oh, his skull was also cracked. That explained why it was so terribly hard to see straight. There, twenty feet away, was Emma. In the arms of a stranger who was busy putting her unconscious form into the back of another vehicle.

No.

That was not how tonight was going to end.

Snarling in rage, he was oblivious to the carnage he unleashed around him on the innocents of the city. The bystanders were screaming and running away. He let those who were fast enough escape. But those who had been knocked down or simply tripped? Chaff. Unimportant.

Bullets embedded in his flesh. The wounds slowed him down. The idiots who were firing at him died quickly, consumed by the many within him. But the damage was *just* enough.

She was gone.

"Emma!"

But it was too late. All the power of the Mirror, of the multitude within the void, and he was helpless to watch the car drive away. He had let himself become distracted. He had focused on making her happy, not safe. He was an utter fool.

The street was in ruins. Blood was splattered along the walls. More than one vehicle was in flames, and a dozen or more victims were now part of the darkness. But Emma was gone.

Then the realization hit him. This was perfect. This played right into his hands!

He began to laugh. No, *they* began to laugh. Yes, this was truly perfect! "Oh, Emma. In trying to stall the inevitable, I fear you have gone and quickened the pace of things." Loosening their tie, they smiled to themselves. "Now I will simply just have to come and save you again. And in doing so, destroy *another* of the Societies."

Yes, fine, she was in danger.

But this was a perfect excuse—no, permission—to destroy the Idol, once and for all.

"Never say we didn't try. We really *were* going to play nice. Oh, well." Undoing his cufflinks, he rolled up his sleeves. Enough was enough. Enough weakness. Enough mercy. Enough compassion.

Enough of being *human.*

CHAPTER ELEVEN

Patrick could not have been happier as he watched Gigi walk across the room. She was tentative and slow, her steps a little unsure. But she was walking. She was going to live. He'd made the mistake of trying to help her across the room and had received a scathing glare and a snippy comment. She didn't need his help.

Not that he had any suspicion that the woman would be stopped by anything short of an act of the Benevolent God. He tried not to think too hard about how he might factor into that, should it come to pass.

She might not want his help, but he stayed close, regardless. Just in case she stumbled and fell. Over the past week, her scalp had healed, and her hair was just starting to grow back, though it was still little more than stubble.

"As charming as this…little game is, I think it's time for me to go home." Gigi leaned against his desk for balance. He had found her some white linen clothes that were usually kept for pilgrims. It was offensive to him, to put someone so beautiful in something so meager.

"Home?" He frowned.

"Oh, don't pout." She sat down in the chair at the desk and let out a puff of air. Walking was still clearly an exertion for her. "As lovely as your…eh…living quarters are, and as charming as your wardrobe options might be, let alone the food—"

"Yeah, yeah. I get it." He smiled faintly. He was sorry to see her go. The past two weeks with her had been stressful, but he had become used to her presence. And sleeping on the floor. Even if his back would be glad to be in his bed again. "I don't suppose I can blame you."

Picking up a small hand mirror he had hunted down at her request, she held it close to her face, touching her skin and pulling here or there as she examined the shadows under her eyes. "Better. But it all needs fixing."

"Fixing." He knew of the power of the Blade—the gift to exchange flesh for flesh. Shapeshifters, for lack of a better word. But it came with a price. "You can heal on your own, you know."

"And where is the fun in that?" Gigi shot him a brief glance before turning her focus back to the mirror. "Like I said, don't pout. Although you are awfully cute when you do. You know who I am, and you know what I can do. If I had the choice to stay like this, injured and weak with—ugh—this lack of *hair*." She ran her hand over the stubble. "Why would I?"

"Oh, I don't know." He threw up his hands in frustration. "Because the other option is wielding dark magic that weakens the veil between you and the void. Between all of us and the void."

"Now you're angry." Putting the hand mirror back down, she turned to him. "And you're very, *very* sexy when you're angry. But I'm still not sure I'm up to ride you like a bronco just yet."

His cheeks went warm. "Gigi."

She grinned in victory. "And if you take me home, I can fix *that*, too."

With a beleaguered sigh, he wiped his hand over his face. "Fine. But I'm taking you there myself."

"What, afraid I'll get into trouble along the way?" Somehow, battered and bruised as she was, broken down and defeated, Gigi still managed to act as though she owned the entire room around her. She draped herself over the back of the chair, smiling at him in that fiendish, playful way that made his stomach twist into knots.

"Precisely." He turned his attention to his living quarters. The walls were painted an austere white. All of the furniture in the room belonged to the Church, not to him. A bed, a desk, and a dresser. The only artwork on the walls was the iron, double-ended cross that represented his faith. Two T's, reflected horizontally, accented with twisting curls. There was one window, though it did little good. It was too small to let in much sunlight, and the walls of the church were three-foot-thick stone. *And* the panes were stained glass. It gave the room an occasional splash of color when the sun hit the building just right.

He had to admit, it was pretty bleak for what she was used to. "This really isn't that bad," he murmured.

Gigi chuckled. "It's fine for what it is, darling. But it's hardly my style, you have to admit." She pushed up from the chair and let out a small hiss of pain as she did.

He fought the urge to rush to her side.

She must have seen him take a halted step forward, judging by the look she gave him. "I'm not the kind of person who appreciates charity, priest. You've certainly given me enough of yours."

"It isn't...I'm not...this isn't *charity*, Gigi."

"Then you're simply nursing your pet cultist back to full health so I can help you weather the oncoming storm." She brushed herself off and tried to make herself as presentable as possible in the white linen clothes. "May I at least have a coat? I look *atrocious.*" She waved her hand. "Never mind. I'm sure whatever passes for fashion around here will simply be the last insult that ends my life."

Patrick smirked at that, but his amusement didn't last long. Walking up to her, he gently placed his hand on her arm. "This isn't charity. And this isn't me nursing my 'pet cultist' back to life."

"Then, I told you not to get attached." She pulled her arm from his grasp.

"I suppose you did." He walked to the coat hook on the wall by the door and slung on his black cassock. "I'll get the car pulled around."

"I might as well start walking to the door." Gigi sighed. "It'll take me an hour to get there at the pace I'm moving."

"You were tortured. You nearly died. Let yourself heal, and try not to blame yourself for the condition you're in." He opened the door.

"I do not—" Gigi grunted. "I'm merely frustrated. Go. Get your car, before I throw something at your head."

"Yes, ma'am." He shut the door behind him, grinning to himself. He knew what would follow next.

"I am not old enough to be a ma'am!" Something smacked into the door. Likely a shoe.

Tucking his hands into his pockets, he chuckled. *Don't get attached.* That's what she had told him. And he hadn't been able to listen. Not before, and certainly not now.

It was clear he was far past that point.

He was attached.

And likely more so.

Damn it.

Emma was sick of waking up feeling like she had been hit by a car. *No, it wasn't me. That was Rafe. He's the one who got hit by the c—*

Shit. Shit, shit, shit!

"Easy, now, easy, there...chloroform can make some people very sick. Take slow breaths. Here, a glass of water." Someone was carefully helping her sit up. Her head was reeling, and for a second, she wondered if she was going to retch.

She had also had enough of retching lately.

Slowly, very slowly, the world came into focus. She was sitting on a cot by a brick wall. The clay looked ancient and crumbling, the surface spackled over in some places but flaking in others. The bricks created arches along the wall. The room was too dark to see all of it, as the only source of light were a few dozen candles flickering in—

Candles.

Thrashing, she pushed away whoever was sitting next to her. She let out a low, terrified, and keening wail that she didn't even recognize as coming from herself. She hadn't ever made a noise like that before. She was suddenly on her feet, panic taking over, though she didn't make it four steps before her reeling head caught up with her body and she collapsed to the ground.

Whoever she had shoved was beside her, carefully helping her back to her feet. "Calm down, Miss Mather. It's all right."

"N—no—Kirkbride—" Fear was sending her heart racing in a tempo that was likely not helping how dizzy she was.

The man sounded confused. "Kirkbride is dead. Dead and gone, you—" He let out a quiet hum. "Ah. The candles. No, Emma. We just don't have electricity down here, I'm afraid." He chuckled. "You're quite safe from them, I promise you."

Kirkbride was dead. She knew that. She was shivering as the man led her back to the cot and helped her sit back down. She couldn't take her eyes off the burning candles along the wall.

"They're simply wax. Normal, everyday beeswax. Nothing to be alarmed about." He knelt at her feet and smiled up at her. It was only then that she managed to shift her focus to whomever was talking.

The first thought she had was, *goodness, he's cute.* In that boyish, warm, Prince Charming kind of way. He wasn't her type—apparently, she went with the dark, stern, brooding, evil, monstrous, murderous ones—but she expected he always had a date to the opera.

He also looked rich.

It was strange that there was a certain level of polish that came with someone's social status. Maybe it was the clothes he was wearing, or the way his hair looked perfect. Or the fact that it looked like he hadn't seen an ounce of sun more than he ever intended to.

He was smiling at her with such gentle warmth that it was hard to be afraid of him.

"Who…" She groaned as her head spun again. She leaned back against the brick wall, shutting her eyes for a moment.

"Tudor Gardner. I'm absolutely *thrilled* to finally meet you, Miss Mather. I'm so very sorry about how we had to bring you here. But you're a hard one to catch, it seems." He chuckled.

"The Idol." She managed to glare at him. "You're with the Idol."

"I am. And I'm afraid we haven't gotten off on the right foot, have we?" Gardner sat back on his heels and placed his hands on his thighs. He looked harmless, but she knew better. "I'm not going to hurt you. I'm not going to torture you. If anything, it seems like you need a place to hide out for a while as you figure out what to do about the professor, hum?"

That was vaguely true. "You want to sacrifice my soul. Rip it out of my body and replace it with *something*. And you want to end the entire *fucking* world. Pardon me if I'm not so enthusiastic about being here."

Tudor opened his mouth to argue, paused, and then shut it again for a long moment. With a shake of his head, he sighed. "I can see why you believe that. I'm sorry that you do. I can explain all of it, if you will let me."

"And if I want to leave?" She narrowed her eyes. Not like she was at all convinced of her ability to stand and walk at the moment.

"Then you're free to go. I recommend you…wait for your dizziness to pass, however." He flashed her a sweet and innocent smile. She didn't buy it. "I would just ask that you let me speak first. Let me explain. I'm sure once you know the reasons behind our actions, you'll understand."

"You've tried real hard to kidnap me to just let me walk out the front door."

"That's true. That's very true. But it has been in an attempt to help you, Emma—an attempt to *save* you." He reached out to take her hand. She quickly pulled away. Frowning at her reaction, he settled his hand back into his lap. "Your brother came to us in dire need. *Dire* need. Voices had begun to plague him, the likes of which he had never known before—they whispered in a language he could not understand. An infinite number of them. And no drugs, or alcohol, or anything else could keep them at bay."

She felt the color drain from her face as she went cold. She shrank away from him. An infinite number of voices…

After all that had happened, she had forgotten that Elliot was Rafe's *student*. "Rafe…Rafe did this?"

"Not intentionally." Tudor smiled sympathetically, green eyes filled with nothing but earnestness. "He didn't mean to hurt your brother. But the darkness can…latch on to those around them. It seems the voices just want you in a very different way."

Now she was fighting not to blush. "For now. They've promised that on my deathbed they'll consume me." Cringing, she fought off the sudden urge to cry. No, she had enough of fainting, of retching, and crying. She was sick of it all.

Rafe was the reason Elliot had been plagued with the darkness. And in his desperation, he turned to the Idol. The only group who could "cure" him.

Cure him by sending his soul to the void.

Shutting her eyes, she let out a wavering breath. "What happened to Elliot's soul?"

"We don't know, to be blunt. It might have been dashed to smithereens. Or maybe it is at peace with the Benevolent God. That isn't our place to say—not yet. Not until the gate to the aether is thrown wide, and all is known to *everyone.* Not just a select few." It was a clear jab at the Mirror.

"I don't want to die. I don't want to go off into the 'aether' or whatever. I am not going to sacrifice my soul for you." She went to stand, instantly regretted it, and promptly sat back down. "You have until I can walk in a straight line before I test out your claim that I'm not a prisoner. Kirkbride said the same thing."

The memory of being strapped to that table, with that awful machine sucking out her blood and replacing it with —with—

She felt dizzy as her heartbeat raced. She never had panic attacks before. And something about this fear was different. It wasn't the *fun,* exciting, dangerous fear she was used to. This wasn't like running from angry animals or crossing rickety bridges.

This fear was deeper. It was disgusting. It was rancid. And it made her want to curl in a ball and make it all go away.

"Shh. Here, please, drink some water." He reached over to a small wooden table next to the cot and picked up a glass. He handed it to her. Taking it tentatively, she stared down into the liquid.

It was probably drugged.

It was really most certainly drugged.

"It isn't drugged." He smiled. She doubted he could read her mind. She was just that obvious.

"Right."

"I want you awake to talk to you. And you aren't trying to claw my face off, so there's no reason to sedate you." He shrugged. "And like I said, if you want to leave, you can leave."

Water would help her get her head screwed on straight. And the chloroform had left a sour taste in her mouth. With a beleaguered sigh, she took a sip. It didn't taste funny, so at least there was that. "I want to go home."

"I know you do. And I wish I could deliver that for you. But I can't. You're in too deep now, Emma. You know you are." Tudor reached out to put his hand on her knee and then thought better of it. "I'm not sure if the professor can leave the city anymore, but even if he can't…he'd find a way to get you back."

"When I was gone, I saw this moldy ink everywhere I went. I was blacking out randomly. I think I would just wander back here on my own." She took another sip of the water. She didn't trust Tudor—not by a longshot—but there was no harm in a conversation.

At the moment.

And he wasn't trying to murder her.

At the moment.

Besides, this was an opportunity she had been dying for since she came to Arnsmouth in the first place. "Tell me more about what happened to Elliot."

"Of course." Tudor shifted to sit on the ground, seemingly having no problem with the gritty bricks of the basement floor and what it might do to his expensive-looking trousers. "He tried every method he could to get rid of the shadows. He went to the Blade, who couldn't help him. He went to the professor and begged to have bits of his mind removed, the same as Saltonstall did to you. But his issue was not a corruption of the body or the mind—but of the soul."

"And that's where you come in."

"Exactly." His smile never wavered. "He wanted his pain to end, no matter the cost. And we were uniquely suited to help him."

"By ripping his soul out."

Tudor wrinkled his nose. "We don't tear souls out, Emma. We allow the soul to *leave*. It's a willing choice. Your brother knelt at the altar and opened himself to the Idol, and it took only what he wanted to give."

Sadly, she couldn't argue that. She knew her brother well enough to know how far he was willing to go to be free. A single tear escaped her eye, and she wiped at it angrily. Damn it all.

"Grief does not make you weak, Emma. Your twin was part of you, as you were part of him. In his own way, he did this in an attempt to protect you. I fear he wasn't successful." Tudor tilted his head with a thoughtful hum. "Are you hungry?"

She was. Not like she was going to admit it. But her silent glare told him enough, and his face split wide in a grin. "I'll have someone fetch dinner. Please. Take shelter here for as long as you wish. The decision to stay or go is yours and yours alone. Get some rest. I fear you might have hit your head in addition to the chloroform."

That last part was probably true. Pulling her legs up onto

the cot, she settled back against the wall. "Fine. I'll eat, then go."

"Great!" He slapped his legs with both hands and pushed up to his feet. "Stay, drink the water, and catch your breath. We'll talk over dinner. Then you can choose whether you want to sleep here or leave."

It was a dangerous plan. But out there in the city was also a very furious Rafe that she had, to be fair, been trying to escape. *Maybe I can talk Tudor into letting me talk to the Bishop. Maybe.*

"All right." She frowned. All her choices were bad ones. But at the moment, she was probably punch-drunk, half drugged, starving, and dehydrated. Taking the opportunity to rest a little wouldn't do her any harm.

Unless he was going to come back and kill her. But she doubted it. They needed her.

"Fantastic." He began to walk away with a cheerful whistle.

"Wait—one question before you go. Where am I?" She gestured at the walls. "What're these lumpy arch things along the walls?"

"Oh. Hah." With the expression of a cherub, he shot her the most dazzling smile she had ever seen. "This is a crypt, Miss Mather."

And there went all her meager comfort.

She'd gone from being held "debatably" prisoner in an asylum to a crypt in less than a month.

Great.

CHAPTER TWELVE

Patrick wasn't sure what to expect as he followed Gigi into her building. The doorman looked extremely concerned at the sight of her, but she held her head high and stormed through the expensive lobby and to the elevator as though everything were perfectly normal.

Never mind her condition, and never mind the fact that she was being escorted by the Bishop of the Church of the Benevolent God. Gigi smirked as she stood in the elevator. "There will be rumors now, you know."

Patrick shrugged. "Never cared much for them either way."

"I've always found them rather fun." She leaned back against the wall, placing her hands on the railing on either side of her. "I do love to hear what they cook up next. Oh, perhaps this time they will think I've been converted. Much more entertaining than the time they decided I was, in fact, a lizard."

He shot her a raised eyebrow. "A lizard?"

She gestured aimlessly. "Idiots are idiots, darling. They can't exist without some pile of nonsense to believe. Otherwise, they have no meaning in life. Rather like religion." His frown made her laugh. "Oh, lighten up, will you?"

"I don't feel like there's much to lighten up over."

"Pah. I've been through worse." The elevator dinged, and the doors slid open. "Trust me." She strolled from the little metal box as though she were walking out onto a catwalk. Nothing about what she had suffered seemed to slow her down. It was impressive, and honestly...he was a little jealous.

He wasn't sure he'd be that strong in the face of the same. With a shake of his head, he followed her, heading down the hallway. The front desk had given her an extra key, since her things were likely burned and buried in the rubble that was the asylum.

She unclicked the door and headed into her dark apartment. Patrick hesitated at the doorjamb, unsure of what to do. Should he go in? Was he welcome? She was home safe, so he should probably just—

"Oh, get *in here,* you big idiot."

The tension left his shoulders a little as he stepped inside her home. He expected everything to be red velvet and taffeta. And it was lavish, that was for certain—especially by his standards. But it was tastefully done, and all in the modern style of thin metal and sharp, angled lines.

Gigi was standing in the center of the room, holding a fluffy white Persian cat close to her chest. "Momma missed you." She kissed the cat's head. The animal was purring loud enough to be heard from where he was and was nuzzling into her cheek in return.

Patrick furrowed his brow. It had been nearly a month since Gigi had been abducted from her club.

"Mykel," she answered his silent question. "We had an agreement. If anything ever happened, he was to go underground. Pretend I never existed. If I didn't make it out, that way the Blade would still have a good leader. I only had one rule—take care of my little baby here." She smiled and buried her face in the cat's fluff.

She was clearly trying not to cry. He couldn't help it. Stepping forward, he placed his hand on her back.

"I'm all right." She lifted her head and inhaled deeply, using the breath to calm down. "Just happy to be home. And —ugh. I am ready to fix this mess." She grunted and put the cat down on the ground.

The purring animal wove between his legs, leaving large swaths of white fur clinging to his black pants. It made him smile. He leaned down to scratch the cat's head.

"I want to show you something." Gigi was headed off deeper into her apartment.

Straightening, he followed, curious as to what she was about to show him. Maybe this was the point she turned a gun on him and shot him dead, though he doubted it. When he found himself standing in her bedroom, however, his face went hot.

"Oh, simmer." She chuckled at him. "Don't look so damn *nervous.*"

Clearing his throat, he mumbled something unintelligible. He wasn't even sure what he had been trying to say.

Gigi went to a large wardrobe that dominated one wall and opened its elegant double doors, revealing mirrors on both sides. The interior was a combination of hangers, revealing long, flowing silk dresses, and a set of drawers. She opened the middle one. Patrick knew what it contained without going any closer. He could tell by all the lace.

"Your Investigators have searched this place at least a dozen times."

That was true.

"And I've had several other uninvited guests over the years. But no one's ever found this." She pulled a knife from the drawer. It was old, the blade rusted and dented. The wooden handle was worn smooth, though it might have once been carved into the shape of the head of a horse or a dragon. It was so weathered it was impossible to tell.

It looked like a piece of garbage, honestly. Patrick blinked. "Is that…"

"It is." She chuckled. "Sitting here in my drawer of undergarments. No one is ever brave enough to search through those." She shut the drawer with her hip. Pulling a dressing gown from a hanger, she tossed it over her shoulder.

He knew all about the power of the Blade. But he had never seen the artifact in question. "What are you going to do with it?"

"Fix this mess, of course!" She gestured at her head. "I can't be seen wandering around this city without *hair*, darling. Don't be absurd."

"What…but…"

"I'm simply just going to cut my palm. A little bit of blood is all it will take. That's all it's ever really taken. Some people just try too hard, that's all." She lifted a shoulder in a half-shrug. "Pity, those who pray so very hard but miss the point."

"And what's the point?"

"That this gift is only for those who truly understand desperation." She frowned down at the blade, and then shook her head. "Anyway." She smiled, her demeanor snapping back. The brief sadness confused him, but he said nothing. Gigi headed toward what was likely a bathroom. "I'll be back in an hour or so. I'm going to soak in some hot water and smother myself in oils to clean the *stench* of that place off of me."

He pointed a thumb toward the door. "Shall I—" He never got the rest of the question out.

"Make yourself at home, darling. If I know Mykel, he knew I was on my way home and has stocked the fridge. Play with Margot. I'm sure she's been frightfully lonely. There's some alcohol hidden in a back cabinet of the kitchen. Or come join me in the bathroom if you like." She winked at him wryly.

His face went warm again.

"You're so shy, it's adorable. All steam and hotheaded when it comes to violence. But a little affection, and you turn into a schoolboy. Men." She leaned against the jamb of the bathroom. "Oh, and if you'd like bigger tits on me, now's the time to say it."

"I—*what?*"

Gigi laughed, her face lighting up with it. It was the happiest he had seen her since he had pulled her from the asylum. "I'm being perfectly serious. Do you like them as they are? How about my ass? Oh—are you a brunette fan, or would you prefer red?"

"I—think—I think you're—you're just fine as you are, and —I—" He was a stuttering mess. And the more he tripped over his words, the happier about it she looked. Groaning in dismay, he put a hand over his face. "I'm not having this conversation."

When her hand touched his arm, he almost jolted in surprise. He hadn't heard her walk across the room, which wasn't too surprising, considering how thick the carpets were. She was smiling up at him, positively beaming, and he was taken once more by how beautiful she was.

"You truly are the sweetest thing." She reached up and placed her palm to his cheek. "Thank you. For all of what you've done."

Guilt wracked him. "I should have—"

"Maybe. But you came before it was too late, and that's what matters." She went up on her tiptoes, though he still had to duck for her to reach him. She kissed his cheek. "I'll be right back. Tits and ass unchanged."

The sound he made was a strangled one, and it sent Gigi back into peals of laughter.

"Oh, you." She patted his arm before turning on her heel and heading into the bathroom. She shut the door *most* of the way but left it ajar. "Margot likes to play with the water," she called out to him. "Before you implode from the scandal of it all."

"Am I that predictable?"

"Yes."

Chuckling, he headed to the living room and sat down on one of the plush, expensive-looking sofas. Margot hopped up next to him a moment later and clearly decided he didn't have enough white fur on his clothes. She proudly stomped onto his lap, rubbed up against him, and purred so loudly that he wondered if she wasn't part car engine.

Smiling, he stroked the animal's back and then scratched her ears. "What is it with psychopaths in this town having cute cats? Ah, well."

The sound of running water from the bathtub distracted Margot instantly. Her ears perked, and he watched the irises of her blue eyes go wide in excitement. A second later, and she was off to join her owner, just as Gigi had predicted.

It wasn't until then that Patrick realized the cat's eyes matched Gigi's in color. Sky blue. He wondered which came first—since Gigi could change her shape at will.

Leaning back on the sofa, he shut his eyes and thought about his insane predicament.

He must have been exhausted, because he woke up out of a dead sleep when someone touched his shoulder. "Hnh—" He jolted.

Gigi. She was standing in front of him, smiling in the way she did when he was acting like a fool. Which was to say, most of the time. She looked just as she did before the asylum. Her hair was down to her chin in platinum blonde curls. Her skin was unmarred from lingering bruises, and the shadows under her eyes were gone. She was also only wearing her dressing gown, revealing very quickly that she hadn't changed anything else.

"Much better, don't you think?"

"I—"

Before he could react, she straddled his lap and settled onto his thighs, spreading her fingers over his chest. "I think it's time to kick some of the rust off. What do you say, priest?" She leaned in and kissed him, slow and with such passion that, without thinking, his hands went to her hips to hold on for dear life.

When she broke away, he was almost breathless. "But—"

"Shush." She put a thin finger over his lips. Leaning in close to his ear, she whispered to him. "I want you to bend me over every piece of furniture in this damn place like we're two drunkards staggering out of a bar. I want you to *fuck me*, do you understand, stallion?"

Another strangled noise left him, for very different reasons than before.

"Good boy." She patted his chest and flashed him a wicked, sinful grin. "Let's get started."

EMMA DIDN'T KNOW what to expect when half a dozen people came down the stairs to the crypt carrying all sorts of random things. A table, two chairs, a white tablecloth—

They were setting up a dinner table?

She pressed her back to the wall. She had been able to get up and wander the basement a little, but her head still felt woozy and detached. The stairs had been a daunting challenge she hadn't been willing to take on just yet.

Because as much as she hated to admit it, Gardner was

right. Going outside meant Rafe would likely snatch her up in a heartbeat. And he was only a slightly safer option than the Idol.

What she needed to do was figure out how to reach the Bishop. Maybe Gardner would let her use a phone. But right now, she was watching a stream of humans in off-white clothing set up for dinner for two. In a crypt. By candlelight.

Gardner walked down the stairs with a warm smile on his face, as usual. "I promise I didn't mean for it to be so oddly romantic."

"If you bring your dates to a crypt, that certainly says a lot about you." She kept her back against the brick wall. "And none of it's good."

He chuckled and waved his hand dismissively. "Sadly, no, I can't say I've ever done that."

"Where did you get all of this?" She figured he was a rich kid, but having a full silver setup on demand was particularly odd.

Tudor walked to the table and pulled a chair out for her. "The hotel across the street from here. I would much rather have just taken you *there*, but...well. You know. The professor. And whoever else is hunting you."

"Seems like everyone in Arnsmouth at this point."

He gestured at the seat. "Seems it. Please, sit. Let's eat. You'll feel better with something in your stomach."

She really hated it when lunatics were right about things. With a breath, she walked up to the chair and obediently sat down. He took the spot across from her and dismissed the people standing by the walls. They left up the stairs to what she assumed was the first floor.

Steak and lobster tail, a baked potato, and green beans. By the hells, it looked and smelled *amazing*. He even had a bottle of red wine, which he uncorked and poured them both a glass. It looked like the strangest date in the world.

Picking up a fork, she started with the potato.

"You always did eat food in the wrong order."

Looking up at him, she blinked. "Excuse me?"

He was grinning as if he knew a secret that she didn't. "I was wondering if you'd figure it out. But you've been through a lot."

She stared at him flatly. "Am I—do I know you?"

"You do. Think back." He picked up his fork and knife. "We were children. There was a rifle over the mantel, you dragged over a chair to get it because you wanted to fiddle with it…"

"Don't do it, Emma! You're going to get us in trouble!"

"Oh, Tudy, don't be such a spoilsport." The voice of her own childlike self rang in her head along with the high-pitched voice of a young boy.

"Oh—" Suddenly, it all connected in her head like lightning forking over the night sky. "Fuck—" She nearly dropped her fork. *"Tudy?"*

He cackled in laughter. "I admit I've grown up, and I look quite a bit different than the spindly child you probably remember."

"Your father and mine used to play cards, and—then you went off to boarding school, and I never saw you again." She hadn't seen him since she was maybe seven or eight. All those memories had been shoved into a filing cabinet in her head and stored away, likely never to be of use again. "I was trying to get the rifle. I was on the chair. Your father came down the hallway, and you panicked and pushed me—"

"You fell! I didn't push you." He waggled his fork at her. "I will die on a hill for that."

"Whatever. I fell and twisted my ankle."

"Didn't shed a tear. Just asked for ice, if I remember right." Tudor shook his head. "Even then, you were ironclad."

"I'm not. I've never been." She frowned down at her food.

"Certainly not anymore. I'm lost and being targeted by cults who want to *suck out my soul.*"

"I don't—we—" He sighed. "We aren't going to hurt you. I know it's so hard to believe."

"That I'm sitting in a crypt eating steak and lobster dinner with an old childhood acquaintance who has kidnapped me in order to remove my soul, summon a demon *or whatever,* and end the world? And that doesn't even touch Gigi, the asylum, Yuriel, or Rafe." She laughed, exhausted. "Yes. It's hard to believe. And if I had a way to burn it all to the ground, I would."

"Exactly!"

She furrowed her brow. "What?"

"That's what I'm trying to achieve, Emma. This world is broken, and on a downward spiral. It's only going to get worse, and I don't believe it'll ever get better. War, greed—the worst of humanity. These monsters you've met—the power of the Great Beast only takes what's within us and corrupts it further. Amplifies it. But the seeds of the disease had to already be planted there." His face smoothed, and he offered an apologetic smile. "Sorry. I get away from myself sometimes." He sipped his wine.

"I can tell." She decided she should eat more before she drank her own wine. If she didn't, she'd get utterly trashed, and she was also over being dizzy. "And I don't eat food in the wrong order. I'm going for the starch to settle my stomach."

"You always ate your veggies first." He smirked. "Don't deny it."

"Well, save the best for last, right?" She couldn't help but smile, but it faded quickly. "Tudor, I'm not going to agree to this."

His expression fell to a solemn one. "I know. But I have to

try." His expression perked up again. "But we'll talk after dinner. Enjoy your food. Relax. You're safe here, I promise."

"Can I use a phone?"

"Why?" He arched an eyebrow.

"To call the Bishop. Rafe is—he's going to go on a murder spree pretty soon, and I need to broker some kind of peace, or else you, the Bishop, Gigi, and everyone else associated in any way with the Great Beast is going to get devoured." She cringed. "And probably a lot more who just get in his way."

When his hand touched hers, she jerked in surprise. He pulled his hand back quickly. "Sorry, I—I've been told I'm too personal in my mannerisms. It's—"

"You've been that way your whole life." She smiled at the memory. "You were always quick to hug strangers." Tudy Gardner had been a nice young boy. They had run around together while their fathers played cards and did their best not to get into too much mischief.

And now he was the leader of a dangerous cult.

Who wanted to hollow her out like a gourd and cook a soup in her.

To end the world.

Tudor shrugged. "We can't fight who we are, or who we were meant to be. You can try to beat it out of a person—and trust me, that boarding school did its damnedest to do just that." He winced and shook his head. "But it isn't how life should be. They—" He paused. "Emma, can I tell you something?"

"I mean, I'm not sure what's stopping you. It's not like we're at a social ball and your reputation will be absolutely scandalized." She grinned.

He returned the expression. "That's very true. Father beat me black and blue around the ears when I was young. And when I went to that school, they did that and more. Much more—and much worse. They used to tease me because I was smaller than they were. They used to..." He stopped, his voice choking.

The implications hung in the air. She fought the urge to take his hand in return. "You don't need to say it. I can guess."

He let out a breath. "This world is an ugly, disgusting, terrible place, Emma. We lie to ourselves every day and claim we can find some specks of light in the darkness. That a bit of love here, and a bit of happiness there, makes up for the rest of it. But it doesn't. We have to end it all. We have to stop the cycle."

She could see some sense in his words. She knew Kirkbride's dark power wasn't to blame for the horrors of the institution in Arnsmouth. Traveling the world had let her see the beauty of it—but she'd also seen the horrors.

But to murder the entire world? To end it *all?*

That was a step too far for her.

At least, she hoped.

"Eat." He gestured at her plate. "Stop staring at me like I'm from space."

"It wouldn't be the weirdest thing I've seen of late," she muttered as she turned her attention back down to her food. "Not by a longshot."

"And no doubt you'll see stranger still before all this has ended. One way or another."

"One way or another." She went for her glass of red wine. She had ceased to care.

He lifted his glass in a toast.

Hesitating, unsure of what she was getting herself into, she tinked her glass against his. Her enemy. The leader of the Idol. The man who had helped her brother end his soul. And a nice man who made a strange amount of sense.

I hate my life.

CHAPTER THIRTEEN

"Little pig, little pig, let us in..." Rafe balled his hands into fists. The old stone church in front of him was bleak and foreboding. Its windows were dark, and it showed no signs of life within. But he knew better.

She was inside.

The Idol was there.

And they were *all going to die.*

There was only one small problem...

His tendrils lashed at the building and hit some manner of invisible ward. They could only go so far. It was as though they truly were made of nothing but shadows. The violence did nothing to change the fact that he could not get inside.

Rage filled him—hatred the likes of which he had never experienced.

Hatred...and fear.

She was in danger. Moreso than even with the Candle. And he couldn't do a damn thing to save her.

No matter how hard he fought. No matter how loudly he screamed out his anger.

The woman he loved was going to die.

"I THINK you made me pull something."

Gigi laughed quietly and took another drag from her long cigarette holder. Patrick was lying on his back on her bed, his arm thrown over his eyes, his bare chest still heaving from exertion. "I'm not responsible for any of that, darling. That was all you." She was reclining on the pillows against her headboard. She felt right as rain. Amazing what a good fuck could do to help set it all straight.

Patrick huffed a single chuckle in response and then let out a long exhale as he struggled to catch his breath. He was something to behold, his bare body on full display. That man was certainly delicious.

She had warned him not to get attached. And she supposed she should have listened to her own advice. But there was something that needed to be resolved first. "Were you planning on telling me?"

"Huh? Tell you what?"

"That you're a Saint."

That got his attention. He flopped his arm down onto the sheets and looked up at her, a line between his brows. "Excuse me?"

"Come off it, priest." She smirked slyly down at him. His head was close to her thigh, and it was probably one of the few times she could ever look down at the mountain of a man. "You killed Kirkbride with your bare hands. No one could do that who wasn't also a Saint."

"I'm the Bishop of the Church of the Benevolent God." His tone was flat, the confusion on his face leaving for something unreadable.

"You are? Well, shit." She flicked her cigarette. "I hadn't noticed."

"I mean to say that my faith affords me certain gifts."

"So does mine."

With a beleaguered sigh, he shut his eyes. "I am not a Saint. And I didn't kill Kirkbride. No one can kill a Saint of the Candle like that. I was just…very angry."

"Are you telling me Kirkbride is still alive?"

"No." He sat up with a grunt. "He is very much dead."

"How did you kill him?"

"I didn't. I told you."

Growling in frustration, she extinguished her cigarette in the tray on the nightstand. Tightening her silk robe around herself, she climbed off the sheets and stormed around to stand at his knees. "Patrick."

He winced and didn't look up at her.

She folded her arms across her chest. *"Patrick."*

"The Investigators took him away." He went to stand, but she put her hand on his shoulder and pushed. It wasn't like she could stop him if he really wanted to leave. Surprisingly, he stayed put. "Gigi, you don't know what you're asking me."

"I'm asking what happens to all the Saints your people have *disposed of* over the years. Because the more and more I see behind this curtain of the Benevolent God, I'm wondering precisely how different you are from one of our Societies. You simply worship the cross, instead." She tried to curb her defiant tone for his sake, as he already looked like a giant, kicked puppy. If he had a tail, it would be firmly between his legs.

He shut his eyes and wiped a palm over his face. "Can I shower first?"

She supposed that was a fair request. He was entirely naked, and the sweat on his body was likely cooling off and becoming uncomfortable. Stepping back, she shrugged and gestured to the bathroom. "Go on. I'll make drinks."

Pushing up from the bed, the springs squeaking as they relaxed under his considerable weight, he headed toward the shower. He did look *good* naked, and she couldn't help but stare at his ass in appreciation. Perfectly firm. She wondered if she could bounce a penny off it.

Once he shut the door, she called after him. "Don't bother trying to escape. You won't fit through the window." Never mind they were on the top floor. Maybe he would simply land on his feet. Or perhaps he could fly. She had no clue.

After fixing her makeup and her hair, ensuring that she looked undone in a perfectly ladylike manner, she headed to the kitchen to fashion them some drinks. She had a feeling they would both need some alcohol.

He came out another fifteen minutes later, wearing his black pants and white undershirt tucked in, but nothing over that. It didn't help the fact that she often found herself staring at his muscles. But they had their share of pleasure—now it was time for business. He sat down on her sofa, reaching out silently for one of the two cocktails she was holding.

She handed him the drink before she asked again. "Are you, or are you not, a Saint? And what are you doing with the others?"

After staring down into his drink for a moment, he downed it in one go, then handed her the empty glass.

Ah. So, it was really going to be one of *those* kinds of conversations.

Gigi braced herself for a long night.

"Another?" Tudor went to open a second bottle of wine.

"No. Please, no." Emma chuckled and sat back in her chair. She studied the young man sitting across from her. He was not, under any circumstances, what she had been expecting. After Kirkbride, she expected the leader of the Idol to be some…terrible monster.

Not a childhood acquaintance with a kind smile and an easy laugh. He was disarming. And that was problematic. She didn't want him to make sense. She didn't want him to appeal to the hopelessness she felt clawing away at her soul. There was no way out of this for her—it was the hungry void in Rafe, or it was the emptiness of having her entire self destroyed or…whisked away wherever Elliot had gone.

"Well, I'm having more." He uncorked the bottle and poured himself another brimming glass. "I'm going to need it."

"What for?" She arched her eyebrow. "I'm the prisoner, not you."

"First of all, you're not my prisoner."

"Uh-huh."

"Go, then. You're probably well enough to leave if you want." He gestured toward the direction of the wooden stairs that headed up to what was most likely a church. She didn't know what other kinds of buildings just had random crypts in their basements.

She wanted to leave. She really did.

But she also knew better.

It was a very sad time when she was afraid of the man she loved, and found the company of another man who was admittedly trying to convince her to kill herself slightly less alarming. If only slightly.

The expression on Tudor's face was one of mournful empathy. As if he understood what was going through her head and felt bad that she was going through it. It didn't help her mood in the slightest.

"I had one of my men phone the Church. The Bishop isn't there right now." Tudor picked up his glass of wine and the bottle and stood from the chair. "I'll have them call every hour. Until they get a hold of him, why don't we talk? I have something I want to show you."

"Why are you being nice to me?"

"First, you look like you haven't slept well in a very long time. Second, Kirkbride is—was—an absolute cretin of a man. Third, you're a sweet girl who didn't deserve any of this. And fourth, well…" He trailed off, clearly not wanting to finish the thought.

"You need me to die so you can see if I can crack open a hole between dimensions for you?" She narrowed her eyes at him.

"More or less." Letting out a breath, he looked deflated. "Come on."

"It's not a creepy human hand-candle, is it?" Emma paused. "A handle, if you will."

Tudor blinked in surprise and then laughed loudly. "Oh, Emma." He shook his head. "You really are something." He started walking deeper into the crypt. "And no, it isn't a creepy handle."

"Great." She stood from the table and picked up her own wine glass before following him. "It isn't another body part, is it?"

"Nope. Just a glowing rock, from your point of view."

"And from yours?"

"The only hope we have at finding lasting peace in this world." He shrugged, aimlessly gesturing with the bottle of wine. "You know, nothing *too* impressive."

Laughing at his dry sarcasm, she shook her head. Damn it. Damn it all. "There's no way I'm getting out of this mess in one piece, am I?"

"Most certainly not. It's just a matter of how you choose to end your story, I think. If you want to join Rafe and his… friends, then so be it. That's your choice. I know you care for him."

"I think I love him."

"Oh." He glanced over his shoulder at her and cringed. "I'm so sorry."

That once more made her laugh, though perhaps more at her own sad predicament than his delivery. "It's all right. I made my decisions."

"When the gate to the aether is thrown open, and we rejoin the universe in a pure state, all the suffering of everyone will end. Including his." They rounded a large brick column. There, resting on a brick shelf in front of another walled-up tomb, was a…well, he told her it was a glowing rock.

It was exactly that.

About the size of her head, its facets were glowing an eerie and unnatural green. It cast strange shadows along the walls, picking up every nook and cranny of the bricks. It pulsed like something breathing, growing brighter and dimmer, making the edges of the space seem even darker.

"Oh." She took a slow step toward it. It was caught in the claw of some enormous lizard, but the base looked…cast in stone, almost. Or carved from it, maybe? But what kind of animal had a claw like that?

You've seen monsters unlike anything you could have ever dreamed of, and you're confused about a giant lizard claw? It was weird what the mind latched on to. Taking a step toward it, she studied the strange writing that was etched along the base. It was all pointed spirals and sharp angles. It looked distinctly unfriendly.

"The language of the Great Beast. We don't have much of the writing from the original Societies. Most of it was burned by the Church or kept in their vaults," Tudor explained. He sat down on a stone lip that was raised a few inches from the ground. Resting his back against the ledge that the glowing rock was placed on, he pointed up at it idly. "That is, in case you were wondering, the Idol."

"I guessed." She sat down across from Tudor, not wanting to turn her back to the glowing rock. She didn't trust it. "Every Society has a totem?"

Tudor nodded. "You met the Mirror."

Cringing, she looked away into the shadows of the crypt. "Yeah. I did. And I met the Candle. I'm sure Gigi has a knife somewhere. I don't particularly want to see it. I don't feel like collecting the whole set."

"You likely won't. Nobody has seen or heard from the Key in…generations?" He shrugged. "Honestly, I think they've been eliminated entirely."

Except for the doorknob that appeared on the stairwell that time she was leaving Rafe's basement. She knew it hadn't been there before. But she kept that to herself. "What happens if the gate to the aether is opened? Do you even know for sure?"

"Of course I don't know for sure." Tudor sipped his wine. "This is religion, after all."

"That's fair, I guess." She took a drink from her own glass. It was helping settle her nerves, if nothing else. "What do you *believe* will happen?"

"We have to start at the beginning. Way back when this world was created, it was made from the aether by two beings —the Great Beast and the Benevolent God. Brothers and twins, they forged this existence in balance. But the Benevolent God betrayed his brother and trapped the Great Beast here, amongst us, in this cage of existence they made." Tudor shut his eyes and leaned his head back against the bricks. "That's why evil is so much more prevalent in our world than good—why the darkness is so much easier to find than the light."

"Do you have any proof of this?"

"The same proof any religion has." His smile turned a little sarcastic. "Old writing."

She supposed that was fair. She gestured for him to keep talking.

"We want to destroy the cage. We want to blow this prison wide open and return to the aether where we, and this entire world, truly belong. And to do that…we need you."

"And Yuriel. And no, I have no *clue* where he is. He did the smart thing and disappeared."

"I have faith that when he is needed, he'll be here." Tudor finished his glass of wine and poured himself another. He offered her the bottle.

Debating the benefits of getting tipsy around her enemy, she decided she would much rather be tipsy than sober at this point in her life. Accepting his offer, she topped off her glass before handing the now half-empty bottle back to him.

"We need a representation of the duality of the divine here on Earth. We need a demon and an angel—a creature of the Great Beast and one of the Benevolent God. That will be enough to shatter the cage." Staring down into his wine, he paused. "We hope."

"You aren't sure?"

"Of course not. It's never been done before." He chuckled. "But it's the best shot we have ever had."

Staring at the glowing rock, she took in a deep breath, held it, and let it out in a long rush. "I'm sorry, but I can't do it."

"Why?" He sounded like a child who was just told that his birthday party was canceled.

"Because the world is more than my suffering. Or yours. Yes, we might suffer from corruption, war, greed, and all the rest—but it isn't my decision to say that everyone else has to die for it." At least she'd be a little drunk for when he turned on her. It was inevitable. It was just a matter of when and how. She downed half her glass of wine, coughed, and reached for the bottle again.

He handed it back to her without complaint. "It isn't death, Emma. It's freedom. It's bliss. The return to the aether, where we belong. Society isn't something worth preserving—it's *mold*."

"And it's still not my place to say it needs to end. I'm sorry." Watching him carefully, she had to ask. She didn't want to, but she had to. "Is now the point where you turn on me, and your friends jump out of the shadows?"

"They won't jump out of the shadows. They're waiting upstairs." He smiled faintly as he let the other shoe drop. "I'm sorry, too, Emma. I was hoping this could be peaceful."

"Why not just start with this? Why the bad lie?"

"Because I didn't *want* it to be a lie. I was hoping you'd understand. That once we talked, you'd agree with me. But… we've waited too long. *I've* waited too long."

She was glad the pretenses were over. "Thank you for the last meal." She downed the rest of the glass of wine and grunted. "Did you ever actually call the Bishop?"

"We did. Believe it or not, I hate lying." He frowned. "This isn't personal, Emma. I'm telling you the truth when I say I wish we could have stayed friends. I'm sorry it has to be you."

"I appreciate that." Putting the empty glass down on the bricks beside her, she braced herself for what was about to happen. Her soul was going to be ripped out of her body. "Is it going to hurt?"

"No. You will only feel rapture. Elliot…was laughing in his final moments. He told me how beautiful it was. And it won't happen here." He stood from the bricks and brushed off his trousers. "Upstairs in the sanctuary."

"I suppose that's appropriate."

He offered a hand up. "Are you going to fight, or are you going to make this easy?"

"I saw only one way out of here. And if you've got a dozen guys up there waiting for me, I won't get far. Even if I do manage to shoot a few of them along the way." She cringed. "Not like shooting you bastards seems to do any good. If anything, it just makes it worse."

Tudor kept his hand extended, waiting for her to make her decision.

"Although kicking you in the balls would be extremely satisfying." She grinned halfheartedly. "Are you sure Rafe won't be along to stop you?"

"Oh, he's already here." Tudor sighed. "He's been out in the street trying to get in for the better part of an hour."

"What?" She jumped up to her feet at that. "How—why didn't you tell me?"

"He's part of the Mirror—the voices tell him things he shouldn't know. But that doesn't mean we're not without our own protections." Tudor lowered his hand. "He cannot get in unless we let him. And I'm sorry, dear Emma, as much as I'd like to let you say goodbye to your lover, the answer is no."

She felt strangely numb to it all. This was the end of the road for her. And truth be told…even if he could get inside, was Rafe any kinder a fate? *At least there's fantastic sex.* That was a definite plus.

"I can make it easier for you, if you want." Tudor stepped up to her. "Something to make this all a little smoother."

It was a kinder way to die. She could at least be grateful for that. "Just don't let it be like Kirkbride."

"Never." He reached out a hand and placed his palm over her forehead. When he whispered something strange, she couldn't quite follow the words.

Her world went dark.

And she wondered if she would ever wake up again.

CHAPTER FOURTEEN

I was a fool to let her out of my home.

We know. We told you, didn't we?

Rafe was seething now. The church was enveloped in darkness—all the power he wielded, and he could not get inside. What was the point of all the crowded void behind him, if he couldn't save the woman he loved?

The Idol knew he would come to save her, and they had planned for it. That was the simple fact. Rafe had *known* the risks. But he had thought that *They* were untouchable. And they were not.

When the front door of the church opened and a young man stepped out, Rafe had to fight for every ounce of control. He stepped forward, taking shape from the darkness, and tugged on the bottom of his vest to straighten it out.

There was a time not so long ago that he was a professor.

He would do his best to keep decorum.

Even if he wanted to *rip the young man apart.* And he would, soon enough. He would. It just remained to see if it was before or after Emma was hollowed out like a pumpkin.

The man smiled at him with a strange sadness. "Hello, Professor Saltonstall. It's an honor to finally meet you."

"And you are?" He arched an eyebrow and glared his best imperious stare at the young man over the rim of his glasses. He didn't need to wear them anymore—his vision was quite fine now that he had sacrificed his humanity—but old habits did indeed die hard.

Hard and frequently, with how we've been tracking.
Please shut up.

"Mr. Tudor Gardner, Esquire." The man bowed at the waist. "And it really is an honor to meet you."

"I'm sure." Rafe tilted his head to one side, cracking it, then to the other, repeating the result. "My proposition is simple—give Emma to me, and I will let you live."

"First, I don't believe you." Gardner chuckled. "And second, I have no intention, nor desire, to survive through the night. If I'm successful, no one, *anywhere,* will be truly alive for much longer. Not in the way we think of it." The man's smile turned to a thinner, far less friendly one. "And you know that was a stupid demand."

It was hard to bargain with suicidal zealots, that much was true. Rafe shrugged dismissively. "It was worth a try, I suppose."

"I suppose." Gardner squared his shoulders. "Well, I fear I must return inside. The ceremony is about to begin. I would let you say your goodbyes under normal circumstances—but you understand, of course."

Normal circumstances. *Yes. Clearly.* Rafe's jaw twitched in fury, but he kept his expression even. "Of course."

"Well! Enjoy your night. What's left of it, at any rate. I suggest if there is anything that remains in this world you have ever wished to achieve, now is the time to do it. You have approximately twenty minutes. Ta!" Gardner turned on his heel and walked back in, his hands clasped at his back.

Rafe hated him.

Yes. He decided he really, quite wholly, *hated* that scrawny little man.

We are going to have a great deal of fun picking him to pieces. Perhaps we'll eat the flesh off his bones. Or perhaps we'll eat the bones from his flesh first...from the inside.

Yes, that's what we'll do.

But how?

He pondered the stone church. His darkness was unable to squirm inside, not even in the smallest of cracks. The wards were too strong and designed specifically with them in mind. So, what was he to do?

The rumble of the underground rail shook the street beneath his feet.

Rafe laughed and slapped a hand over his face.

Oh, he was such an idiot!

We know.

He tried not to swear at himself. There was no point. The old stone church might not yet be wired for power—but he was certain it *was* plumbed. And while coming up through the sewer drains was hardly exactly going to be the highlight of his life...what must be done, must be done.

Now it just remained to be seen if he would make it in time.

Hold on, Emma. We're coming.

Emma was sick of crying, sick of being kidnapped, sick of retching, and so much more. But what she decided she was sick of the most, above all, was being tied down to a table like a sacrificial lamb.

Because there she was again.

Tied to a *fucking* table.

There really should be a quota on this kind of thing.

At least this time she wasn't gagged, though she couldn't think straight. It took a long while for her vision to clear. It took a longer while for her to figure out where she was, exactly. Someone was stroking her hair, quietly talking to her, trying to soothe her. For a moment, she hoped it was Rafe.

But it was Gardner.

Her arms were over her head, her wrists bound with rope that kept her lashed to the altar of the church. The stained glass windows above her were dark and foreboding, eerily uplit by the glowing green Idol that sat upon a second table closer to the wall. It was where the cross of the Church of the Benevolent God would have been placed but had likely been taken when this particular church was closed.

Gardner wasn't alone. A dozen people stood by the walls, heads bowed in prayer.

Emma thrashed, but it was no use. Her ankles were tied together, another rope securing her to the bottom of the table. Letting out a frightened whine, she kicked and tried again.

"Shhh, Emma. Shush. It's all right." Tudor smiled down at her gently, stroking her hair. "It's all right."

"Let me go—please, let me go—" She knew it was useless to beg. But there wasn't anything else she *could* do.

"I'm sorry. I hoped you would have understood. I know why you're scared, but once you see the beauty of it all, you will know such peace. Elliot could be waiting for you."

There was some small hope that when she died, he would be there. But she wasn't ever the kind of person to live her life on the belief that something *might* or *might not* be waiting for her once she died. Poppa always tried to teach her to live in the moment.

Oh, what she wouldn't give to have Poppa there.

Suddenly, she missed him with such vehemence her eyes began to water. She wanted to hug him. She wanted him to make everything okay. To tell her all of this was just an elaborate hallucination.

But none of that was going to happen. Taking in a deep, wavering breath, she struggled not to cry. Again. "Please, Tudor…"

"I am so very, very sorry. But I can't. I promise this won't hurt. I promise you'll know nothing but joy." He moved from where he was by her head to the side of the table, facing the glowing green rock. Shutting his eyes, he muttered what must have been a prayer, before turning to face the sanctuary of the church.

It was then that she realized they really, *really* weren't alone. There were at least a hundred people gathered in the building, maybe more. She couldn't see far into the dimly-lit space, illuminated only by a few candles here or there. But she could see the shadows of people moving up in the balcony, and as far back as the entrance some hundred and fifty feet away.

"Blessed brothers and sisters." Tudor began to deliver a sermon.

Honestly, she couldn't be bothered to listen. She now had one goal—get her hands free. She glared up at her wrists, as if they were the problem, and began to twist and turn her hands every which way. She was surrounded by people, and one of them was going to stop her before she made any real progress. She knew that.

But she had to *try*.

Unfortunately, one of them must have gone to the Scouts, as the knots that were holding her in place were perfect. With a snarl of frustration, she thrashed one last time. *"Fuck!"*

Tudor paused in his speech.

Someone in the room snickered.

He kept talking.

With a long sigh, she stared up at the ceiling. She was going to die. This was it. Her soul was going to get ripped out of her body, and then...poof. Off to wherever ripped-out-souls went.

Rafe, I'm so sorry. I'm so very, very sorry.

She wished she could say goodbye. She wished she could kiss him one last time. And the thought of him mourning her death put tears in her eyes once more. This time she didn't bother to fight them. Yes, the two of them were doomed. Literally and figuratively.

But she loved him. Murderous eldritch monster or not. *If only he hadn't been out to destroy the entire city...if only I could just sit still for ten minutes when I'm supposed to.*

If only, if only, if only.

But none of it mattered now.

Tudor was done with his speech. He turned to her, placing his hands on the table beside her. "Thank you for your lovely addition to my moment." It was clear he was trying to hide a laugh.

"I can shout a lot worse if you prefer." She glared up at him.

"No, no. That's quite all right. I'd hate to have to gag you." He rolled his shoulders, stretching his back as he let out a breath. He looked nervous. "Are you ready?"

"No."

"Neither am I. But here we are, all the same." Shutting his eyes, he held his arms out at his sides. It was time.

The words that left him were strange and foul. She never thought a language could make her want to throw up, but there it was. It twisted in her stomach and seemed to coil in her blood, rancid and wriggling. Every time she tried to focus on what he was saying, it was like her mind forced her not to listen. It was only a sound after a while—a sound that made every fiber of her being feel *wrong.*

Tudor opened his eyes once more. She pulled in a startled gasp. They were glowing bright green, pulsing in the same pattern as the stone on the small table beside her. Terror filled her. She opened her mouth to scream.

It was then that he looked at her.

And the scream stopped before it truly began. There was something in that pulse of light in his eyes. Something that took hold of her. Her muscles went slack. The fear and anguish in her fled like the last vestiges of night before the dawn broke.

He smiled. "Do you see?"

She did. She truly did. In his gaze, in the power he wielded, she could see all of eternity laid out before her. A simple harmony—a single way of being. No more duality, no more darkness, no more light. Simply *existence.* Peace. Unity. Purity.

No Benevolent God. No Great Beast. Only beauty. And oh, it was *breathtaking.*

He held a hand over her heart, palm down. "Are you ready now, Emma Mather? Are you ready to deliver us from this corrupt world?"

"Yes," she whispered. She was. Why hadn't she listened to him? Why had she been so afraid of this? There was only kindness and warmth within Tudor. He was her friend. He only wanted what was best for her—for the world.

The tears that left her now were tears of joy.

She would see Elliot again. Or perhaps they wouldn't be individuals at all anymore—but only energy, devoid of identity, together in the whole. And that would be fine, too. Her other half would rejoin her. And Rafe would be there, too, soon enough—when the world came crumbling down. "Yes," she repeated.

"You are saving us. Now, we shall be *free!*" Once more, he began the chanting that made her mind simply turn away from the words. His hand lowered, and his palm touched her chest over her heart. At first, she didn't feel anything at all, save the contact. But when he lifted his hand—she went with him.

Or part of her did.

Emma suddenly felt as though she were floating. But she was light. Small. Intangible. It felt like she did when she was dreaming—like her mind was all that existed, and her body was just a manifestation.

Somewhere, distant and far away, she could hear the others in the room chanting with Tudor as he *lifted* her soul from her body.

It felt like freedom.

It felt like rapture.

No. It *was.*

Something else touched her mind. Something that was not Tudor Gardner, or his terrible chanting. Something that felt like a single finger, perhaps—long, and painfully thin, pointed like a claw. She couldn't see it. But she could sense it.

It was like the creature from the Mirror, the first time she had snuck down to see it.

"Free us, Emma Mather. Free us all."

But its plea was not like Tudor's. It was asking for something different, she didn't know what. But it didn't matter. She wouldn't be able to help the shadowy, whispering darkness.

Or maybe it knew something she didn't.

Everything came crashing down.

Everything shattered with the sound of a single gunshot.

CHAPTER FIFTEEN

Emma's soul slammed back into her body.

That was all she could think of that could have happened, because in one moment she was floating, free of constraints, and the next she was very much not. And it *hurt*. Her vision went white in tiny spots, and she shivered in a cold sweat that covered her almost instantly.

It took her a second to remember the gunshot.

Trying to swallow down the pain, she looked up at Tudor. The young man was standing there, stock still, staring ahead at the glowing green Idol.

A small, round hole had appeared in the center of his forehead that had not been there before. The glowing in his eyes hadn't dimmed. Crimson began to ooze from the hole, running down the bridge of his nose and by one of his eyes.

The church had devolved into chaos. She heard people screaming and running—that particular sound of a crowd of people who had all been spurred into panic in a singular moment.

Turning her head, she tried to see what was going on. Standing in the center aisle of the church, gun still raised, was a man in a long oilskin coat. She recognized him immediately. "Yuriel!"

Her ex-twin, now-a-something-else, said nothing in reply. Just kept his gaze fixed on Gardner. Who was still standing there, unmoving, staring ahead. For the longest moment…nothing happened.

Tudor's knees buckled, and his body collapsed to the ground with a quiet thump.

His body fell.

But his soul did not.

Like a double exposure on a piece of film, Tudor remained standing where he had been, only now ghostly and translucent. But something had changed—his face wasn't the same. The thing that stood there had strange, sunken features, like a corrupted version of a face, with deep sockets like those of a skull, the still-glowing green eyes like candles set in shadowy windows.

The thing laughed. The sound of it sent fear crawling up her spine, and she redoubled her effort to escape, even though she knew it was pointless.

"There you are," the creature that had once been Tudor said, its mouth lacking lips but composed only of jagged points like a jack-o'-lantern. Its voice was all at once a hiss and a shout, and it made her head hurt to hear it. *"Yuriel, my brother! So good of you to join us."*

"Let the girl go." Yuriel kept his gun trained on the ghost. Though Emma really wondered what a bullet was going to do something that she could *see* through, she wasn't going to really argue.

The ghost turned to face Yuriel. *"Still keeping your promises to that whimpering child?"*

"And stopping you from this mad crusade of yours." Yuriel grimaced. "We don't belong in this world. We never have. What you're trying to do is madness, and it'll never work."

Emma desperately wanted to ask what was happening, but for the moment, Yuriel was distracting the thing-that-was-once-Tudor-Gardner, and she kind of wanted to keep it that way.

"I want to go home!" The creature took a step toward Yuriel. *"I was left here—abandoned by our creators—like a spurned dog. I will do whatever it takes to escape this shithole of a world, even if it means I have to tear it all apart, piece by piece."*

Yuriel sighed. "I don't know why they left you here, brother. But what you're doing—dragging more and more of us here to suffer with you—it's not going to help."

"Oh, yes, it will. Each soul I tear from the aether weakens the veil. I will keep punching holes in it, like you did to poor Gardner here, until there is nothing left. Until it all comes crashing down." The creature laughed, its voice tinged in mania.

Oh. Great. It was insane. And it had been masquerading as her friend the whole time. Now she *really* needed to know what was going on. Even if it was stupid to speak up. "Excuse me?"

The ghost turned to her, eyebrow raised in a silent question.

"What's happening right now?"

The creature sneered. *"Poor little Emma Mather. Always a penny short and a minute late. The girl of the hour who can't catch a break and seems to be all the void's new favorite plaything!"*

She frowned. "I resent—"

It wasn't listening to her. *"I am V'inth'y'varl, summoned here by those mortal cretins who founded this putrid city. Left to rot by my gods. And I will tear apart the fabric of reality itself, if it means I can return home. And I will do it one pathetic mortal at a time."*

"But…I thought you needed me because of Elliot."

"No." The thing laughed again. *"I hate to tell you this, but you aren't special. Why did I fight so hard to get you? Because I*

knew it would annoy Yuriel. And he is a traitor who sided with humans *and needed to be punished!"*

"I won't become a Saint so you can blow a hole in reality, V'inth'y'varl." Yuriel finally took a step toward the altar.

"See?" It pointed at Yuriel while looking at her. *"See how he betrays me, the Idol?"*

"I thought…" She glanced at the glowing green rock.

"Oh, this thing?" It walked to the table that held the glowing green rock. Picking it up, he tossed it to the ground. She watched it shatter as it hit the marble—it had just been made of glass. It laughed. *"Humans love to have a prop to worship. Give you all a piece of metal and gold paint and you'll stand there staring at it and drooling on yourselves. Just because you think, what, it resembles the divine? You know nothing of what it means to be divine!"*

The creature turned back to Yuriel. She was now between the two of them, and she didn't know if she liked that in the slightest. *"Yuriel, my brother—let us make a deal. Take her soul. Become a Saint. Consume her and give her peace, like you did with the other sniveling child. Together, we shall rip this place apart."*

"What? No—no, no—" Emma thrashed.

"Will you shut up?" The thing clapped its ghastly hand over her mouth. Its touch was like the arctic air. The searing cold shut her up immediately. When it removed its hand, she felt sick to her stomach. He hadn't just touched her body—that thing had touched something far deeper. It had touched her soul, and it was easily the most uncomfortable feeling she had ever experienced.

"I won't do it." Yuriel took another step toward the altar. "And I won't let you do it, either. She goes free. This ends now."

"And what will you do, hm?" The ghost stepped through the altar, and her, and came out the other side.

No, *that* was easily the most uncomfortable feeling she

had ever experienced. She groaned in pain and squirmed, trying to escape the sensation of pins and needles that was all at once an agony and yet left her feeling numb.

"You cannot fight me, brother. You cannot stop me."

"I can. I will."

"With what? That little cap gun of yours? You only killed my Host. You know that won't do a damn thing to me." The thing took another step toward Yuriel, and soon the two were only a few paces apart.

"I know."

"Then why're you still pointing it at me?"

"Just waiting." Yuriel pointed his gun at the altar and pulled the trigger. Emma squealed as the gun went off, and waited for the bloom of sharp angry pain she was certain would follow being shot.

But nothing came. Instead, when she went to curl into a ball to flinch away from the pain, her hands moved. He'd shot through the rope that had tied her wrists to the table! They were still lashed to each other, but at least she could move her arms. Sitting up, she immediately began trying to untie her ankles. If she could get those free, she could—

That terrible arctic cold grabbed her by the throat and slammed her back down to the table. *"No!"*

The ghost dug its fingers into her throat—literally into it—and squeezed. The feeling of it felt like death—felt like dying. And seeing as thanks to Kirkbride she had something to compare it to, she knew precisely what it was.

"Little rich girl, playing with the darkness, you cannot begin to comprehend what it is you think you understand." It snarled down at her, its twisted features a mask of rage.

Her vision blacked out for a second from the agony of the thing's touch. When she could see again, there was shouting and sounds of shattering wood. Blearily turning her head, she tried to wrap her head around what was happening.

Yuriel had just been thrown through a wooden pew and was picking himself up from the splintery mess. Emma could only watch as the creature and Yuriel continued to trade punches, brawling it out like they were in nothing more than a bad bar fight.

Even if one of them was a ghost and the other was… whatever Yuriel was. And that both of them were strong enough to send the other one sailing through the room and through furniture.

I have to get free. I have to escape.

Yuriel was buying her time, if nothing else. Sitting up, she groaned and fell back again. It took her two more attempts before she succeeded. She could barely focus on what she was seeing. Her fingers felt too small and useless as she weakly tried to undo the knots that lashed her to the table.

When the monster screamed loud enough that the windows near her cracked, she desperately wished she had her hands free to cover her ears. She couldn't do anything but wail in pain as the sound left her ears ringing.

Yuriel had the monster pinned to the ground and was… she didn't know what he was doing. Something was leaving the creature and flowing into Yuriel's body.

The creature was clawing at Yuriel, leaving pale tracks on the Host's skin, as if he was being touched by ice that instantly left him frostbitten. But Yuriel didn't flinch in pain. His expression wasn't even angry. He was just staring down at the monster with a mix of determination and…pity.

Yuriel was speaking to the monster, but she could barely make out the words. All she could understand were the words "I'm sorry, brother. Forgive me."

The creature screamed again…and was gone.

The silence was deafening. Emma's ears were still ringing from the sounds of its screeching. Yuriel was left on his hands and knees, his head lowered. He was bleeding from several cuts that she could see. He pushed up to his feet slowly, leaning heavily on one of the few remaining wooden pews.

"Yuriel...?" To say she was confused would be to put it mildly. "What just—" Her words choked off as he looked up at her.

His eyes were glowing that same, terrible green.

Expression contorting in pain, he lowered his head and snarled. "Shut *up!*"

She got the distinct impression he wasn't yelling at her.

When he looked at her again, the glowing had stopped. But it was clear something was still very, very wrong. He shook his head numbly and let out a tired laugh. "I understand now. *Shit.*"

"Can you please tell me what's happening?"

He shook his head again and took a step back. "I'm sorry, Emma. I'm so sorry. I—I have to go. I know what needs to happen now."

"Wait!" She yanked on the rope around her ankles. Nothing made sense. Not a damn lick of it. Growling in frustration at the rope, she tugged on the knot holding her down. "Wait, Yuriel—"

"I'm so—I'm so sorry." The creature inhabiting the body of her brother turned and limped from the building as fast as he could, ignoring her continued shouts for him to come back.

Before she knew it, she was alone.

Alone, and still tied to a *fucking* table.

"Damn it!" She kicked and struggled, but without the ability to separate her hands, she couldn't get enough leverage on the knot to pull it apart.

Taking a break to lie on her back, she put her palms over her eyes. Complaining to no one, she whined, "You couldn't have at least untied me first?"

Tudor had been a host for the creature Yuriel had fought

and then…absorbed? She tried to process everything she had heard. It was a thing from the aether, like Yuriel. And it had told Yuriel to consume her soul "like the other sniveling child."

Did he mean Elliot?

She could get her answers if and when she got free of the table, even if she had no idea where Yuriel was going. That was the second thing to solve. Step one was getting out of the damn church.

"Well, well, well…what do we have here?"

The voice cut through the silence like thunder through rain. Fear once more took hold as she went from one problem right into the next.

Something grabbed hold of the rope around her wrists and yanked it back up over her head, stretching her out once more on the altar.

The room had somehow grown darker.

She couldn't see the person approaching, but she could hear his shoes on the stone floor. Not that she needed to see him to know who was coming. Nor did she need to look up to know what was pinning her wrists over her head.

Stepping from the shadows into the dim light of the few remaining candles, Rafe wore a sick, sadistic grin on his face. And his eyes were as black as the void.

Her stomach felt like it fell off a building. She wasn't sure where it was going to land, but she knew it wasn't going to be good when it did.

Frying pan, fire.

Oh, no.

CHAPTER SIXTEEN

Patrick was a little drunk.

That was good. That was fine. He felt like an ass for having drunk so much of Gigi's liquor, but...she had hit the bottle pretty hard as well once he got into the thick of his story. She was sitting in the chair across from him, staring blankly down at the coffee table.

No, he wasn't a Saint.

He was the Bishop.

Though from her point of view, they might as well be the same thing. From *his* point of view, they couldn't have been farther apart. He was the Benevolent God to their Great Beast. The opposite side of the coin.

But he understood why Gigi couldn't see it that way. That wasn't what was upsetting her, however. That wasn't why she was sitting there, numbly processing everything he had said. It was because of the other part of her question—what did he do with the Saints that he captured?

Where did they go?

And why?

And why did the entirety of Arnsmouth depend on it?

He had to say something. Had to explain why they were all sitting on top of a literal ticking time bomb. Reaching out, he went to take her hand. Shockingly, she didn't pull away, though she didn't precisely react. "Look, I—"

There was a knock on the door. A hard one. Gigi gestured her hand dismissively and pulled her legs up onto the chair beside her. She was clearly not going to answer it.

With a sigh, he pushed up from the sofa and headed to the door. When he opened it, he was shocked to see one of his white-masked Investigators standing there silently. They never spoke. Not even to him.

The man handed him a note. It was from the front desk of the apartment building, but it was addressed to him, not Gigi. Furrowing his brow, he unfolded it. It didn't take more than a few words before Patrick was swearing.

Storming back into the apartment, he grabbed his cassock from the back of the sofa and pulled it on. "I have to go."

"What's wrong?" Gigi frowned.

"It's…Yuriel is at the church. He's demanding to see me. Something terrible has happened." He shook his head. "Stay here, where it's—"

"Are you insane?" Gigi was already on her feet and headed into her bedroom. "You're going to stand right there and wait as I get ready."

"But—"

Gigi was already gone.

Patrick put a hand over his face and let out a long sigh.

"Oh, don't be a grump. I'll only be a minute!" she shouted from the other room. "Yuriel can wait a little longer. He's likely been waiting hours."

The world might be ending. The city was in grave danger. And Gigi wanted to do her hair. Well, at least she was consistent. He couldn't exactly claim he was surprised. And something about it made him chuckle.

When she emerged a few minutes later, he did have to admit she looked wonderful. But then again, she always did. Opening the door to the hallway, he folded his arm in front of him like he was a doorman. "After you."

"Why, thank you." Her smile was beaming as she stepped into the hall with all the panache of someone who was about to walk the runway at a gala event, not confront the terrible truths he had unveiled to her just a few minutes before.

She knew what was about to happen.

And she did it with her head held high.

Damn it all.

Damn it to smithereens.

I love her.

"Let me go!"

Rafe chuckled as Emma thrashed. She must know she couldn't win. She must know she couldn't even muster much of a fight. But she struggled all the same, and he *reveled* in it. "Do you know how miserable it is to travel up through the sewers? That was an experience we're not looking forward to repeating anytime soon. But this? This makes it worth it."

"Rafe—"

"This is what happens when you try to escape. This is what happens when we let you out of our grasp." They stepped over the crumpled body of Tudor Gardner. Shame that Yuriel had beaten him to murdering the little idiot, but at least the job was done. A tendril or two slithered forward from the shadows and made quick work of the corpse.

The dead body was going to cramp the mood.

For her, anyway. Not for them.

They wouldn't mind having her on a pile of bodies. And

the way their night was tracking, that might just be in the cards.

"Yuriel is—he's in trouble—something happened. He *ate* a soul or something, and—" Emma was babbling. The look on her face was wide-eyed and pale. She had been through a lot. And she was about to go through a lot more.

They were in a *mood,* and they were going to have their pound of flesh.

One. Way. Or. Another.

"We need to go—go save him—I don't know where he's going but he's—he's in trouble—Rafe!" She thrashed again, kicking at the tendrils that had now replaced the ropes that bound her to the altar.

"Interesting." They couldn't care less. Stepping up to the side of the wooden table where she was lying, they took in a deep breath, held it, and slowly let it out. The scent of her fear, of the blood that had been spilled, of the chaos and destruction…it sent a shiver through them.

"Rafe, please let me up—please—"

"And give up on this?" They chuckled. Lifting a hand, they trailed their human fingers slowly up her leg to her knee, rolling the fabric of her dress as they went. Her skin was soft, and the silk of her stockings felt so wonderful. "Do you know how perfect you look? A sacrifice, all laid out, just for us. Shame all the onlookers fled."

"Technically, it wasn't for—"

"Shush." They grinned. Cheeky girl. Always with a snappy comment or a swift joke. They loved her for it. "Let us have our fun."

"But what about Yuriel? Please, Rafe." Her thrashing turned to a wriggle as one of their tendrils slowly wound its way up her ankle to her calf, squeezing and pulling her taut. The sight of her stretched out, vulnerable and exposed…

They were going to have her like this.

There was terror in her eyes. But there was the glitter of excitement as well. Good. She did so much love to be afraid —up to a point, like most humans. But her unique reaction was particularly advantageous to them.

"We know where he's going."

"You do?" she shouted, lifting her head. Her struggles redoubled. "We—"

Grasping her hair in their fist, they pulled it back down to the table. Her words cut off to a startled squeak. Grinning like the fiends they were, they leaned in close. "We know where he's going, and we know how this is going to end. Yuriel will be dead within a few hours. And for those hours, we're going to be *very* preoccupied."

Her gaze flicked between their eyes. They knew they had gone as black as the void they came from. It was likely part of the reason she looked so very afraid. "I don't understand what's happening," she whispered. "Please."

That much they could sympathize with. What were they, if nothing but the collection of knowledge, and the desire for more? With a long sigh, they opted to amuse themselves with the tie of the front of her dress, slowly unlacing the bow that held the split of her neckline together. They would take their time.

"Tudor Gardner ceased to be the moment he sacrificed himself to the Idol. It was a soul, same as Yuriel, who has been trapped here in Arnsmouth since the original members of the Society summoned him here. He has bounced from body to body, flesh to flesh"—they squeezed her breast roughly, causing her to arch her back from the table with a gasp—"ever since."

Human bodies were strange things. Limited things. Fragile and weak.

But they had their benefits.

The tendril around her calf slowly wormed its way

higher. They were going to have her this night—all of her. But they could take their time. She deserved to know, they supposed. She had been through enough.

"He wanted to go home." Her words were tiny and distracted. Her cheeks were beginning to flush red, and her heartbeat was beginning to quicken.

Good, yes, that's it…

"He did. And he was going to do it by ending the world. The rest of his followers believed they were *saving* it. Peh. Idiots. He did believe that the more hosts he pulled through the veil, the weaker it was. Although we're unsure if the duality of you and your former twin was really as important as they pretended to be." They shrugged. "Doesn't matter anymore."

"But what about—" Her words choked off as one of his tendrils wound around her throat. Not squeezing. Not yet. Just making themselves known.

"Yuriel consumed the Idol. Took it into the flesh they share. I suspect he's having a bit of an argument in his head right now." They laughed. "We sympathize. The action has likely made him a Saint. And knowing how stupidly *noble* he seems to be…he's likely off to end his life."

"No!" She kicked harder, trying to yank her wrists free of the tendrils that only squeezed harder. "No, please! We have to stop him—we have to—"

"If only you understood the price of what you're asking." They let out a sigh. Some things were better left unsaid. Because if Yuriel had to die for being a Saint, then very clearly so did what was left of Rafe's mortal form.

They were working on a solution to that, but *humans* kept getting in the way. Best not to overburden her. Not at the moment.

"Rafe, *please.*"

"No, pretty girl. Yuriel has to die." *It stalls for time. Time we need to figure out a way to destroy the Bishop first, now that you're safe.* "We're sorry."

"No, you're not."

Oh, her glare was delicious. They cackled. "You're right. We're not. We're not in the slightest!" They knew their grin was vicious as they sent their tendrils to work undressing her. They would rather have just ripped her clothes clean off, but they doubted they could find a new set of clothes for her in the building.

"You can't be serious right n—" Emma's words broke off in a startled gasp as they wormed a tendril against the heat they could feel gathered at her core. She bit back a noise and tossed her head to the side. "Damn it, Rafe!"

Chuckling, they walked around to stand by her head. Leaning over her, they kissed her ear before whispering, "Go ahead. Struggle. Fight. We want to feel it, and we know you do, too. You're enjoying this little game just as much as we are, aren't you?" They brought the lobe of her ear between their teeth, grazing it with his teeth before biting just perhaps a little painfully.

Emma couldn't stifle the moan that left her, though she tried.

She snarled in rage and thrashed against the shadows that bound her to the table. *"Rafe!"* she screamed, her fury cracking her voice as she desperately tried to escape. But it was useless. All it did was pull a groan from them. The feeling of her struggling with all her might against them?

Delicious.

They caressed and fondled her, swarming her body with their many tendrils, even as she resorted to screaming insults at him in several different languages. Chuckling, they kissed her cheek and watched as she fought and writhed.

Reaching down with their mortal hand, they grasped her

breast before toying with the pert nipple, pinching the bud between their fingers.

She moaned, her back arching.

They took the opportunity to slide one of their shadowy limbs up between her thighs and into the heat of her core. Her moan turned to a wail. It was a tapered, narrow thing, no thicker than a thumb—at the moment. But it was enough to send her eyes slipping shut. She turned her head to rest on her cheek.

"No, we want to watch this. No hiding." Shrugging out of their coat and vest, tossing their suspenders over their shoulders, they climbed up onto the altar. Wrenching her legs apart, they laughed at her startled little squeak.

Resting between her knees, they knelt and once more could not help but bask in the sight of her. "Emma, you are so beautiful—so perfect." They leaned down and kissed her slowly, ignoring her muffled protests. But they could feel her sink into the bliss of the embrace, and soon she was returning the gesture with equal fervor.

It felt good, this *kissing* thing.

Perhaps they could get used to owning a human body.

Especially when they got to share it with her.

As they broke off from the kiss, they smiled down at her, carefully grazing their fingers along her cheek. She was blushing, her lips were parted, and she looked up at them with what they could only describe as fearful adoration. The joy within the terror she loved so much.

And oh, how she was clearly *petrified* of them.

It was only fitting.

They kissed her again, slower that time, before parting. Pushing up onto their elbows, they rested their thumb on the hollow beneath her chin. "We love you, Emma Mather."

"I—"

"Shush. You needn't say a thing. We know how you feel.

We can sense it. You love us. Even if you can't bring yourself to admit it."

Now her glare was annoyed. "I just think this is exceptionally bad timing."

They had to turn their head to laugh so as to not deafen the poor girl. Pushing up to sit back on their ankles, they grinned down at her. "You truly are a treat."

She squealed as they drew her closer. "Rafe—please—we need to save Yuriel."

"It's too late for him. And even if we had time to try, we wouldn't. He's making his choice, and we cannot fight both him and the Bishop. Not yet. And besides…" They drank in the sight of her naked flesh as they peeled her clothing from her body, one piece at a time.

They donned their best sinister grin before they spoke again.

"We're a little busy right now."

CHAPTER SEVENTEEN

Emma wondered, yet again, if this was going to be the moment she died. She didn't *think* so, but with Rafe —or what Rafe had become—she couldn't ever be sure.

They said they loved her.

And she believed them.

It remained to be seen what the consequences of that love would be, however. Like the murder of hundreds, if not thousands of people, let alone the destruction of her own soul. Well, not destruction—consumption.

And it certainly felt like she was being devoured right now.

He kissed her with such a desperate, hungry passion that it was hard to focus on anything else. The shadowy tendrils that had filled the darkness were all around her. It felt like she was being eaten by snakes. The strength and number of them left her unable to move. They were even winding between her fingers, squeezing as if they were trying to simply hold her hand.

It'd be sweet if they weren't also pinning her down.

When one of those powerful limbs pushed itself inside her body, she moaned against Rafe's lips. She couldn't help it. It felt so damn *good*. He growled at her response to his invasion, his hand at her breast squeezing harder. The tendrils that surrounded her tightened and relaxed in waves.

It was dizzying. When he parted from her, she could barely breathe, and it had little to do with the cord of muscle that had circled her throat.

"We are going to have you in every way a man can have a woman, Emma. It's finally time to show you all that we are capable of." He grinned, a sick and sadistic expression that promised as much pleasure as it did violence.

But Yuriel needed her. She needed to stop him from doing whatever suicidal act he was about to commit. "Pl—" She never got the word out of her mouth. One of the tendrils took the opportunity and filled her mouth. She gagged at the sudden invasion and tossed her head, trying to dislodge it. But it was pointless. So, she did what any sensible woman would do. She bit down as hard as she could.

He chuckled. "We like the pain, silly girl."

Damn it.

The tip of the appendage curled around her tongue, squeezing and caressing her, exploring her mouth and leaving nothing untouched before pushing into her throat. Rafe moaned, his eyes sliding half shut. He lowered himself down her body, his lips taking the place of his hand at torturing one of her nipples.

"And so do you," he murmured against her skin before biting down.

He wasn't wrong. She cried out against the invading tendril as it began to pump in and out of her mouth, mimicking the familiar dance. She couldn't even imagine what she must look like, stretched out on an abandoned church altar being ravaged by shadowy, inhuman monsters.

But she knew what it felt like.

And it felt like bliss.

"That's it, pretty girl." His other hand slid down her body, his fingers joining the presence that was exploring her core, writhing and slithering about inside her body. The added girth stretched her, but she needed more.

As if he could sense it, he kissed a trail back up her body before pushing up onto his hands on either side of her. The expression on his face was dark and feral as he watched the tendril push in and out of her throat.

With one hand, he freed himself from his trousers. And with a single, vicious thrust, he rammed inside of her. The sound that left him was a mix of human and not, part growl and part rumble that shook the building around them.

She could feel the other tendril still there with him, winding around him, making his presence all the more unnatural. It felt astonishing, and she couldn't do anything but whimper and gasp as he began to rut her like an animal, his hips impacting hers with a vengeance.

The cords around her thighs lifted her, easing his approach. But that wasn't the only reason. When another tip of a tendril pressed against the entrance to her ass, she shrieked against the one in her mouth.

He laughed, fiendish and cruel. "We warned you."

It pressed inside, the taper of it making its entrance impossible to fight. She could feel it, worming its way inside her, stretching her carefully. Not too far, not far enough that the sting was unpleasant.

It was too much.

Her pleasure peaked, and she was glad for the tendril that muffled her scream of ecstasy as her vision nearly went white from it all. Muscles tightening and spasming, her moment of bliss didn't even slow Rafe down.

No, if anything, it spurred them on.

He was going to leave bruises with how hard he was slamming himself into her, his impacts slow and brutal. Each one jolted her against the wood, and each one sent sparks of pleasure and pain flashing through her like lightning.

And all the while, the tendrils writhed. Claimed her, took her, ravished her. There was no escape, and now escape was the farthest thing from her mind. *Yes, please, Rafe—more—harder—*

She would be begging him if he weren't still pressing down her throat.

"Ours—you are *ours*—do you understand now?" He grunted with each stroke, each collision. "Now and forever—your body, your soul, your mind—"

Yes—

Again and again, over and over, she came undone from the onslaught. It was more than she could handle. Being touched *everywhere,* fondled *everywhere,* filled *everywhere.* It was going to empty her mind permanently, that blinding bliss. And she couldn't think of any better way to die.

If this would be what it meant to be consumed by the void?

Let it have her.

The appendage in her mouth abandoned her abruptly, but she had no time to catch her breath before his lips were on hers again. He kissed her, his tongue eagerly dancing with hers.

His hand twisted in her hair and yanked it back, stinging her scalp. Glaring down at her, the rest of the onslaught never ceased. Never slowed. "Say it."

She could only gasp for air and let out a sharp, tiny mewl each time he thrust into her, stretching her in such a perfect way. She could feel the tendril that was now quite at home inside her ass, thrusting and pressing against the rest of his presence.

"Say you understand. Say you belong to us! Tell us you are *ours*."

"Yes—" She could barely form the word. "Yes—yours—"

His expression was a grimace of pleasure as he sped his tempo, the strokes inside her body now feeling more like the piston inside a car engine than a man inside a woman.

She felt like she was going to faint. And maybe she did. She wasn't sure when he had flipped her onto her stomach, her arms still stretched over her head. He was standing beside the table, using it for leverage.

He had threatened to take her in every way a man could take a woman. And it seemed he was a man—and monster— of his word. They were everywhere, the tendrils—the man— the sensation of him. Of Rafe.

She was his. And now was the time to stop pretending she hadn't been his from the very start.

His hands had her hips in a viselike grip, and she knew if she lived through the experience, she'd have bruises in the shape of fingertips in the morning. But she wasn't sure as she really cared.

Yanking her head off the table by her hair, he arched her back. "We have to admit, this human *fucking* thing—*nnh*—is quite something. We think we could get used to this. But you are still so little, so fragile…so easily broken."

A second tendril pushed inside her ass, tangling with the first, and she screamed against the one that had resumed filling her mouth. She saw stars—but not from pain. He really was going to hollow her out like the Idol had planned to, just in a very different way.

"Have you had enough?" He yanked her up from the table, arching her back, her knees still supporting her weight on the wood surface. The cord of muscle inside her mouth left, and all motion ceased.

She could only sob. It was too much. All of it was just too much. "Please..."

"Please, what? Hm?" He chuckled close to her ear as the appendage around her throat squeezed and then relented. "What is it that you want?" He drove his hips against her body, pressing himself into her as far as he could go, trying to find a way even deeper inside her.

The pressure of it forced a choked moan from her as her body surrendered to the pleasure once again. She didn't know if she could take any more. The pleasure was overwhelming.

"Well? We could go forever. And we mean that *very* literally." He stroked her thighs with his hands, kneading the flesh, spreading her legs even wider. He began to pull out of her, very slowly, until just the head of him remained.

"Mercy—" she said through a gasp. "Please, no more—"

His laugh echoed in the cavernous room. It was the sound of victory, of triumph, of a predator sinking his fangs into his prey. "Mercy! You are asking *us* for mercy?" He sank himself into her to the hilt. "Beg us some more. We like how it sounds."

"Please—Rafe—I can't—I can't take any more..." She moaned, her head reeling. She might faint again.

"Poor little mortal human...don't worry. We're going to fix that." He lowered her back down to the table. "We told you we're going to keep you—and we meant it. But now, we think we have a new plan. You are too fragile. Too easily threatened. Even if we murder every *damnable fool* in this entire city, you might still get sick and die. Or...we might fuck you to death." He chuckled, clearly enjoying the notion. "That has to change."

"What're you—" She mewled as he began to thrust inside of her again, slower than before, but no gentler. She couldn't finish the words. She was too overwrought.

"You will become like us. A Saint. You will have your choice of which Society you wish to pledge yourself to, seeing as you and I are well on our way of emptying their ranks." He snickered, his hands sliding back to her hips. "You will ascend. You will become corrupted, like us. We will rule Arnsmouth together—we will rule the *world.*"

His tempo snapped, and whatever control he—*they*—were showing on her, dissolved at the idea of reigning supreme. He slammed into her with an inhuman force, and once more stars danced in front of her eyes. "Rafe—"

"Say yes—say you belong to us—say you will join us."

All she knew was the pleasure. All she knew was him. He was promising her safety, a way out from all the fear, all the death, all the darkness. She was sick of crying. Of being the victim. Of being the *poor little mortal human.*

There was no escaping Rafe. There was no escaping the Great Beast. And there was no escaping Arnsmouth.

"Yes!"

They cradled her spent body against theirs. They were sitting by the wall, their back up against the cool stone, and she was sitting on their lap. What a beautiful girl, hair matted from sweat, chest still heaving from the exertion.

They had ridden her raw. They knew they had been unkind. She would be sore—and likely very grumpy with them—come the morning. But she had also run away from them. Now, there would be no more running. No more escape.

They were going to make her like them. Perhaps she would like to become the Saint of the Blade? Control her physical body to whatever whim she desired? Or perhaps she would prefer the Idol, to let her soul wander free from her flesh and possess whoever she pleased.

She would be a glorious monster.

Or perhaps…they grinned. Yes, that was the direction she would go. It made such perfect sense. Once more, they would have to lay her out as a sacrifice. Once more, she would have to suffer. But only once. Then they could be together. Truly together.

They understood why she didn't wish to join them in the writhing emptiness of the dark. They understood why the whispers of the unknowable many were not for her. But they could no more let her go than they could embrace the sunlight. She belonged to them, now and forever.

And there were other ways to make sure she never, ever abandoned him.

It would take time. They had never attempted to contact another part of the darkness. But the Great Beast wanted Emma, that much was clear. They were certain the Beast would come for her when called.

For now…they would take his ravaged prize home. They would tend to her bruises. Then they would begin preparations. The spell would take some time.

They smiled in joy and kissed her forehead. The Dark Society of the Key had been dormant for so very long.

But they were about to change that.

CHAPTER EIGHTEEN

Patrick stormed into the sanctuary of the Church, throwing open the doors. He wasn't mad, per se. He was anxious. Whatever had happened that had sent Yuriel to the Church spelled trouble. Very serious trouble.

It wasn't long before he spotted the Host. He was seated in a pew, his head down, wide-brimmed hat obscuring his features.

Patrick slowed his steps and gestured for Gigi to stay back. The woman huffed and rolled her eyes but leaned up against the end of a row and obeyed.

He approached Yuriel, careful not to take his eyes off the other man. If what had happened was what Patrick suspected…the Host was now extremely dangerous. "Yuriel?"

"Mostly." The man sighed. "I think so."

Yep. It was exactly as Patrick suspected. His shoulders slumped. "I'm sorry."

"What for?" Yuriel leaned back in the pew and took off his hat, wiping his hand over his dark hair. It was only in certain moments that Patrick could see the resemblance between him and Emma. In times like these, when there was hopelessness but defiance etched on their features.

The Mathers were doomed. Both of them. In similar but different ways. "Is Emma all right?"

"Think so. I had to leave, once—" Yuriel grabbed half his face and winced in agony. For a moment, there was a flicker of green energy within his eyes, but it faded. "Once I wasn't alone anymore. Speaking of multitudes, Rafe was right on my heels. I expect Emma is—eh—safe might not be the right word. But alive."

"Safe enough for now." Patrick shook his head. He had to deal with the professor. And the professor was one Saint he would regret disposing of more than any other.

Including the one in front of him now.

"I can see it. The whole of it." Yuriel shut his eyes and let out a tired breath. "I remember what I am." When the Host turned his gaze to Patrick, it was beleaguered. "And you've known it all along."

He didn't bother denying the accusation. Nodding once, he walked up to the pew and sat down beside the Host. "Arnsmouth sits in a very delicate balance. Each piece could throw all the rest out of whack and bring it all down. And if that happens…if this city falls…"

"The world ends." Yuriel fished about in his oilskin coat and pulled out a package of cigarette papers and a tin of tobacco. "Do you mind?"

"No. Go ahead." Usually, Patrick hated it when people smoked in his sanctuary. It left such a terrible odor for days. But in this instance, he couldn't figure he could fault the man. Especially with what was coming. "Are you going to fight me?"

Yuriel snorted.

"I'm glad for that." Patrick smiled faintly. "You're one of the good ones."

"No, I'm not. I'm really not. I just know when I've reached the end of the road." Yuriel began rolling up a cigarette, licking the paper to carefully adhere it to itself. "I remember the Civil War. I remember the Revolutionary War. I remember…I remember so much death, Bishop. I think I was there for all of it."

"The roots of the Great Beast's corruption travels deep and wide. I wouldn't be surprised. That is why it must be kept contained. The lock must *never* open." Patrick turned his gaze to the cross over the altar. The double-sided shape was a constant reminder of the terrible secret he was burdened with. A secret he had promised to protect.

"I hear it. The ticking. I hear it wherever I go—I think that's why I liked the clocktower so much. It makes so much sense now, but, shit, I thought it was going to drive me insane." Yuriel tucked the finished cigarette between his lips and fetched his lighter from another pocket. With a click, he lit the paper, and another click had it shut and tucked away again.

"Do you need any time? To say goodbye?"

Yuriel huffed an exhausted laugh. "No. Just let me finish this cigarette." He paused. "I don't need to see her cry again. It's brutal. She knows the truth now—about what I did, about Elliot. I don't know if I can face that."

Patrick nodded solemnly. "Let's make it quick. She has a way of appearing out of nowhere."

"Tell me about it." Yuriel took another drag from his cigarette and let out a long puff of smoke. "I have to ask one thing, though."

"Of course."

"You and Gigi?"

Patrick let out a sad chuckle. "Yeah."

"Shit."

"Yeah."

"Good luck."

"Thanks." Patrick smirked at the other man's sarcasm. The luck was certainly needed.

No, he wasn't a Saint. He was the Bishop. And while, from Gigi's point of view, they really were one and the same, there was simply only one difference—Patrick wasn't out to open the cage to the monster that would end the world. He couldn't say the same for Kirkbride, Saltonstall, or even Yuriel.

They sat in silence as the Host smoked his cigarette. He flicked the ashes into his pocket, which Patrick found oddly endearing. The man didn't want to leave a mess on the floor of the Church. It was thoughtful of him.

"At least the Idol will finally get to go home." The Host pushed up from the bench with a grunt. "At least he'll finally have some peace."

"You're a good man, Yuriel." Patrick stood as well and tugged on his cassock to straighten it out.

"I'm not a man. Not sure if I ever even was." Yuriel shook his head. "It's like a magic trick. It's a mystery until you know the secret. And then once you see how they palm the cards, it's like the answer was there the whole time."

Patrick placed his hand on the man's—or whatever's—shoulder. "I don't care what you are, or were, Yuriel. You don't deserve what's happening to you."

"I don't deserve anything at all. I'm just an illusion. Just a —a piece, peeled off the whole." The Host's face contorted in disgust pointed squarely at himself. "I'm just a fuckin' magic trick."

"Well, this world could use more illusions like you." He began to walk toward the back of the Church. "Come on."

"There's going to be stairs, isn't there?" Yuriel put out the rest of his cigarette on his sleeve and put the extinguished butt into his coat.

"At least you won't have to walk back up them, Idol." Gigi huffed as she approached, ever looking somehow defiant and yet extremely bored at the same time.

"I'm not—" Yuriel went to argue before stopping. "Whatever."

"Just make sure *it* doesn't start driving." Gigi poked Yuriel in the middle of the forehead, nudging the man's head back. "Or else I might have to put a bullet in you."

"I did that already. Trust me. Doesn't work." Yuriel grinned, not taking the woman's goading seriously. "Only one way to end this, and that's where we're going."

Gigi smiled back, revealing that it was all in jest. "Good." Her smile faded. "Sorry to see you go."

"I appreciate that."

"The last Host was not *nearly* so nice to look at." She shrugged, pulling her fur coat tighter around herself. She waved her hand dismissively at Patrick. "Well? On with it."

Patrick chuckled as he turned his back on them to lead the pair through the back of the church. Fishing a key from his pocket, he went to the heavy iron door that blocked off the stairs that led deep down beneath the city.

I hate stairs.

I especially hate these stairs.

And by the Benevolent God, I hate the ticking.

To the mechanism that kept the world teetering on the balance.

To the lock.

To the Tenebris.

EMMA WOKE UP IN A DAZE. She groaned, feeling like she had run a marathon. And she supposed she did, of sorts. She didn't remember sections of whatever had transpired—just the overwhelming presence of *Rafe*. He had been everywhere.

Someone stroked her hair and kissed her shoulder. She let out a small hum at the press of familiar lips. Turning, she blinked herself awake. "Wh…"

"Home. You're safe now. And we're going to make it so that you will *always* be safe."

They were lying in bed, her back to his chest, and he had an arm draped over her. It felt so good with him there, his knees tucked against the backs of hers, his other arm beneath her pillow. The bed smelled like him—like crisp cologne.

It was so easy to shut her eyes and forget that he was threatening to murder everyone he believed was in their way. And he didn't care whether or not it was true. It was also easy to forget that he had vowed to consume her soul. At least until…

Wait.

She rolled onto her back, not surprised to find his eyes were still as pitch as the void. Chances were, they would never turn back. It was all right. Reaching up, she placed her palm to his cheek. "Is he still in there, somewhere?"

"Of course." He smiled back at her gently. Or *they* did. There was probably only *they* now. They leaned into her touch, the corner of their eyes creasing in happiness.

God above and below, they did look so perfectly *happy*.

"I love you. All of you," she whispered. And it was true. Even through it all, she couldn't imagine him not being there. "I just wish…"

"We know. But it's all right. We have a solution we think you'll like much better than the previous one."

"That's what I was about to ask you." She narrowed her eyes at him in a somewhat-playful, mostly-sincere annoyance. "What did I agree to last night?"

They chuckled. "Nothing we would keep you to. You

weren't precisely in the position to agree to much of anything in your right mind."

"No, I don't think I was. Considering you were trying to screw all the thoughts out of my head entirely." She stretched and groaned again. Everything was *sore*. "I think I'm done being abducted for a while."

"We would hope so." They combed their fingers through her hair gently. Almost sweetly. It was so strange to have such a terrible monster be so gentle with her, especially now that she knew what they were capable of doing to her. And she'd put money on the fact that they were likely still holding back. "No, we have a new plan."

"Which is?"

"You shall become a Saint. Like us. We will sacrifice you to one of the Dark Societies, and you shall become a beautiful monster. One we can cherish and one *no one* could challenge." They grinned, so very pleased with themselves. "That is, once the Bishop is out of the way. But he wouldn't be able to stand against the two of us."

"I—" She moved to sit up, but the arm they had draped over her tightened, keeping her pinned. So much for no more abductions. "Rafe."

"It will take us a little time to prepare for the ceremony, so you'll have to get comfortable and actually *sit still* for once." Now it was their turn to look annoyed. "We think we know just the Society, too. We think you'll love it."

"Which one?" She very much didn't like the idea of being sacrificed. To anybody. Ever. She'd had enough of that.

"The Key." They grinned in triumph. "The masters of sanity. Isn't it just too poetic?"

It wasn't. "Rafe, no. Please, no."

They frowned and let out a sigh. "We figured you would refuse. But it doesn't matter. We're doing this, with or without your consent, pretty girl." They leaned in and kissed her cheek. "Because you're ours. Don't forget that."

"You would really do this to me against my will?"

"Yes." They squeezed her tight in an embrace that she was sure was meant to be comforting. "Because this way, you'll be free. You'll be our *equal,* not our pet human. Don't you see? It's for your own good." They had the same tone of voice her Poppa used to take when she didn't want to finish her vegetables.

"But—" She stopped herself. There was no point. They wouldn't ever understand. And from their point of view, she could see why it made so much sense. There was an allure to it that she couldn't deny. To have power—real power? To finally be able to stand up to the monsters that had threatened and tortured her for *months* now?

It was tempting.

Very tempting.

But everything came with a price. How much of herself would she lose in the process? What would she become? Would she turn into something like Kirkbride or whatever had been inside Tudor?

Or would she only become one voice in an unfathomable crowd, like Rafe?

What did it matter if she said yes or no? It was happening anyway. "I'm not going to grow extra eyes or limbs, am I?" She wrinkled her nose.

Laughing, they kissed her before rolling onto their back, taking her with them. She squeaked as she wound up lying on his chest, their lips still firmly planted against hers. When they parted, Rafe was still smiling up at her. They looked almost silly, with a lopsided, lovesick expression. They were an eldritch monster, after all. "No, you won't grow eyes or limbs." They combed their fingers through her hair, tucking the curly strands behind her ear. She did love it when they did that.

"What will happen to me? What's the Key like?"

"They control sanity. The minds of those around them. And therefore, pretty girl…they control reality itself. Because how we perceive the world around us is all that matters in the end. There hasn't been a Saint of the Key since the very beginning when the first Societies formed." Rafe definitely was still in there. No matter how lost in the multitudes he was, he couldn't ever resist a good lecture.

"Why not?"

"I suppose because they would be too dangerous. Or, perhaps, the Key itself is lost. Or, most likely…no one wants to willingly throw themselves into the arms of madness. But you're halfway there already, aren't you?"

"Don't be an ass." She jabbed them in the side.

Chuckling, they blew a strand of dark hair out of their eyes. "That was low. We're sorry."

Her stomach growled loud enough that she worried it might be another monster coming to eat her. No, it was just her body trying to remind herself that, for the moment, it was still human.

Rafe's expression was bemused, before it seemed they remembered the same thing. "Yes. Right. Food." They slipped out from under her, kissing her forehead. "We'll make something for you. Stay here, shower, do what you like. There is no escape, however. We've secured the doors and windows."

"I figured." She rolled onto her back and stretched, feeling her bones crack. Hells, she was going to have a sore neck for a while.

Rafe was halfway out the door when they paused. They looked back at her with another quirk of a smile. "We also promise we're a better cook than Rafe."

"How's that?"

"We've eaten a few chefs over the centuries."

Of course. Naturally.

She threw her arm over her eyes with a grunt. Laughing, Rafe left her alone to go make them whatever it was that eldritch monsters made for their lovers. It would probably be steak. Rare. She didn't want to know where he was going to get it.

"Just don't cook the cat!" she shouted after him.

"We aren't *that* evil," he shouted back.

Small favors, she supposed.

Taking a quick shower, she basked in the hot water for as long as she could before it began to run cold. But feeling clean and wearing a fresh set of clothing did wonders for her mood. Surprisingly, the bruises she'd earned weren't too bad.

They were definitely worth it.

Looking at her reflection in the mirror, she let out a breath. What was she going to do? Yuriel was probably dead already. Even if he wasn't, there was no way to reach him in time. Rafe was certainly not going to fall for the "let's go for a walk" trick again.

"I hate being helpless." She was talking to herself; she knew it. But she couldn't help it. The words needed to get out. "I hate being *trapped*. I feel like I've been locked in a cage, and no matter what I do, I can't get out. I want to be free. Truly free."

But how?

Shutting her eyes, she snarled in frustration as tears slipped free and ran down her cheeks. She lowered her head, pressing her palms against the bathroom counter. She wanted to break something. She wanted to smash everything in this damn house. She wanted to bash Rafe's head in with a heavy object—*again.*

It didn't matter. She was out of choices. Out of options. And out of plans. This was the best path she could see leading forward. The loss of her humanity in exchange for some semblance of agency returned.

Whatever.

It was time for dinner.

There had better be booze.

Turning to leave the bathroom, she pulled up short.

The door had changed.

The previous door was normal, just like all the rest in Rafe's house. It had been wooden with a glass doorknob, and somehow both modest and elegant—refined was probably the word for it.

But now?

Now it was made out of *cast iron*. The black of the metal had turned to various shades of orange-brown, flaking in its rust and age. Emblazoned on the door was a cross she recognized as belonging to the Church of the Benevolent God. The double-sided T with its curling leaves looked to be made of copper, not iron, as it had turned to mottled shades of blue and green.

Swallowing down the sudden rush of fear, she slowly stepped up to the door. It was the only way out of the otherwise normal-looking bathroom. "Um…hello, Mr. Door. Nice to meet you." The door might wear the cross, but the doorknob had an equally familiar symbol attached to it—the multi-edged geometric symbol of the Great Beast.

Just like the door that had appeared in the stairwell that led from Rafe's mirror.

"Nice to meet you again, I suppose," she corrected herself. Reaching out, she poked the door with a fingertip, wondering if it was just an illusion. Maybe Rafe's spell had already been done, and now she was hallucinating large, extremely heavy doors.

She wouldn't put it past herself.

Nope.

The door was there. Solid to the touch. Slowly getting braver, she placed her palm against the metal. It was cold and rough, like the weathered fencepost of a cemetery.

Well, now she supposed she had *two* options. Sit in the bathroom like an idiot and wait for Rafe to come rescue her from a suddenly-appearing and rather meddlesome door, or…open it and see where it went.

Maybe it was trying to help her.

She snorted at her own naivety. "Well, Mr. Door. I guess all I can ask is that if you're going to kill me, just do it quickly. I've had an extremely terrible few months. I'd rather not have the pattern continue, if you please." *No point in being rude.*

The door didn't answer.

Thankfully.

With a shrug, she threw up her hands and gave in. "All right, then. Magic door it is." Turning the knob, she pushed it open.

The other side was pitch black. Not that the space beyond was dark, per se, but that it simply didn't exist. Or that whatever was in front of her was a veil. Cautiously, she reached through the darkness, and sure enough, once her fingers passed through it, she couldn't see herself anymore.

But she also felt nothing on the other side except a slightly cool breeze.

"Here we go."

She stepped through.

CHAPTER NINETEEN

Emma half expected to fall to her death. Again. Or wind up strapped to a table. Again. Or be under siege from some other combination of terrible or invisible monsters. *Again.*

Instead, she was…standing in a hallway. She was underground, wherever she was. The walls were brick and arched overhead. It looked old—maybe as old as the city itself. Turning back to the wall, she wasn't entirely shocked to find that Mr. Door had abandoned her.

Touching the clay of the bricks, she found them crumbling but otherwise solid. No door to be had. "Thank you?" She wrinkled her nose. "I think?"

The tunnel was lit with electric lights, which struck her as odd. The wires were strung from point to point in lazy u's. She was grateful for not being left in the dark, even if she had no flipping clue where she was. She also had none of her personal belongings. Which meant no weapons.

She was a sitting duck if anybody came after her. But… hey, she *had* just been complaining about being trapped.

Now, which way was she supposed to go? She looked left

then right and saw nothing appealing in either direction. Just brick tunnels illuminated by faintly-buzzing amber bulbs. Shaking her head, she picked left, though she wasn't sure why. "Why not" was probably just as good of a question.

"Remember, Emma. If you're ever lost in a maze, keep your hand on the left wall and simply follow it, no matter how silly it sounds. You'll find the way out eventually." The voice of her Poppa chimed in. Ah. That was why. She had forgotten about that. They had been in Greece, and she had asked how anybody was ever meant to get out of a labyrinth.

Luckily, this maze seemed like a really simple one, as it only went on in one direction. It was about five minutes into her walk when she heard it. Quiet and low. Almost too far—or too deep—to really register at first.

Tick.

She felt it more than she heard it, to be fair. Frowning, she pressed her hand to the brick wall and waited. And waited.

And waited.

Maybe she was honestly losing her mind. Had she—

Tick.

It reminded her of the clocktower. The sound of some enormous piece of machinery as it went through the movement of its gears. But she was *underground.* None of it made any sense. Not that not understanding what was happening was anything new for her. She kept walking, sticking to her direction of choice.

Tick.

She couldn't tell if it was growing any louder. It was another ten minutes or so of walking with no noise except the buzz of the lights and the ticking that vibrated through the packed dirt floor beneath her feet, when she came to an intersection.

And smashed right into someone. It felt like she walked

into a wall of flesh, and the impact would have sent her sprawling to the ground, if it weren't for hands that caught her by the upper arms.

She screamed.

They screamed.

She stopped.

They stared.

She couldn't believe her eyes. *"Bishop?"*

He swore. *"Fuck."*

W<small>HY</small>?

Why?

Why was Emma Mather *always* exactly where she shouldn't be?

Patrick stared down at the girl in disbelief. How had she managed to get down here? There was only one door to the Tenebris. One, and one alone. And he had come down the stairs to the winding underground passageway that led to it. No one had passed them. And she certainly hadn't been down here all this time.

He was about to ask her when she wriggled out of his grasp. "Yuriel! Oh—oh, *Gigi!*"

"Strawberry, is it really you?"

Patrick just stared as the two women embraced. Gigi kissed the girl's cheek, holding her tight in an embrace. Yuriel had pressed his back to the wall and looked for all the world like he was going to be sick.

"Of course," the Host muttered, barely loud enough that Patrick could hear him. "Of course, she's here. Of course, this couldn't be easy."

Patrick put his hand on the other man's shoulder. Partly to comfort him. Partly to make sure the Host didn't turn and run. Patrick was great in a fight, but *not* a quarter mile dash. He'd never catch the Saint if Yuriel made a break for it.

As if sensing his concern, Yuriel just shook his head.

Gigi kissed Emma's cheek, then chuckled and wiped some lipstick off where it had left a mark. "Oh, strawberry, don't cry. Don't cry. I'm all right."

Emma bent her head to the other woman's shoulder and simply held her. Gigi glanced up to the two of them and gestured for them to wander off. "Can we ladies have a moment of privacy, please?"

The world might end. They had nearly reached the Tenebris. Yuriel was about to die. And she wanted a moment? Patrick's expression must have clearly displayed his disbelief.

"Girl talk," the jazz singer snipped.

With a heavy sigh, Patrick turned. "C'mon, Yuriel. Let's give them a minute."

Yuriel followed just a little too quickly, clearly eager to get away from Emma before the moment went from strange to uncomfortable. Stopping about fifty feet away, Patrick leaned against the brick wall, though the arch of the ceiling was just a little too low for him to be comfortable.

Yuriel mimicked his pose across from him, folding his arms across his chest, and glared down at the dirt between his feet.

"She's here to save you, you realize." Patrick smiled. Emma was a lot of things, but a quitter wasn't one of them. "She's not here to push you off the ledge."

"I...lied to her, Bishop. I *lied.* About her *brother.* Her *twin.*" Yuriel cringed. "How is she not going to—" He pulled his hat from his head and ran his hand over his hair. "Damn it."

"I know." Patrick let out a single weary laugh. "If there's one person in this world who understands the consequences of not telling someone something to protect them, it's me. Believe me."

"Have you told Gigi? About…" The Host gestured at him aimlessly.

"She knows everything. About the Tenebris, about the Saints, about…me. About it all." It was Patrick's turn to cringe.

"And she hasn't tried to murder you?" Yuriel arched an eyebrow. He began to make himself another cigarette. Patrick considered complaining about the smoke in the enclosed space, but he opted to let the man have his relief.

"Not yet. To be fair, she didn't have the chance. I had just finished explaining it all to her when we got your note."

"Ah. Well, watch your back down here." Yuriel finished rolling the cigarette and stuck the end between his lips. It bobbed as he talked. "One shove, and off you go."

"I…" Patrick turned his attention to Gigi and Emma. They were still embracing, talking in hushed tones. Emma was wiping at her cheeks, trying to get rid of the tears that were still flowing. Gigi was stroking the young woman's hair, smiling with such tenderness that it made his heart warm. "I trust her."

"Then you're either a fucking idiot, or you're in love." Yuriel snorted. "Or both. Not mutually exclusive, I suppose."

"I suppose you're right." Patrick paused. "On both counts."

"Shit." Yuriel grunted. "First the professor, now you? Now I'm feeling left out. I guess it's for the best."

"It is." Patrick was beyond relieved that Gigi had not ascended to Sainthood. And from her own admission, she had zero desire to do so. He was spared the pain of having to…no, he wouldn't even think about it.

"This isn't the end of the Idol. Something will come back and take his place." Yuriel sighed.

"I know. The Societies can't be eradicated. They can only be controlled." Patrick shut his eyes. "That's why I never bothered to try. They always come back."

"I never really considered how damn tired you must be." The Host lit the cigarette with a click of his lighter. "Don't you ever just get sick of it all? The constant fighting, the constant *watching,* waiting for some little shit like me to show up and ruin it all?"

"You're not the problem." He glanced over at Emma. "You're not the one who I think is going to end the world."

Yuriel chuckled. "Point." His amusement dropped like a badly made paper aeroplane. "I don't want to do this."

Patrick wasn't sure what the Host was referencing. Facing Emma and her knowledge of what really happened to Elliot's soul—or sacrificing himself. He assumed both. "But here you are, doing it. And that's what matters."

"That's what we like to tell ourselves, isn't it? That it matters. I don't know as it does, in the end. But I guess I'm about to find out."

"I guess so."

They fell into silence as they waited for the girls to finish their conversation. And in the silence, Patrick could feel the ticking of the enormous mechanism beneath them. And with each reverberation of the movement of the gears, he could see Yuriel wince.

"You all right?" he finally had to ask.

Yuriel snorted.

That was fair. He had no clue what it was like to hold two souls inside one body, nor did he have any interest in finding out. "For what it's worth, Yuriel…I'm sorry."

"Me, too." The words left him with an exhale of cigarette smoke. "Me, fuckin' too."

Silence fell over them again. Except for the sound of the mechanism that was calling the Host home with each twist of the gears. He knew it was. Because Patrick could feel it, too.

Tick.

Yuriel snickered.

"What?" Patrick looked up and followed the other man's gaze over to the women.

Who were kissing.

Well, more accurately, Gigi was kissing Emma, who looked more than just a *little* startled, her hands flailing to the sides as the jazz singer held her head in both hands.

"Well, if I'm going to die today, at least I get to go out on that pretty picture." Yuriel continued to laugh.

Patrick cleared his throat. And couldn't find the words to argue.

EMMA CLUNG to Gigi as if the other woman were a life raft. Everything she had been holding inside her came bursting out in a tear filled, ugly flood. "Gigi, I thought—oh, by the hells, I thought—I hoped—And now Rafe, and then the Idol came, and—"

"Calm down, strawberry." Gigi chuckled as she rested her forehead against hers, stroking Emma's hair as if she were a child. "I'm all right. Look at me. I'm just fine."

"H—how?" Emma sniffled and rubbed her hand over her face. Sure enough, Gigi looked…perfect. Her hair was back. She picked up the woman's arm and turned it over, and all the bruising and wounds from the needles were gone. They should have left scars. But there was not a single trace left of what Kirkbride had done to her.

"The Blade, you silly girl. What do you think it's for?" Gigi lowered her voice, her smile turning coy. "How do you think I managed this *beautiful* visage in the first place?"

Right. That. Emma had almost forgotten. She shook her head numbly. "It's been a rough patch for me lately…"

"Oh, aren't you just the absolute sweetest?" Gigi pulled her into a hug again, squeezing her as if they hadn't seen each other in twenty years. "Now you're going to make *me* cry."

Emma rested her head on the other woman's shoulder, just glad for the moment to hold her friend—she supposed they were really friends now—and appreciate the fact that she was safe. For now.

But everyone was only ever safe *for now,* weren't they? There were no promises about tomorrow. Or even in the next thirty seconds. Especially not when she was involved.

"I think I'm afraid of candles now," Emma muttered.

"Tell me about it." Gigi pulled away to watch Emma, her thumb running back and forth over her cheek, occasionally wiping away her tears. Gigi, despite her complaint, wasn't crying at all, though her eyes did look a little damper than usual. "You saved me."

"I didn't do anything. I got caught. He almost killed me. He—" Emma had to stop before she got sick or panicked. She wasn't used to having panic attacks. But after Kirkbride and his machine, she figured she was owed a few.

"I know. Sshh. I know." Gigi kept gently stroking her cheek. "No, you *did* save me. I don't care if the boys had to come clean up the mess. But you charged on into that wretched, disgusting place, with nothing but a damn fire poker." She paused. "I've been wondering all this time—why did you have that, anyway?"

"I had just murdered Rafe with it. Again." Emma smirked. "Not like it sticks."

Gigi laughed, pulling her tight into a hug again. "My strawberry—the fire poker murderer. You poor thing. You've certainly been through the wringer, haven't you?"

"And you haven't?"

Gigi huffed, as if offended. "Please! I've been through so much worse than what that giant, waxy anus tried to do to me."

Emma couldn't help but make a face and laugh at the terrible visual.

Cheering her up had clearly been Gigi's goal, as her expression bloomed into one of pride. "There we are. That's better. I want my impish friend back."

"Are we friends?"

"Darling. I don't say those kinds of things lightly. Of *course* we're friends. Don't be absurd." Gigi's expression went serious, even perhaps a little mournful. "Did you tell anyone?" she asked, her voice low. "About what you learned about me?"

Emma shook her head. "Not my business. Besides, I'm not sure how you measure this kind of thing, but." She laughed, somehow, through her tears. "I'm pretty sure you're more of a woman than I am, and—"

Gigi grabbed Emma's face and kissed her. Full on, to the lips, kissed her.

Emma squeaked in surprise, her eyes flying wide. She didn't want to push the other woman away, but certainly didn't want to encourage the action. So she did the only thing she could think of—do neither and both at the same time, which resulted in probably less-than-graceful-looking flailing.

When Gigi finally broke away, the jazz singer's pale blue eyes were smoldering. "I am jealous of the professor, you know. Not that I haven't come away from all this with my own pleasures."

Emma stammered.

Reaching into her fur coat, Gigi pulled out a compact mirror and a tube of lipstick. Even in the dim light, it seemed she was intent on looking perfect. After touching up her makeup and ensuring every hair was still in place, she snapped her mirror shut with a loud *click*. "Well! Enough of that nonsense."

Emma stammered.

Gigi chuckled, her gaze flicking over Emma's shoulder to where Patrick and Yuriel were waiting. "If you enjoyed that, I'm sure we could give the boys *quite* a show."

"N—no, I think—I think I'm fine, thank you."

The beautiful blonde shrugged and walked past her toward the gentlemen. "You're right. Too dirty here. Maybe later. A victory lap, perhaps."

Emma put her head in her hands and let out a whine. What had she done with her life? Truly, what had she done?

"Chop chop, strawberry! You can tell us all about your mysterious little arrival on the way." Gigi snapped her fingers.

There was one thing Emma was glad for, amongst all the rest of the chaos. She wasn't alone in the darkness anymore. She didn't know who had brought her down here or why, but she was grateful for that.

And here were the two people in Arnsmouth she needed to talk to the most. Yuriel and the Bishop. She should be ecstatic. But even through her relief, all she could feel was a climbing sense of dread.

Someone was listening.

Someone was doing her favors.

And favors never went unpaid in this town.

CHAPTER TWENTY

Rafe had felt it the moment that Emma had vanished.

By all that was and would ever be, they were *sick* of hunting that girl down.

But maybe we can fuck her senseless again?

Please shut up.

One moment, she had been there. The next, she had simply not been. She was a mortal—tiny, weak, fragile, powerless! There was no way she had managed the stunt on her own. So *how?*

Rafe was the Mirror. They were every secret, every lie, every mystery uncovered. And yet not a single one of the whispers in their mind could find her. Not a single one of the multitude in their mind had the answer.

So, they were left to *guess.* To take a look at the likely subjects and whittle them down one by one. The Candle was dead—snuffed, for the moment.

Robert would someday become a problem, they knew. The little urchin pretended to not be the master of the Candle, but Rafe knew better. Had always known better. But for now, Robert and the rest of his ilk were likely lying low to lick their wounds and see how the chaos played out.

Rafe would murder him later.

The Idol was also disposed of for the moment.

The Blade was with Gage. And Gage had no powers like the one that snatched their Emma away.

The Bishop could do nothing of the sort.

So that left one option—only one. And the realization made them laugh. Oh, how utterly perfect! "You should have waited. Only a few more hours, maybe even a day, and you would have *had* her, you fools." Rafe swiped a hand down their face. "I would have cracked her open and let you in."

The Key.

The Key had come for her and taken her away.

But to *where?*

That was a question they could answer. Shutting their eyes, they focused. They were in every shadow, every crevice, every corner. They were the voices that listened. They were *everywhere.*

Find her.

"Yuriel!" Emma jogged to catch up with the group ahead of her.

Yuriel was some twenty feet ahead of Patrick and Gigi. As she tried to brush past the Bishop to get to the Host, Patrick caught her arm and shook his head.

"I need to talk to him, I—"

"You will. You'll get your chance. But he's..." The Bishop sighed and shook his head again. "Give him some time to think."

Frowning, she fell back in step with Gigi. "Where are we going?"

"I'll tell you that if you tell me this—how did you get down here?" The Bishop was smiling, if a little bit like her dad used to smile when she fell out of a tree and somehow managed not to break both her legs in the process.

"I don't even know where 'here' is." Emma folded her arms across her chest. "I was trapped in Rafe's house. He wouldn't let me leave. Then…there was a door."

"A door," Patrick repeated.

She nodded. "Big, metal, had the cross on it. I opened it, and here I was."

Patrick let out a long, heavy, dreary groan.

"What?" She looked up at him. "What is it?"

"I knew they would come back eventually. Figures it would be *now*." The Bishop looked furious, then frustrated, then resigned. "That particular talent belongs to the Key."

"Oh." Emma chewed her bottom lip, debating whether or not to tell the Bishop everything. But that was what she had been trying to do this whole time, wasn't it? Find the Bishop. Tell him everything. Beg him to call a truce with Rafe.

A truce she knew Rafe would never accept now.

"Rafe was planning to sacrifice me to them."

"What?"

Everyone stopped walking at the sound of the Bishop's shout that was made far louder in the small space. It made Emma shrink back against the wall and try to do her best to hide in a place where there was literally nowhere to go. "Look—it's not my plan. They made the plan! They were going to eat me—like they ate Rafe, and I said no, so they— they picked a second way forward. I figured they were going to try to kill everybody *first,* so I might have some time to get to you, but then the Idol and Tudor had to show up, and then —then that changed. They were going to make me a Saint to keep me safe, and—"

"Emma, Emma—slow down." The Bishop reached out and

gently placed a heavy hand on her shoulder. "One thing at a time. Breathe."

She tried to focus on the last bit. Breathing was important for not passing out. Putting a hand over her eyes, she filled her lungs slowly, held it, and let it out in a gradual rush. "Rafe is going to murder everyone. You. Gigi. Everyone in the city who might stand in their way. I wanted to talk to you, to try to come to some sort of truce—to—to save everyone's lives. Even theirs. But now I think they're past the point where they would listen to reason."

"They?"

"Rafe is…isn't Rafe anymore." She dropped her hand to her side. "Not really. He's in there somewhere. It's why they won't let me go. It's why they love me. Or they say they do, anyway." She looked down at her palms and wondered what they might look like when she wasn't human anymore. Or if she'd be dead and it wouldn't matter. "I believe them, though. They don't seem to know how to handle it." She chuckled. "Poor things have never been in love before."

Gigi had wandered a few paces away to swear under her breath. Yuriel had even wandered a few paces closer and was doing the same thing, only louder. Patrick was staring at her, expressionless.

"Look! I'm sorry!" She threw up her hands. "I know this is entirely my fault, and I'm sorry. If I had just listened to a single one of you *once,* none of us would be in this mess. I certainly wouldn't be left trying to decide between—" Oh, great. There were the waterworks again. Cringing, she dropped her head, fighting back the tears that inevitably won the fight. "I love Rafe. I love them. I know I shouldn't, but I do. They're sweet, when…when they aren't trying to…they nursed me back to health. Do you know how weird it is to have them feed you soup?" She huffed a laugh.

"The sex must be *fantastic.*" Gigi cackled and wiggled her fingers at Emma.

Emma tried not to laugh. She failed. Even if her cheeks did go warm at the same time.

The jazz singer grinned. "I knew it!"

"I hate all of this and all of you." Patrick put his hand over his face. "And that was way more information than I needed." Emma wasn't the only one who was blushing.

"We're all about to be ripped apart by a shadowy monster or the world itself is about to be cast into oblivion. Do try to have a sense of humor about it, won't you, darling?" Gigi withdrew a cigarette from her silver case and fitted it into the end of her long cigarette holder. Even down here, even in the ticking tunnels beneath the city of Arnsmouth, she had to have class.

"If Rafe is out to destroy Arnsmouth, or murder hundreds if not thousands, you know I have to stop him—stop them." Patrick's expression was grim when he fixed his gaze back on Emma. "You know I have to do what needs to be done."

And that was the terrible thing. She knew. She truly knew. Rafe was…they were too far gone. She didn't know what she would do without him. Maybe she would lose her mind again. Maybe she would kill herself. And maybe that was okay.

Because the monster he had become wouldn't ever stop. She knew that, deep down inside. The hunger in them would never abate, even if they were convinced she was finally safe and the threat was over. Even if she became a Saint like him.

"Maybe we can…" She trailed off. No. There wasn't a point.

"It's worse than you know, Emma. Come. Let's walk and talk." He glanced behind them down the stretch of dimly-lit tunnel. "I get the sense we won't be alone down here for long. They'll find you, sooner rather than later."

He was right. Nodding, she pushed from the wall and headed toward Yuriel. The Host had stopped to listen to them, but upon seeing her, turned his back and lowered his head as he stormed forward, keeping his distance. He didn't want to talk to her.

He ate Elliot's soul. She'd have her chance to sort it out with him. Patrick had said as much, and she trusted the Bishop.

"Where are we going?" she asked again.

The Bishop was silent for a long time before he finally began to talk. And for a moment, she didn't wonder if Rafe had taken over his body, for how much like a professor he sounded. "This city was founded three hundred years ago by a group of religious zealots who were kicked out of England for their beliefs."

"The Church of the Benevolent God. I know. I went to school." She smirked.

"No. They were not holy souls. They were the Dark Societies. They were driven away because they worshiped a darkness that seemed to plague the city of London. And burning them at the stake or hanging them never stopped them. Not for good."

Patrick's hands balled into fists for a moment before releasing. "That's why I never tried to eradicate the cults. It did no good. The darkness always found a way back. But the people of England kicked them out, instead. Told them to go infest a new so-called 'uninhabited' land, instead. If they couldn't eradicate the corruption, perhaps they could quarantine it."

"There were already people here."

"Do you think they didn't know that?" He huffed. "Do you think they cared?"

"Point…" Emma frowned.

"Six cults came to the Americas and founded Arnsmouth.

It was meant to be their sanctuary—where they could unwind the fabric of humanity and the world around us to their whim. No one would challenge them here."

Emma blinked. "Six?" She counted off on her fingers. "The Mirror, the Blade, the Candle, the Idol, the Key…" That was five.

He smiled sadly. "The Cross."

Her eyes went wide. "O—oh."

"I just want the record to show that I called it," Gigi chimed in from behind them.

Emma laughed once and smiled over her shoulder at the jazz singer who looked remarkably bored, considering the circumstances.

Patrick rubbed his temple with his hand. "They wished to break a hole through our world into the aether, to release the Great Beast they all worshiped. But to do this, they needed to pull pieces of its power from the aether into ours. And to hold that power, they needed vessels. And simple tools wouldn't suffice."

"Saints."

"Exactly." He sighed. "And they almost succeeded. Until the Saint of the Cross turned on the others. A crisis of conscience, maybe of greed, I don't know. But the damage was done. The hole was already forming. So, he fashioned…a mechanism. Something that kept the Great Beast trapped where it belonged. The Church of the Benevolent God was created in the aftermath. A constant reminder that we must strive to be like the Beast's brother—to stand within the light, not the darkness. To strive for something greater. Because the darkness is always waiting to take us."

As if on cue, the thing she could hear let out a *tick* that was much louder than it had been before. They were going toward the mechanism, whatever it was.

"But the presence of Saints in the city weakens the lock.

The longer they exist—we exist—" Patrick cringed at the admission. "The more of us there are, the more damage it causes. One of us is all it can withstand for any length of time. All the rest must be...returned."

"Returned," Emma repeated blankly.

"The corruption of the Beast that beats within all of us must find its way back to the whole. One way or another, or else it will continue to grow stronger. So we...return them as we must. And that is my duty, as Saint of the Cross—as Bishop—to see that the rest are dealt with."

Emma felt the color drain from her face. She looked up the path at Yuriel. "Oh, no—" She tried to run forward, but Patrick caught her arm. "Let me talk to him!"

"You will. But he's...this is his choice, Emma. Not mine. He knows what's about to happen. Let him talk to you when he's ready."

Emma growled and then sighed. "Fine." She turned over the Bishop's story in her head. Only one Saint could exist outside the...whatever-it-was. Ticking-lock-thing. Something told her Rafe knew that. Something told her Rafe knew *all* of this. And it was just a matter of how much Rafe the professor had known before he became Rafe the monster.

By her count, there were three in the city. The Bishop, Yuriel, and Rafe. And if Yuriel was out to remove himself from the board, she could see what was coming. She would have to pick between the Bishop and Rafe.

Between light and dark.

As if he could read her mind, Patrick spoke up again. "He won't stop. They won't stop. They are creatures of knowledge—but more than that, the hunger for it. The unstoppable, unwavering *need* for more. They've found you, and I would have believed they could be contained and amused for a time. But that was when Rafe was even somewhat behind the wheel. Now that they've taken over…they won't stop with me. Or anyone else, for that matter."

"I know." She did. She agreed. She just didn't want to. "But you're…asking me to turn on him."

"No. I wouldn't ask a woman to turn on the man she loves. I'm just asking you to try *real* hard not to put yourself in the position where you have to make that choice." He chuckled. "Although asking Emma Mather not to get in the way is like asking winter not to come this year."

"Har, har." She rolled her eyes.

"But I also know that Emma Mather also does the right thing. Every time. And follows her heart wherever it goes." He reached out and placed his hand on her shoulder again, squeezing it. "I have faith in you."

"I just wish I had faith in myself."

"That part, I can't fix. Sorry."

They fell into silence for a few moments as a bend in the tunnel brought them slowly around a corner. Light was pouring in from a sharper turn in the path, and Yuriel was standing in the amber glow, staring ahead. The mechanical sound was much louder now—not only the large, heavy *tick* of some gigantic gear, but now the higher-pitched *click-click-click* of dozens of smaller ones.

Yuriel's eyes were wide, his cheeks wet with tears. He took a step forward and out of sight. Emma went to run after him again and was once more caught by Patrick.

"My predecessor named it Tenebris. It means *darkness*. Be careful, Emma. And remember that everything that comes from it must return to it in time. Including me. Including all the poison inside all of us. Yuriel is doing the right thing. He is trying to save innocent lives."

With that, he let her go. She turned and ran after the Host. "Yuriel!"

CHAPTER TWENTY-ONE

Emma turned the corner to follow Yuriel. The ground beneath her feet switched almost instantly from packed dirt to metal grating. The sudden shift, along with what she saw before her, had her reeling backward and nearly falling onto her ass.

The ground was moving.

She had to grab on to the wall, the shifting presence under her feet too much to handle at first. The floor beneath her was indeed grated metal, suspended over a circular room that she could only guess was several hundred feet in diameter. Cables tied into the stone of the walls, hammered in and fastened off, supporting the weight of the metal. Electric lights provided the only glow.

The catwalk ran around the room along the edges, some three feet wide. Thankfully, there was a railing, though it was far too thin for her liking. The room was bisected by another thin walkway that stretched out over the entire room from one side to the other.

But it wasn't the railing that was bothering her. It was what was *beneath* it.

The bottom of the room was some fifty or so feet below her. And at first, it was too much to even make sense of. It was like staring into the inside of a clock with a magnifying glass. Enormous cogs, gears, escapements, springs, and wheels spun at various rates. Some were so slow that it almost seemed as though they were not moving at all. And some so quickly they were nothing but a blur.

Tick.

The main gear rotated one notch with such force that it shook the catwalk. Squeaking, she pressed her hands against the cold stone wall, staring down at the mechanism beneath her in horror.

This was the Tenebris. This was what kept the city safe from the Great Beast. This was the thing that must be *fed* the Saints to stay closed.

Patrick stood next to her, a dreary expression on his face. "You get used to it."

"Do you?" Her voice was more of a shriek than she had expected it to be, though she couldn't say she was surprised.

"No." He chuckled. "I suppose I lied."

Through the maddening sound of ticking and the spinning floor that made the whole thing wobble in her vision like a funhouse, she finally managed to find Yuriel. He was standing in the center of the crosswalk that stretched over the clockwork. There was a gap in the railing, and he was gripping either side of the gap, staring down into the whirling depths.

"No—no—Yuriel!" She ran forward, nearly tripping as she grabbed hold of the metal rail to try to keep her balance. It was cold beneath her hands, flaking like the rusted metal door that had led her here. "Wait!"

The wind created by the movement beneath her swallowed her words almost entirely. She kept shouting as she made her way across the room, trying very hard not to look down. The clockwork seemed to dip in the center, each successive layer of copper, brass, and iron, one jump deeper than before. She couldn't see down into the pit in the middle. She was glad for that.

"Yuriel!"

He turned his head to look at her briefly but said nothing before staring back down into the abyss. It seemed like an eternity before she reached him.

"Please—wait—"

"You can't stop me, Emma. You can't." His cheeks were streaked with tears. "I have to do this. I have to take this thing inside me and bring it home. Bring us both home."

"I—" She reached out and put her hand on his arm. "I know."

His shoulders drooped. Something about her acknowledgement of it all seemed to hurt him worse than if she argued and fought for him to turn away. When he let go of the railing to face her, the agony in his gold and silver eyes broke her heart.

Maybe she'd fall to her death. Maybe she'd lose her balance and tip over the railing and plummet into the giant whirling meat grinder of gears beneath her. It didn't matter. She threw herself at him, hugging him as tightly as she could.

He returned the embrace, clutching her tight. He was still sobbing, his chest heaving with each exhale.

Lifting her head to look up at him, she smiled as best she could. "I just wanted to say I forgive you. And to say thank you. For saving me. For being a good friend."

"I..." He laughed, sad and exhausted, and shook his head. "You are a strange girl, Emma Mather."

"I know. That's what people keep telling me."

"I—about Elliot, I—"

"I know." She shut her eyes, not fighting her own tears that slipped down her cheeks. "Is he...a part of you, now?"

"I suppose. Though I'm not—I'm not *real,* Emma. I'm just a collection of memories that were yanked out of the Great Beast and tricked into thinking I was something else. I'm not an angel. I'm not a demon. Those things don't exist. I'm just… muck. Leftover muck." Yuriel shook his head again, his words cracking as he cried. He looked away from her, trying to hide his pain, however useless it was.

"You're the best leftover muck I've ever had the honor to know."

He snorted.

Placing her hand on his cheek, she turned him to look back to her. "You're a friend. You've saved me so many times. You're *family,* Yuriel—with or without Elliot's body." She tried to smile. Tried to be brave. Tried to do it for him, even if she wanted to collapse to the ground and weep until the stars burned out. "I am just so, *so* sorry."

"No. It was only a matter of time. This isn't your fault. The Idol is unstoppable. They all are. It's just about…keeping the evil at bay. They would have gotten to us both eventually. But that doesn't matter now."

She hugged him again, resting her head on his chest. He smelled like lamp oil and cigarette smoke. Nothing like her brother had ever been. "Is he still there, somewhere inside you?"

"I don't honestly know. I wish I could tell you more than that." He rested his cheek atop her head. "But I can tell you that he loved you *so* much. And maybe a little bit of that rubbed off on me."

That pulled a sob out of her chest, and she squeezed him tighter. She didn't want him to go. Not just because he was all she had left of Elliot—but also because he was Yuriel.

"I'm glad you're here. Thank you. For understanding and for…saying goodbye. At least I won't die alone." Yuriel laughed like a man standing on a gallows. "If this could even be called a life." He pushed her back from him gently, urging her to take a few paces away. She obeyed, though she wanted nothing in the world more than to fly over to the Bishop and beg him to find another way.

But there wasn't one.

She took his hand and squeezed it tight. She could barely see the gears through the blur of her tears. "Yuriel—I—you're my friend. Not because you're—not because of him. But because of *you*. You've saved me. Helped me. I just wish we had more time…"

"That means more to me than you can ever know." He squeezed her hand in return before releasing it. "Goodbye, Emma. Maybe we'll meet again someday, if I was ever real enough to have a soul of my own."

Yuriel tipped over the edge.

Emma screamed and reached for him.

But it was too late.

The flutter of an old oilskin coat as he fell was swallowed by the cacophony of ticking, whirling metal, and wind.

Falling to her knees, she wept.

Patrick waited a minute before going out to retrieve Emma from where she collapsed on the catwalk. He hated this. He hated every damnable stinking piece of it. He scooped the girl up into his arms, not even waiting for her to fuss. She didn't bother and just let him carry her back toward the entrance as she sobbed into his shoulder.

He couldn't say as he blamed her for a second of it.

He didn't know what they talked about. It wasn't for him to know. But the tragedy of it all broke his heart. He was crying as well. And Gigi had to leave the room, complaining of motion sickness. But he knew better. Gigi was just visible inside the pathway, swearing and cursing and wiping at her eyes.

Couldn't blame her for that, either.

He set her down gently on her feet on solid ground. She leaned up against the brick wall, and Gigi was instantly at her side, stroking her hair and offering her a silk handkerchief to wipe her tears.

Emma stared down at the ground by her feet for a long time. Patrick didn't know what to expect.

"We should get back to the Church before the professor catches up to us. This isn't exactly a defensible position." He kept his voice low, gentle, not wanting to sound scolding.

Miss Mather did the thing he least expected. She laughed. It was broken and grief-stricken, but it was there. "Is there even a Benevolent God?"

What was the point in lying anymore? The girl had been through enough. The girl had suffered enough. He was done. Done with it all. "No. Or if there is, not the way the Church pretends."

"So, my brother—and Yuriel—and the Idol in there with them?"

Patrick stayed silent until Emma glared up at him with all the ferocity of a lion. He sighed. "Are with the Great Beast."

Emma swore. He didn't know what language she was swearing in, but it sounded colorful. Placing both hands over her eyes, she looked as though she were going to begin to cry again. Once more, she laughed. "I'm done. That's it, I'm done."

"That's my girl. Jaded already." Gigi took a drag off her cigarette. "You'll be just like me in no time."

Patrick shook his head. "Let's go."

They turned the corner down the long brick hallway that led back up to the church. Him in the lead, Emma in the middle, and Gigi behind her. Likely to make sure the poor girl didn't run off and leap into the Tenebris after Yuriel.

His day went from bad to worse very quickly. Stopping abruptly, he felt Emma bump into his back.

"Hey!" she whined. "Warn me, you wall of flesh."

"Isn't he, though?" Gigi chuckled before peeking around him. "Oh. Well, *shit.*"

Well, shit, indeed. Patrick gritted his teeth. There, down the end of the hallway, some hundred or so feet away before the tunnel turned once more…was nothing.

Literally *nothing.*

An empty, dark void from which no light and nothing at all could be seen. And it was coming toward them. The darkness subsumed each electric light as it passed, surrounding it with shadowy, slithering tendrils until it was gone.

There was only one way out. Only one way back to the Church and relative safety.

And behind them was the Tenebris.

Taking a deep breath, he held it for a long time, then let it out slowly. Fantastic. He was going to have to deal with *this* now.

The darkness slowed to a stop some twenty paces away.

Emma was now hiding behind him. Gigi was quietly trying to console the girl, telling her it would be all right. But they all knew the truth. No, it wouldn't.

Someone wasn't going to come out of this alive.

And unless the Benevolent God burst into existence and gave him a miracle, it was probably going to be him. And Gigi. And the rest of Arnsmouth.

Gritting his teeth, he rolled his shoulders, cracking the knots in his muscles as he did his best to prepare himself for the fight that was about to occur.

"Hello, Professor Saltonstall."

"Bishop."

From the darkness stepped the man he recognized. He still wore the thin, wire-rimmed glasses, though Patrick wasn't sure why he bothered. His eyes were an inky blackness that matched the void behind him. His clothes were rumpled, as though he had dressed hastily. Or he didn't care at all how he looked.

Not the stern and exacting man Patrick had met.

But he wasn't a man anymore at all.

Patrick stalled for time, though he wasn't sure why. "Should I keep calling you that? 'Professor Saltonstall?' Or do you have another name?"

"He is still within us, so call us what you like. We have no true names, though she's tried to give us a few." He chuckled, a sadistic, cruel grin spreading over his features. "We delight in her so very much." He held out his hand. "Come here, Emma. Let us keep you safe."

"If I do, you're going to murder them both." Emma made no move to step forward.

The professor furrowed his brow as if that were somehow a confusing statement. "Of course. And?"

"I can't—I can't let you. This is *wrong,* Rafe. All this death, all this—all this loss, I can't do it anymore. I can't! You need to stop, please."

"Stop?" He cackled. "Love, we're just getting started." Slowly, Rafe began to roll up his sleeves. "No. This grief of yours shall pass. You don't need these ingrates. You need us and only us. The Bishop and Gigi will die tonight. Then we will hunt down whoever from the Key has decided to start playing games." He sneered. "That was a lovely little trick, but in the end, we must say we're grateful. It's saved us a lot of time."

"Emma, Gigi, run." Patrick ground his foot into the dirt, firming up his stance. "I can stop him."

"In case you haven't noticed, darling, we're trapped." Gigi laughed once, incredulously. "Run *where?*"

"I know that." He fought the urge to turn to face Gigi so she could see precisely how annoyed he was. "I need *distance*."

"Fine, fine. Come on, Emma. Let's go back to the ticking whirlwind pit to the hells, hm? It's such a comforting view."

"Emma. Come here. *Now.*" Rafe snarled. "You belong to us, and you are only delaying the inevitable!"

Patrick felt a hand on his back. It was the girl of the hour. "Please be careful, Bishop."

He smiled down at her. "I've faced worse." That was a lie, and a bad one. But he had to have faith. If not in his nonexistent god, then in himself. "Go."

"Just…just don't…" She broke off.

"You would pick them over us?" Now the monster sounded crestfallen. "Come here, Emma—we didn't mean to scare you. But you're so fragile, so…so little. You're like an egg made of glass to us. We can't let you break. We can't. We *need* you. Please, come here." Rafe reached out to her again.

Tears ran down her cheeks again. "I…I love you, Rafe—all of you—but I'm sorry—I can't…"

Gigi tugged her away. "Let's go, Emma. I have a flask in my coat and a mind for us to empty it."

Patrick loved that woman so damn much.

He just hoped he had the chance to tell her.

"Emma!" Rafe's pain instantly turned to rage. *"Come back!"* He snarled, and the darkness around him writhed as it seethed along with him. "Well…then we suppose this makes it simple, doesn't it, Bishop?" The fiendish grin was back.

"It does."

"You're standing in our way."

"I am."

"Good."

The darkness came for him.

CHAPTER TWENTY-TWO

Emma wondered when she'd run out of tears. Leaning against the jamb of the doorway that led into the Tenebris, she kept her eyes off the whirling room beside her. It was nauseating at best, and extremely upsetting at worst.

"You've had a terrible time of it, haven't you, strawberry?" Gigi sighed. They both also did their best to ignore the sound of the fight raging some few hundred feet away down the tunnel. Neither of them looked thrilled, though Gigi was doing a much better job of pretending everything was fine.

Emma watched the other woman for a moment. "When're you going to admit you love him?"

Gigi barked a laugh. "Admit it? Darling! You never *asked.*"

That made Emma smile, despite everything. Damn that woman and her ability to cheer Emma up. "All right. Do you love him?"

"That's personal." Gigi's bright blue eyes sparkled in momentary mischief before her demeanor faded. Only sadness and worry were left behind. Suddenly, Emma was very sorry she asked. "I do. Damn it all, strawberry—I do. And what kind of future would there be for us? None at all."

"I don't know. He just admitted he's a cultist. At least there's that out of the way."

Gigi rested her head against the wall behind her and laughed. "Oh, Emma. I adore you." She opened her arms, offering Emma a hug. And who was she to refuse? Emma crossed the hallway and hugged the other woman, resting her head on the soft fur of Gigi's coat.

"Our boyfriends are beating each other to death right now." Emma wasn't sure why she felt the need to point out the obvious, but there she was. "One of them is going to win."

"I know, strawberry. I know." She kissed the top of Emma's head.

"For what it's worth, I…hope it's Patrick." Emma shut her eyes. It was a terrible confession to make. But it was true for many reasons. "I don't want you to lose him. Even if it means Rafe is gone."

"Well, I have to definitely agree with you. But if we don't get our way, don't cry over my loss. I'll be dead shortly after him." Gigi chuckled. "But I appreciate the sentiment."

She had a point. Losing Patrick meant losing Gigi as well. And a whole lot more. She held Gigi tighter and waited to find out who would die. "I'm sorry I'm an idiot."

Gigi laughed. "It's been an exciting ride, I'll give you that much."

Emma had to smile. "Never a dull moment around me."

"I won't argue with you there." Gigi paused. "Can we try for a few dull moments if we survive this? Maybe just a few?"

She chuckled. "I'll do my best."

Patrick's face collided with the brick wall. The ancient clay crumbled to dust, skittering to the floor at his feet. Of all the things he'd impacted in his life, he had to say it wasn't the worst. Even if the gritty texture did feel a bit like sandpaper.

Grabbing the shadowy tentacle that had done the deed, he wrenched it forward and, bending it, snapped it like a string attached to a kite. He tossed what was left to the ground, watching it disintegrate like the smoke from a candle.

Rafe snarled in pain and staggered back. His dark eyes were wide in shock. "How—"

"Do you think I survived all this time on luck?" Patrick wiped the back of his hand across his lip. He was bleeding. Oh, well. Wouldn't be the worst of it before he was done. Cracking his neck, he took his stance in the middle of the hallway again. "I am the Bishop of the Church of the Benevolent God."

"Your god doesn't *exist,* you pompous fool." The professor sneered at him in superiority.

"That's not the point."

Rafe blinked. "What?"

Pulling a bandage from his pocket, he wrapped the knuckles of his right hand, then did the same for the left as he talked. "I stand for what the Church *represents.* For hope, for dignity, and the war against the darkness that would consume us all. I don't care what power backs me. I don't care if I don't have any power at all. The point is that I am here to stop things like you from destroying the world. And that's all that matters."

"You are a leech and nothing more. Feeding off the darkness only to turn your back on it and claim you stand above it. That you're *better* than us." Rafe grimaced. "You disgust us."

"And you're a disease. A parasite, consuming its host. You won't stop until you've eaten every living soul on this planet.

And you can't help it." Patrick cracked his neck from one side to the other and finished tucking the bandages. "For what it's worth, Rafe—if you can hear me in there—I didn't want to do this. I hoped your love for Emma would change things."

"We love her. We will protect her!"

"By corrupting her." He huffed. "You want to make her a Saint. Do you know what that'll do to her?"

"She is human!" Rafe clenched both his fists, and the dark tendrils surrounding him squirmed around each other in their impatience and anger. "We would break her if she stayed the way she is. We—it'd only be a matter of time." His shoulders dropped a little. "We wouldn't be able to help it. But soon, soon she'll be like us—powerful. Unbreakable."

"The girl seems pretty fuckin' unbreakable to me, but I guess we have different standards." He shook out his arms. "All right. Are we going to do this or not?"

"We agree, muscle bag. Enough talk." Rafe held his arms out at his sides.

The shadows lunged at him, each tendril wrapping around a limb. Fine. Let 'em. It wasn't his first dance with the darkness. As strong as they were, he was stronger. Yanking an arm free, he ripped another one of the tendrils off from its source, and then another. And then another.

Several banded together to slam him into the opposite wall, then drag him to the ground by his ankle. Snarling, Patrick clapped his hands together in front of him, and then pushed his palms towards Rafe. Light exploded from his hands, driving the shadows back and all that went with them.

The professor—or what was left of him—howled in pain, reeling back and covering his eyes with his arm. Patrick was on his feet in an instant. Balling up a fist, he drove it into the back of Rafe's head, knocking the smaller man to the ground.

"Not just a bag of muscles." He smashed his fist into Rafe's head again, splitting the skin of his temple. The blood that oozed from Rafe's head and covered Patrick's knuckles wasn't red. It was black. And it *wriggled,* as if it was a million tiny maggots. He flicked his hand, sending the thick goop splattering to the dirt floor. "Ugh."

"Cute trick." Rafe coughed. "Very cute."

But if there was one thing about light, it was that it was impermanent. And the blast had only lasted a second, long enough to knock the professor down. Patrick had only another second before—

A tendril wrapped around his throat, cinching down like a snake, almost impossibly strong. Patrick gagged and yanked at it. Before he could react, the thing had him flying through the air. It released him, sending him tumbling down the hallway end-over-end.

Patrick finally came to a stop with a groan. He hadn't felt every impact. If he was lucky, he'd get to feel all the bruises in the morning. But for now, he had to get up. He had to fight.

He had to win.

Or else all was lost.

A SECOND BLAST of light hit them, but they were prepared for the pain that time. The first had caught them off guard. Now they knew the searing agony that chased them away would only last a brief moment. The Bishop was strong. He had gifts. But he was *slow.*

And they were fast.

The *Bishop* was one.

And *they* were many.

They understood why Emma was afraid. They understood why Emma wouldn't understand that what they planned for her was a good thing. That she deserved to be on her own feet, powerful, able to defend herself against all the interlopers and threats that seemed to follow her around wherever she went.

No more Kirkbrides.

No more twisted lost souls.

She could even leave them, if she chose. She would have that power. That right. She would no longer be a little mortal bauble. They wanted that for her. To elevate her to the status that she *should* own. But there was just the triviality of the death of the Bishop and the singer. And then they could force her to understand. Force her to see the truth.

First?

Kill the Bishop.

Then the singer.

Then take their Emma away from here.

Unfortunately, the Bishop was being more annoying than he had any right being. They were starting to become frustrated as Rafe's head bounced off the ground or met the Bishop's fist again, and again, and again.

When Patrick cracked open the skull of Rafe and the body could not move, they watched as a sense of relief and victory crossed over the Bishop's face.

"I'm sorry, professor. I'm sorry it had to be this way," the Bishop muttered down to the unmoving body that was Rafe.

Oh. He doesn't understand, does he?

Isn't this just glorious...

They laughed.

Though perhaps the Bishop could not hear it.

PATRICK SIGHED as he pushed himself up from the ground. He was bloody, he was bruised, but he had won. Rafe was dead, skull split open and left bleeding that dark ooze all over the ground. Maggots in tar, that was what it looked like.

He knew the bastard would put himself back together in a few moments. He knew he didn't have much time before the other man woke up and the fight began again. But a few moments was all he needed to throw him into the Tenebris and be done with it.

Gigi would have to restrain Emma. But he trusted the jazz singer to do what needed to be done in the moment.

Wiping the blood from his hands, he paused.

There were voices coming from all around him. Quiet and whispered, in a language he didn't understand.

The darkness hadn't faded.

I was fighting the figurehead. Not the ship.

"Fuck."

EMMA COULDN'T HEAR the sounds of fighting anymore. Maybe it was because the whirring, ticking mechanism was drowning it all out. Or because there was a winner. Gigi went rigid, sensing the same thing.

Pushing away from the other woman, she faced the hallway and waited to see who, or what, came down the darkness toward them.

"Patrick?" Gigi took a halting step forward. Because at first…it looked like the Bishop was walking toward them down the darkened hallway.

At first.

But something seemed wrong. For a moment, Emma couldn't tell what it was. And then she realized…his legs weren't moving. The man was *floating* down the hallway, his feet just an inch from the ground, toes barely brushing the dirt.

He was being carried. Carried by limbs of shadows that

writhed and tumbled over each other, each one crawling just a little closer.

They threw Patrick the rest of the way, sending the big man to the ground with a *thud* at Gigi's feet.

"Patrick!" The singer fell to her knees quickly, searching for a pulse. The Bishop groaned. "Oh, thank *fuck* you're alive!"

For now. He was bloody. A dark ring circled his neck, and wounds covered him. He looked like he should be dead. It was then that Emma remembered. "He's a Saint. He can't die like this."

"Correct, Emma. You aren't such a bad student after all." Rafe stepped from the darkness. Blood, black as pitch, ran down his temple. His glasses were missing, likely broken or lost in the fight. "We cannot kill him in a brawl any more than he can kill us. There is only one way to be rid of a Saint. And it is to return us to our maker."

Patrick rolled on his side, spitting red blood onto the dirt.

"But we can be beaten." Rafe sneered. "And we have won. Say your goodbyes, love. These two must be disposed of."

Gigi stood, pulled a pistol from her purse—a tiny little white-handled derringer—and unloaded the bullets into Rafe.

The professor sighed. "Do you feel better now?"

Gigi grunted and lowered her hand. "Did it hurt?"

"A little."

"Then, yes. I do."

Rafe shook their head. "Say goodbye, Emma. Now."

"No." Emma stepped around Gigi and Patrick and moved to stand in between them and Rafe. "I won't let you hurt them."

"You won't *let* us?" He laughed. "Oh, sweet girl. Don't you understand how little we care for what you'll *let* us do? You're weak. Small. Human. If you had just listened to us and let us make you a Saint, perhaps we would be having a very different conversation." They took a slow step toward her, one after another, stalking her. Calling her bluff.

She stood her ground. "Stop this, Rafe."

"Do you think the Bishop will stop hunting us? You know the truth now! He will never stop unless he is the only one allowed to wield power. Why, because he thinks it'll unbalance the world?" Rafe spat dark blood onto the ground by their feet. "Another lie."

"It's—true." Patrick couldn't stand. His ankle was shattered, by the looks of it. Gigi crouched and helped him prop himself up on his elbow. "The more of us there are in this city, Rafe, the more unwound the Tenebris becomes. And if it opens, it gets free. And then not just Arnsmouth is doomed— but the whole *world*."

"We don't care!" Rafe threw up their hands. "Let it be free. Let the world end! We do not care. We will have the only thing in this world that we find we desire. Her." They pointed at Emma, before turning those pure-black eyes back to her. Their voice softened. "Emma. Please…we love you. We have never *known* love."

"It shows." Emma glared at them.

"Then teach us. Teach us what it means to be loved. Teach us how it is that we are willing to give everything we are for you." They took another step forward, and another, slowly approaching.

"I can't love you if you kill them, Rafe. I can't. I can't let you destroy everything. Not even in my name." Emma wiped angrily at her tears. Damn them, why wouldn't they stop? "If you can't let them live, then you'll have to kill me, too."

"Don't say that. Don't ever say that again." Rafe was standing in front of her then, covering the last few paces in a blink of an eye that was so sudden that she jolted in fear. He grabbed her by the upper arms. "Don't even *think* it!"

"I'll hang myself with the bedsheets." She levied her best glower up at him. "I'll slice open my tongue with a steak knife and drown myself in my own blood."

"Then we will envelop you in nothing but shadows and ensure that there is nothing you can do to harm yourself." He grimaced in anger.

"I'll claw out my eyes."

"We'll tie you down."

"You're not going to win this fight, professor," Gigi interjected. "Not with a woman. Not with her."

"What kind of life would we have then? What kind of love is that? I'd be a goldfish in a bowl. Is that all I am to you?" Emma reached up and took his head in her hands, ignoring the stickiness of the pitch-black blood under her palm. "That is *not love,* Rafe."

Their expression flickered. Then hardened. "You will understand when we make you Saint of the Key. Then you will see. But first…they die."

Tendrils wrapped around her waist and yanked her into the shadows.

She screamed.

CHAPTER TWENTY-THREE

F*ree me.*
And I shall free you.
Emma didn't know where she was. Was she standing? Running? Sitting? Lying down? Floating? Falling? She couldn't say. She was nowhere. Absolutely *nowhere*. But in the darkness, there was not nothing. There was everything. Everything that she was, pulled apart to its smallest component.

Every memory of sitting at her dining room table with her family played before her eyes. Laughing. Smiling. The tense conversations between Elliot and Poppa. Her mother's gentle, knowing smile.

The times she spent in the dark holding her twin as he wept and prayed for death. Begged her to kill him, to let him die. To let him *go*.

Every breath. Every meal. Every step she had ever taken, every sight she had ever seen. It was all there—Emma Mather. Every speck of existence she had ever been, wound and unwound, small and large.

And she wasn't alone.

Free me.

And I shall free you.

Suddenly, her thoughts weren't her own. Her memories weren't the ones she recognized. They were strange and warped, as if they were fever dreams. Her hands were not hers, but she *made* them hers.

She was in someone else's memories.

She felt them cram her inside a tiny box. Felt them bury her beneath rock and stone and ticking mechanisms. Felt them force her to be small, small, small. To fold in on herself until she could barely breathe. She could hear them laughing above her, celebrating their victory.

Let me out!

Please, let me out!

It hurt. It hurt so very much to be so very small, to be buried so tightly where she couldn't even move. Couldn't even see. Could only hear them above her. She screamed, she threatened, she cried. And then she began to beg.

She offered them all that she could give and more, promised the sun, the moon, the stars. Whatever it was that would make them happy—just *please* let her out!

But they never did.

No matter what she gave them. No matter how much of herself she peeled away and gave to them as gifts. They took it and cursed her name. And never, ever, *ever* let her out.

She felt each second like an eternity. Each tick of the clock like another nail in her coffin—in her flesh. And it never, *ever* stopped ticking.

With every ounce of her being, all she wanted to do was go *home.* Home! Home to that safe place where she could be with her family. To laugh with her Poppa. To mourn her brother's loss together with him. To make new friends, to be with her lover, to live her life. Safe. Home. *Out.* Away. Away from this terrible place that was so small, so tight, so cruel.

Her mind was her own again. Her hands were hers again. She felt packed dirt beneath her hands.

Free me.

And I shall free you.

Patrick was about to die.

He knew it was inevitable when he took the role of Bishop. Every Bishop before him had been murdered by another Saint. It was just how it went. He would have been at peace with it if it weren't for one thing.

Gigi.

He loved her.

And now he would never get a chance to tell her.

She was unconscious by the wall, thrown there by Rafe's shadows. She was alive. For now. But there was no point in shouting at her, telling her how sorry he was. How he wished he could have protected her.

Rafe was dragging him down the catwalk toward the center of the Tenebris. Soon, Patrick would be thrown into that darkness. It was only fair, he supposed. How many cultists had he hurled to their deaths in that very same way?

He'd lost count.

A dozen? Two?

Did it matter? Were those deaths weighing on his soul? He supposed it didn't matter. He was going to die and be swallowed up by the Great Beast. He had borrowed power from the monster he dedicated his life to keeping at bay. He knew this was how it would end for him. It had only been a matter of time.

There was no point in fighting anymore. He had lost. But at least he could take some solace in the fact that if he had to finally bend the knee and accept his defeat—it was for love.

There was no doubt in his mind that the darkness had fallen in love with Emma.

It was just a matter of what would happen now because of it.

He supposed it wouldn't be his problem in a few moments.

"Rafe! Stop!"

The man dragging him down the catwalk whirled, void-like eyes going wide in surprise. "Emma? How—"

Something shifted in the air. Something simply *changed.* Patrick felt the cords of shadows wrapped around his leg give way. They vanished as quickly as they had arrived, slithering back into every dark crevice.

Rafe collapsed.

Patrick rolled onto his side, trying to take advantage of whatever had just occurred. But his ankle was shattered, he was definitely punch drunk, and the whirling Tenebris beneath him coupled with his reeling head made it very hard to move.

Very hard and very nauseating.

Emma ran up to him, crouching beside him. "Bishop—"

He waved his hand to shoo her away. He felt flushed and wondered if he was going to throw up *into* the Tenebris. How disgusting. "Ignore me." He needed to focus on not being sick.

Emma stepped over him carefully, holding on to the railings to keep from falling into the pit below. The walkway was only three or so feet wide. It didn't leave much room for his girth and her. Or his girth and anything else, for that matter.

He felt woozy again and shut his eyes. That might've been a mistake.

Yep. Definitely a mistake.

Emma watched as the Bishop went limp, his head falling back to the metal grate with a quiet thunk. The poor man looked as though he'd been in a train wreck. She'd have to worry about him later. If she got the chance.

"Rafe!"

The professor was lying on his side, one arm draped over the edge of the catwalk, his eyes shut. She ran to his side and, kneeling there, gently pulled him into her lap. "Rafe, wake up!"

When he groaned and blinked his eyes open, she pulled in a gasp and held her breath. His eyes weren't black from lid to lid. They were…human. Still as dark as the night sky in a storm, but *human.*

"Rafe?"

"Emma…I…" He cringed and carefully put his hand to his temple. "What happened?"

"I wish I could tell you. I don't honestly know." She threw her arms around his neck and held him tight. She clung to him like a child. "I'm so sorry—I'm so sorry, Rafe—about Patrick and Gigi…"

He chuckled weakly and held her in return. "I know. You did the right thing."

"But…"

"Shush." He kissed her temple. "Help me stand, please."

It took some effort, but she finally got him there, even if he had to lean against the railing for a moment before he could stand on his own. Gathering her into his arms, he kissed her. It took her breath away. Not from passion but from the emotion he put behind it.

When he broke away, he rested his forehead against hers. "Have I told you that I love you, Emma Mather? I honestly can't remember."

"You *specifically?*" She couldn't help but tease him.

"Yes, me *specifically.*" He smiled though it was clear he fought it.

"I don't remember either. But I knew." Resting her head against his chest, she hugged him. She didn't ever want to let him go. "Come on. Let's go home. You get the Bishop's arms, and I'll get his legs, and we can drag him back." Taking Rafe's hand, she turned to leave. "We'll leave him in the hallway and get Gigi out of here. We'll come back for him later. He'd—"

"No, Emma." Rafe didn't budge.

Turning to face him, she felt whatever meager hope that had begun to bloom in her heart begin to crumble away. "What?"

He slowly let go of her hand and took a step back. "I don't know how much time I have before they come back." Cringing, he looked away. The updraft from the mechanism blew a few strands of hair in front of his eyes. "And they will come back."

"It...are you sure?"

"I can feel them. Something yanked them out of my head, but they're already worming back in. I am still a Saint." Shutting his eyes, she watched as a tear slipped free and ran down his cheek. "Emma..."

"No! No, no, no! I won't accept that. This can't happen!" She stepped toward him and grabbed his hand again, yanking him forward. He didn't budge. She forgot how strong he was compared to her. "We're leaving. We're leaving *now.*"

Instead of successfully pulling him down the catwalk, he pulled her close, wrapping her up in his arms again and holding her tight. "Forgive me. Please, forgive me. For all that I've done. I tried to protect you, and I failed at every turn. I love you, Emma Mather. I love you."

"No—you can't be serious!" She pulled out of his grasp.

"I will tear this world apart if I stay. I'll make you into a monster, or worse. And who's to say 'we' won't change 'our' mind and kill you if 'we' get bored of it all?" He cradled her head in his hands. "Listen to me, Emma. You know there's no other way."

"There *has* to be. There has to be! I can't lose you—I can't. I lost Elliot. Now even Yuriel is gone. I can't—" She choked off. She couldn't form the words through the sob that wracked her chest. "Please, no…"

He kissed her again, firmer that time. She could taste the salt of their tears on her lips.

It was a goodbye.

He was saying goodbye.

And it was going to kill her.

When he parted, she clung to the front of his vest with both hands, her knuckles turning white. "I'm going with you, then. I'll jump in after you, and—"

"No." He glared, that fiery rage of the man she had fallen in love with coming back to the surface. His word was final. "You shall do no such thing."

"I—I can't live without you, Rafe."

"This is the only way to ensure that you *can* live without me. Besides…" He smiled thinly, though it didn't stay on his face for long. "Who's going to take care of Hector when I'm gone?"

"You aren't funny."

"I know." He stroked his hand through her hair, tucking some of the unruly strands behind her ear. "I love you, Emma. Do take care of that cat of mine, will you? Believe it or not, she'll get to like you in time."

"No—I won't. I won't have this conversation!"

"Promise me."

"Of—of course, but—Rafe, *please.*" But she knew there was no use. She knew that no matter how hard she begged, how hard she pleaded with him, he had made up his mind. And besides that...she knew he was right.

They were going to come back.

And when they did...everyone would die.

Maybe even her.

He kissed her again before taking a step back. "Despite it all, despite what it's come to...I would not trade away having met you." He looked down at the whirling mechanism beneath him. "I would perhaps look away."

She shook her head. She wouldn't hide from this. She didn't want to miss any second she had left with him. "I don't know how I'm going to live without you."

"You'll find a way. Nothing stops you when you put your mind to it." He smiled faintly. "Goodbye, Miss Mather."

Emma screamed as he jumped from the catwalk.

She would have even perhaps gone after him, if a pair of delicate hands didn't pull her back from the edge.

Gigi silently pulled her into the hallway.

Emma collapsed to the ground and wept in the other woman's arms.

Professor Raphael Saltonstall was dead.

And she knew her heart had gone into the machine with him.

CHAPTER TWENTY-FOUR

"How long are we going to go on like this?"

"*Mrraaaaack.*"

Emma sighed from where she lay on the sofa. Hector was sitting on the coffee table, glaring at her, ears folded back and tail swishing menacingly. The cat was pissed. As usual. And still clearly blamed her for Rafe's disappearance.

Even though it had been almost three months. Maybe it had been four. Honestly, Emma couldn't be bothered to track the time as it went by. What was the point? What was the point in *any* of it?

"*Mrrrrrrrack,*" Hector complained again.

Shutting her eyes, she rolled onto her other side. "I've fed you. I've changed your box. You have water. You hate me, so you won't let me pet you, so it isn't that. I try to play with you, and you hiss at me. And for the last time, *I'm sorry.* He's not coming home."

The heavy thump of the cat hitting the floor signaled that Emma's lecture had worked. But unfortunately, it wasn't without its cost. Because it, like the sofa she was on, like the house she was living in, was a constant reminder of what she had lost.

Rafe was dead.

The first few days after the incident with the Tenebris had been a blur. Gigi had offered to take her in. So had the Bishop. But she had made a promise to the professor to take care of Hector, and she kept her promises. And after four attempts to wrangle the fat animal, each one resulting in blood loss and wounds that might leave scars, she gave up trying. And it felt...somehow right, to stay in Rafe's brownstone home.

Here, she was surrounded by his things. His personality. This place was all that she had left of him. This place and a cranky animal that she was convinced would *never* like her. But that was fine.

The Bishop had called her poppa and explained everything to him the moment her father had come back from his trip. Poppa clearly didn't believe it all, but he had seen enough strange things during his years of travel to accept it. He asked her to come home but understood when she explained why she had to stay.

The phone call had gone as she expected. He began with one simple question. "You love him, don't you, Emma?" Her father could see through anything. But especially her.

"I do. I did." She had sniffled through her tears. He had come down to Arnsmouth the next day and cooked her an enormous dinner in Rafe's kitchen. He had always been an amazing cook. It had been Ethiopian food, his specialty.

Patrick and Gigi had joined them, and the four of them went through in detail again. Except she left out a few details —Gigi's personal history and how Rafe's corruption had been...eh...rather touchy-feely with her.

There were certain things parents really shouldn't ever know.

She had laughed, she had smiled. But it had only ever really been in the moment. Her happiness felt more like fireflies than anything else. Brief. Fleeting. Pretty to watch, but… not much else.

After that, there were only a few phone calls before it turned out that Emma was the owner of Rafe's house. He had left it to her. It had been a shock, but…also not a surprise. It seemed like the exact kind of thing that Rafe would have done without telling her.

Still, she decided to sleep in the guest bedroom on the top floor, the one he had given her the first night she had stayed in his home.

The main bedroom was *his.* Not hers. They had shared it for a little while, but it didn't change the fact that she had no claim to it. She made the bed, however. Tidied up. Dusted from time to time.

Hector slept almost entirely on his bed, curled up against his pillow. And each time Emma found the fat animal like a furry decoration snuggling with what probably smelled the most like her former owner…Emma sobbed.

She was slowly becoming inured to her tears. She didn't even notice them anymore. Not until they fogged her vision or wound up leaving small dots of precipitation on one surface or another.

Although she did keep a pair of Rafe's glasses sitting on her nightstand. It was just a little piece of him.

It might have been week four when someone came to her door. A little, bespectacled man who reminded her a little bit of a weasel with his pinched features and tiny eyes.

He had asked about "an antique of some importance that he wished to buy."

She had slammed the door in his face.

When he returned the next day, she greeted him with her pistol pointed squarely at his face.

He didn't come back a third time.

Talking to Rafe as she went about her day kept her from feeling too crushingly lonely. But even if she wanted to sit in his house and wallow in her own misery all day every day, she wasn't given the option. There was no stopping Gigi Gage.

The jazz singer dragged her out on the town a few nights a week, bringing her out to the other clubs and bars in the city. The Flesh & Bone was still destroyed, and Gigi said she wasn't sure if she wanted to bother rebuilding it, or if it was time for a change.

Emma just felt like a passerby to her own life. Like she was just watching the world go by from the other side of a train window. It felt like she had her memories removed again—only this time what she was missing she had no hope of replacing. The longer it went on, the more embarrassing her grief became. Shouldn't she be moving on with her life? Doing something?

Shouldn't it hurt just a little bit less, each time she picked up a piece of his clothing and smelled the crisp cologne he had worn? But she *had* done one thing she was proud of.

She had managed, every single day, to ignore the damn door that had appeared in Rafe's hallway.

A door that had no business being there.

While the trim and wood paneling looked identical to all the others in the home, and might have tricked someone visiting the house into thinking it was sensible and had every right to be there, there were two things that stuck out to her immediately.

The first was that the other side of the wall it was attached to was several layers of brick and belonged to the neighboring townhome.

The second was the doorknob.

She knew that symbol anywhere now. The one Rafe had

put beneath his skin as a ward. The one her brother had scrawled on the note in blood. The symbol of the Great Beast. For a while, she had tried to figure out how the "sixth cult" factored into the image. The Church of the Benevolent God had once been the Society of the Cross, after all.

When she had seen it—two of them, actually—hidden in the overlapping symbols, she had smacked her forehead with her palm. *You're an idiot, Emma Mather.*

But she was an idiot who wanted *nothing* to do with Mr. Door who had once more shown up to haunt her. She did the only sensible thing; she pretended she didn't see it.

It worked.

Right until about month five.

And then it seemed Mr. Door was entirely done with her shit.

First it tried appearing on every floor, as if the problem was that she honestly hadn't noticed it. That seemed to be its new favorite game for a week or so before it escalated the issue.

It was late one night that Emma got out of bed and shrugged into her nightgown to go fetch herself some water. Filling the glass from the tap, she turned down the hallway to climb the stairs to go back to her bedroom.

And pulled up short.

There, in the middle of the hallway, facing her perpendicularly to the other walls was that damn *fucking* door. Blocking her way, pretending to be part of a wall that cut her off from accessing the stairs. She sighed. "No."

Turning to go the other way—there was a back stairwell, after all—she jerked in surprise.

Another door. Exactly the same as the first, also facing her and blocking off her path. Glowering at the second door, she gritted her teeth. "No. I'll stand here until somebody comes and finds me or I starve to death. We're not—"

Something brushed against her arm. She yelped and jumped away from the first door. It had moved closer to her in an instant. Taking a step away from it, she bumped into the second door.

Each time she reacted to one, the other moved closer without her seeing it. But soon, she was wedged in such a tiny space that she thought she might scream. "Okay! Okay!"

The doors were ten feet apart again, as though they had never moved.

She let out a wavering breath. "I *hate* you. I want you to know that." She downed her water and put the glass on the floor by the wall. She'd get it later, if she was alive. "We have to do this now? I'm in my damn nightgown."

The doors didn't disappear or move. Nor did they, thankfully, talk.

"Whatever..." She wrapped the gown tighter around herself and cinched the belt before tying it off into a bow. "You're an ass." She paused and glanced between the two doors. "Do you have a preference?" Teasing an eldritch creature of unknown motivation was exceedingly stupid. But it's not like it ever stopped her before.

Silence.

Shrugging, she went to the first one that had appeared. It seemed to make sense. Grasping the glass knob with the etched symbol upon its surface, she sighed and gave it a twist.

There was nothing but darkness on the other side. She reached her hand through the veil. She half expected something to grab her and yank her through, but at least Mr. Door seemed patient. Patient up and to a point.

It has been five months, to its credit.

Nothing grabbed her, and nothing felt particularly offensive about the air on the other side. Test two was reaching out with her foot and tapping on the other side for solid ground. She'd been pitched head-first into the void a few times, and she really disliked falling.

It felt firm enough. She couldn't identify what it was, but it was there.

"All right. Well, here we go. Sorry I don't have my face on," she said with a smirk. She'd been spending too much time with Gigi. The woman's sarcasm was wearing off. "But something tells me you've seen me at my worst already."

She stepped into the darkness. And, like one would expect, couldn't see anything.

The door slammed behind her with a *WHAM!*

The sound of it startled her. She jumped forward.

And *then* promptly fell into the void.

Emma screamed.

Or maybe she hadn't fallen? She couldn't tell. Maybe that was just what it felt like to move through whatever she passed through into wherever she was now. Because she could have sworn she had been falling, but now she was standing with her feet on…something.

It was pitch black around her. She couldn't see a damn thing.

But she could hear something.

Tick.

The sound of the Tenebris reverberated through the space around her. The ground beneath her shuddered with it. And she shuddered as well. The mechanical noise had haunted her nightmares ever since the incident with both Yuriel and Rafe.

Tick.

It sounded far away, but…wait. Was it coming from above her? If it was coming from above her, that meant only one thing. "*Fuck.*"

Something laughed.

But she knew it wasn't a noise she heard like the ticking

of the mechanism. No. She *felt* it. Felt the sound inside her head—inside her soul. Yet somehow it managed to be absolutely deafening. She grabbed her head and wailed in pain, the sensation of the laughter threatening to pull her apart at the seams.

"Ah. Yes. Sorry. I forget."

The pain ceased. When Emma looked up, she was no longer standing in a dark void. She was standing...in Rafe's living room. Everything looked perfectly normal and as it should. The sun was streaming in through the window, dappling the red and black carpet beneath her feet.

For a moment, she wondered if she had just hallucinated the whole incident with the doors. It wouldn't have surprised her. That was until movement caught her eye.

Turning, she pulled in a breath and held it.

Rafe was leaning against a table, half-sitting on it, smiling at her. He looked just as he had the day she met him. Sure, there were dark shadows under his intense eyes, but not like there had been toward the end.

"You aren't—" It took her two attempts to get the words out without choking on them. "You aren't real."

"I'm very real. Is this real?" He gestured at the space around him. "No. But it might as well be. It will feel real, taste real, smell real. So I ask, what's the difference?" He pulled out some cigarette papers and a tin of tobacco from his coat pocket and began to roll himself one.

Emma narrowed her eyes. "You aren't Rafe."

"Correct. I'm not." He paused and then looked at her with a furrowed brow. "But what gave me away?"

"He doesn't smoke."

"Shit, that was the other one, wasn't it?" False-Rafe grunted and put the two items down on the table. "You're all so easy to get mixed up. Ah, well." He smiled at her. "Hello, Emma."

"You're…" She didn't know how to say it. "Am I where I think I am?"

"Yes on both counts, I suspect. Your true physical body is currently located several miles beneath the city you call Arnsmouth, trapped within a chamber where no light has ever shone."

"Beneath the Tenebris." She felt the truth begin to settle on her like bricks.

"Beneath the Tenebris," he confirmed. "I really don't know why Rafe insisted on thinking you were a fool. You really are quite clever. Men." He shrugged.

"That makes you…" She trailed off, not believing it. She shook her head. "Not possible. I've hit my head. Or finally lost what's left of my mind."

"Both are possible, I suppose." He folded his arms across his chest. "And as much as I'd love to stand here and debate the merits of whether this moment in your mind is *real* or *fake*, we have business to deal with."

"What business?"

"Did you forget our bargain?" He arched a dark eyebrow at her. "I set you free. Now, Emma Mather…it's time for you to return the favor."

Free me.

And I shall free you.

In a rush, the voice echoed through her mind like being overtaken by a wave in the surf. It filled her thoughts, just as it had before. And then she understood. Rafe's corruption had been driven away by some strange force, giving him enough time to leap into the Tenebris. And now she knew what had been responsible.

The Great Beast.

It wanted to be free.

It had bargained with her.

And now it had come to collect.

CHAPTER TWENTY-FIVE

"No."

Oh, she was going to get in real trouble for saying that.

He laughed. It wasn't a cruel or vicious thing. It was more like how her father used to sound when she told him she wasn't going to eat her broccoli.

False-Rafe pushed away from the table and walked toward her. It wasn't until he was a few steps away that she lost her nerve and took one back. He smiled, and it was the friendliest she'd ever seen him look.

Because, quite simply, it wasn't Rafe. It wasn't Rafe at all.

She braced herself for the *Great Beast* itself—*himself?*—to murder her.

"No?" he repeated.

"No." She tried to sound more confident than she was. It didn't work.

His expression turned almost mournful for a second as he watched her. Not only mournful—but pitying. "Humans. Why must you all break your promises? Why must you all be so very duplicitous? We made a deal, Emma Mather. Doesn't that mean anything to you?"

"I…" What in the name of the hells was going on? Taking another step back from him, she watched him warily. "You're going to destroy the world if I do."

"Is that so?" The Beast shook his head, walked to the sofa, and sat down. "That's news to me." He gestured to the chair across from him, clearly intending for her to sit.

Hesitating, not knowing what else to do, she carefully sat in the chair across from the Beast. "I don't understand."

"If I were to give you a speck of dust and ask you to take care of it, what would you do?" He was still smiling in a kind and tender way that confused her. This wasn't how she expected this to go at all.

She pondered his question for a moment. "I'd probably sneeze and lose it in the first two seconds."

The laugh that left him startled her. She felt like a skittish deer. She probably looked like one too, what with her wide eyes and rigid posture.

He leaned back on the sofa and kicked up his feet beside him, getting comfortable. Something Rafe never did. It looked bizarre at best. "I love your honesty, Emma."

"Thanks…?"

"I am not human. I never have been. I never will be. I have been the expanse of all that exists between the worlds—the void. But I was not alone. There were many of me, thousands of me, all together and apart at once." He shut his eyes as he talked.

She did her best not to run for the door. She knew where she was—trapped beneath the city in the Tenebris—and all this was just an illusion. Running was pointless. So, she sat and listened. It wasn't every day one got to talk to a god, after all.

"I heard the prayers of some specks of dust. Little, tiny

things. Interesting, though—very different from everything I'd ever known. They wanted power. Power I could give them. So I, like many of my kin have done, came down from the darkness to play within existence."

"Play?"

He opened one eye to peer at her. "The eternity of the sentient nothing gets very boring."

"Oh." *Ask a stupid question...*

He shut his eyes again and lay down on the sofa, fluffing the pillow behind his head, as if he were honestly enjoying being there. "So I answered their prayers. I thought I would be loved. Instead, they *hated* me for what I gave them! They despised me for it. I let them peel off pieces of myself and watched them use my power to fight each other like children. But I only did what they wanted."

She cringed when he got angry, shrinking back into the chair, worried he'd lash out at her.

"Then...they did this to me. They locked me away, deep down inside the earth. I'm not meant to be here, Emma. I'm meant to be free. I want to go home."

Oh, how she could empathize with that.

"They prick me with needles, they fight me, they rip parts of me free and then blame *me* for what they do with it. That man who tortured you—what was his name?"

"Kirkbride."

"Right. Him." The Beast snorted. "I gave him eternal life, and *that's* what he does with it?" He threw his hands up in frustration. "Tortures people. Decides he's better than they are. Hurts them. That poor creature he hurt—the friend of yours."

"Gigi."

He snapped his fingers. "That's her name." Chuckling, he folded his arms behind his head. "You all run together sometimes. You are so very brief and tiny." He felt so...normal.

Like he was just lying on a lounge in a psychoanalyst's office, regaling her with all his problems.

"What happened to my brother?"

The Beast took in a deep breath, held it, and let it out in a long rush. "I'm sorry."

Her shoulders slumped. That was the definitive answer.

"The Idol—the thing that was possessing that boy—wasn't a real soul. Not like you, your brother, Raphael, the rest, and so on. He was an amalgamation of bits and pieces of all the humans who have died and become part of me." The Beast frowned. "I can't make *souls,* Emma. These people, these worshippers of the soul, asked me to make new ones for them. They wanted to summon 'angels' or 'demons' so they could use them for their own ends. What the *fuck* was I supposed to do?"

She had to laugh. He sounded so frustrated. She certainly hadn't expected him to swear.

He smiled at her, just a little playfully.

Oh. He was trying to make her more comfortable. He was talking to her at her level so she would relax. It was kind of working. She shook her head and looked away.

"They asked me to give them souls. So I did the only thing I could do—I took what I had, rearranged it, glued it all together the best I could, and gave it to them. The one you liked…uh…" He snapped his fingers again, searching for the name. "Yeg…"

"Yuriel."

"That one. When he was made, I had to take the soul of your brother, combine it with bits and pieces of other humans I had kicking around, and rearrange it until it was whole." The humor left his expression again. "I'm sorry, Emma. He's still here within me, just…in pieces."

"Can he be put back together?" Hope blossomed in her heart.

"Perhaps. I'm not sure what condition he'd be in if I did. Human souls are finicky."

She knew better than to ask for it. She knew better than to beg him for her brother's soul to be put back in one piece. She knew what he'd want in return.

They sat in silence for a moment as he let her process the truth. Putting her head in her hands, she rested her elbows on her knees and gave herself some space to think.

"I want to go home, Emma. I want to be free of this cage they put me in. It's so very small. I can't—you would feel suffocated. You humans have a fear of being buried alive. That's what they've done to me." He shifted, and she looked up to see him sitting once more on the sofa, his elbows also on his knees, watching her intently. "I don't want to destroy the world. I just want to leave it."

"How can I trust you?"

"Haven't I done everything I could to help you? To make you happy?"

"You're the reason all these terrible things happened to me!"

"No, I'm not. The humans who used my power were responsible. I tried to give you a path out of every moment you were in danger! Sometimes you didn't even see it." He smirked. "There were two of my doors in the asylum. But you were panicking too hard to notice."

"I—" She stammered for a moment. Leaning back in the chair, she watched him warily.

"I knew you and this one—Raphael—would fall in love. I tried to put you both together as much as I could. I wanted him to be happy. I wanted *you* to be happy."

"Why?"

"What else do I have to do around here?" He gestured at the house around him, but she knew that wasn't what he was really gesturing to. "I'm trapped in a hole! So I play with the specks of dust. Sue me."

Again, he made her laugh. But the reminder of Rafe broke her heart all over again. Having him—the vision of him, anyway—sitting there in front of her brought tears to her eyes, now that she had a second to really think about it. The sound of his voice…

Wiping at her cheeks, she sighed.

"Set me free, Emma."

"How?"

"Become the Saint of the Key. The Bishop won't be able to stop you when you can warp the world around you to your whimsy. Reality is only what we make of it. And if you control what people perceive? Well?" He huffed a laugh. "They never let the Key gain purchase. The 'Church' they built hunts them down. There has never been a Saint of the Key before because they knew what they could do. You will take the little totem of power that I will give you, and you will use it to blow open this *awful* thing above me. Let me go home."

Tick.

The room vibrated with the sound of the machine, reminding her just how fake this whole experience was.

"What'll happen to me? To everybody? To Arnsmouth?"

"Oh, I'd get in a car and get out of here if I were you." He hummed thoughtfully, looking up at the ceiling of the living room and squinting at it. "I expect it'll get messy. Warn as many people as you can. Once I'm gone, you will be human again. So will the Bishop and everyone else. My power will leave this place."

"I…don't know." She couldn't trust him. He was the Great Beast.

"This world will be cured of my so-called 'corruption' once and for all. Otherwise, this pattern will just keep repeating. Someone will take too much of me, become my Saint, and then the Church's Saint will chuck them back into me like garbage down a chute. Again, and again, and again…"

Tick.

He snarled. "I can't take it anymore!"

Shrinking back from his anger, she felt her fear come back instantly.

"Every second. Every *millisecond.* I hear it pass, the ticking of the gears, the movement of the springs. Please…Emma *please.*" Standing from the sofa, he moved to kneel at her feet. Before she could react, he had her hands in his and was clutching them tight. "Let me go home. Help me."

"I—I can't—I don't know—I need to talk to the Bishop, I—I don't think I can do this. I can't trust you."

His expression became unreadable. Once more, he got to his feet. But the slowness of his movement scared her more than if he had been angry with her. "Humans. Pathetic, weak, tiny little things…fine. Do you need me to sweeten the deal? Do you need me to appeal to your selfish greed? *So be it."*

The world dropped away from her. She was sitting on the stony ground, not a chair. The illusion shattered as if it had never been there at all. She was back into the darkness and the emptiness of the cage the Beast was trapped within. The stone beneath her hands was cold and rough.

For a moment, she wondered if the Beast was going to leave her there. But slowly, something around her changed. She couldn't tell what she was seeing for the longest time, or if it was just her mind playing tricks on her, like the time she went into a cave and turned off the lights.

Trees.

Bare, dead trees against a background of a sky that was such a deep blue it was nearly black. It was only because the silhouettes that were even darker that she noticed the sky at all.

Something moved in front of her. Something was coming toward her. They looked like branches. But it wasn't until they were nearly hovering over her that she could recognize them.

Hands.

Enormous *hands.* Long, pointed, dangerous, inhuman fingers reaching through the world around her, coming toward her. One on each side. A left and a right.

The sound that left her was one she barely recognized. She scooted backward, terror catching what was left of her whimper in her throat and choking it off.

The hands formed fists, hovering some fifteen feet in the air and half a dozen paces in front of her.

Slowly, the hands unfurled, their claw-like fingers blending in with the jagged bare branches of the dead trees around her.

From their fists fell two bodies.

They jerked before they hit the ground.

They were hanging on nooses, the rope dangling from the monster's hands like a child's toy, creaking as the bodies swayed from the force of the drop.

She could see them clearly, lit as though from some unknown source that cast nothing else on the world around her.

On the right…was Elliot.

And on the left?

Rafe.

One word echoed in her mind like the ringing of a terrible bell. Or perhaps the ticking of a maddening clock.

Choose.

CHAPTER TWENTY-SIX

Choose.
Choose to free the Great Beast.
Choose who to save.
The city? Or Rafe? Or Elliot?

Kneeling on the ground, sitting back on her ankles, Emma simply wept. She pounded her fist into the stone beneath her until her knuckles stung and got that sticky sensation that told her they were bleeding. She didn't care. That'd been the point.

Save the man she loved.
Save her twin brother.
Save the world.

The problem was that she knew the right answer. She knew what she was *supposed* to do. She was supposed to deny the Great Beast and leave it trapped beneath the city, even if that meant she starved to death in the dark because of it.

Starving to death down here was the best possible future for her if she went that route. What was the other option? Living like a phantom in her own life, same as she had when Rafe had taken her memories away? She loved him. She needed him. How much more was she supposed to sacrifice? How much more was she supposed to lose before she had given enough?

"Take me instead." Looking up at the hands that dangled their two corpses, she begged. "Please. Let them both live. Take me instead. I don't want to do this anymore!"

Silence. She wasn't expecting an answer. The time for talking was done. It had given her that chance. No. She could either kneel there forever…or she could choose.

Pushing up from the ground, she ignored how the bits of rock stuck in her bleeding knuckles. She walked up to Elliot first, looking up at his gaunt features. Reaching out a hand, she carefully, tentatively, touched his.

His skin was as cold as the corpse he resembled. He didn't respond to her presence. Picking up his hand, she placed his palm to her cheek, not caring how tepid and unnatural he felt.

Someday she would stop crying.

Today was not that day.

Maybe she wouldn't ever stop until she died.

"You used to make fun of me for always being so cheerful. Look at me now." She sniffled. "I miss you so much. I love you, Elliot—I love you." She slowly dropped his hand from her cheek and simply held it. But he was at peace now. He had hated his life. And who was to say that being "put back together" would return him to life any better than he'd been before?

Who was to say he wouldn't come back worse?

The Great Beast had the power to give her both of them. She knew it did. But it wanted to *play*. It wanted to spin its stories and amuse itself as it watched her stumble her way forward.

Looking up at Elliot, tears blurred her vision. "I just—I just wanted to say I'm sorry I wasn't there for you more. I should have been home helping you with your shadows, not off on some continent exploring the world with Poppa. We didn't know how to help you…so we hid from you. Him worse than me. I understood, but when I knew there wasn't anything I could do to make things better, I…I'm so sorry, Elliot. I wish I could go back. I wish I could do a million things differently."

She wiped her nose with the back of her clean hand. "I never meant to drive you away. And I'll regret leaving you behind on those trips every single moment I live. I look back on all the chances I had to be there for you as we got older, and I hate myself for all the times I wasn't there."

Smiling weakly, she could almost hear him mocking her for being the melodramatic one for once. She could see him in her mind's eye, sprawled out on a sofa, smoking something or other, sarcastically calling her *mom*. He hated being fussed over. But the other alternative was where they had wound up.

"You would hate me if I dragged you back. And maybe someday you would forgive me. And maybe someday you wouldn't. But you wanted peace. And…at least here, you have it. I can't take that risk. I love you, Elliot." She kissed his cold fingers. "I hope someday we meet again."

Lowering his hand, she turned her back on him one last time.

She got to say goodbye.

There was that to be grateful for.

Wiping at her tears with a frustrated snarl, she had enough. She had enough of it all. Enough of the torture, of the terror, of being pushed about and toyed with by creatures and monsters and men she couldn't contend with. First it was Rafe. Then the Bishop and his failed "exorcism." Then Kirkbride. Then the Idol. Then Rafe a *second* time.

Now this.

Maybe the Great Beast was lying. Maybe setting it free would destroy the world. Well, then she'd have a mighty bit of egg on her face, wouldn't she? Or maybe the thing that had been inside Tudor Gardner was right—maybe the world deserved to burn.

She turned toward the darkness from which the arms extended. "We have a deal."

Rafe woke up to the sensation of a purring ball of fur headbutting him.

Mumbling something about wanting five more minutes, he buried his head back into the pillow it was resting on. But the ball of fur wouldn't let up, nuzzling his face and purring loud enough to be mistaken for an automobile engine.

"Yes, Hector—" he muttered and nudged the animal away. "I'll feed you in a minute."

"She missed you."

The voice he heard confused him. Why was…? Lifting his head, he squinted. He wasn't wearing his glasses, and the shape sitting at the end of the bed took him a second to recognize. "Emma? What're you doing here?"

Her quiet laugh didn't answer his question. The look on her face was grief-stricken and faraway, glazed over as if she had been weeping and had simply lost the energy for it. Her skin was pale. Her eyes were red as if she had been crying. And sure enough, she wiped at her cheeks halfheartedly. "The symbol on your back is whole again."

He knew then, with a doubt, that he had missed something important.

Sitting up, he groaned as the world spun around him. Pressing his hand to his head, he shut his eyes and waited for it to calm down. He was in his underwear, and despite the reeling in his head, it would have been a normal morning.

But something was very, very wrong.

"What's the last thing you remember?" Emma sounded exhausted, like she hadn't slept in days.

Rubbing his hand over his eyes, he was relieved when the world finally decided to stay where it ought. Blinking the sleep away, he could finally focus. Emma still looked like a ghost of the young woman he knew, with dark circles under her sorrowful eyes.

Focusing on the question, he paused. Rubbing at his chest and frowning, he shook his head. Flashes of strange things. He had taken her memories and sent her away. Then she came back, and...then everything was confusing. "I think you shot me?" Looking down at his skin, he saw no mark where the bullet had gone in. Shouldn't there have been a wound. "Did I die?"

She laughed. It was the sound of someone who had long since had enough but was expected to deal with one more thing. Her laughter turned to tears.

"Oh, Emma." He couldn't help himself. Climbing out from under the sheets, he shifted to sit beside her. Pulling her into his arms, he cradled her against his chest, feeling her tears against his skin. Kissing the top of her head, he waited until her sobbing stilled, and she just rested against him silently. "I forgive you for shooting me, if that makes you feel any better."

The snort of sarcastic laughter that left her confirmed his theory that yes, he had missed out on something important, and that yes, something was terribly wrong. "I'm unsure what time of day it is, but I believe a drink might be in order."

He got no argument there.

It took two drinks before Emma finished telling Rafe all that had happened. He was sitting in a chair in his study—not the one she had shot him in, he dutifully avoided that one—with the expression of a man who had just been slapped in the face with a cricket bat.

But that wasn't the worst of it.

The worst of it was apparently the fact that she had disliked the color of Rafe's walls in this room. They had been burgundy. Now they were eggplant. And she couldn't stop staring at it. It really had been burgundy this morning.

Now they were purple.

And she knew it was her fault.

The Key controls sanity. That's what they told me. The Great Beast had said she could control the perception of reality. And what was reality other than our perception of it? What did it matter if the walls were supposed to be burgundy when everyone saw it as purple?

"And you are now…" Rafe began but trailed off, as if he couldn't believe it. "You are…"

Fishing out the necklace she was wearing from between her breasts, she dangled the small object on the end of the chain from her finger. She had just woken up wearing it after the incident with the Beast.

It was a key. She had been expecting something big and fancy, maybe even scary, but it looked no more threatening than the single post key that might go to a desk drawer.

Small, brass, a little tarnished at the edges, and utterly benign looking.

And she was going to use it to end the world. Maybe. Possibly. If the Beast was lying to her.

All the air fled Rafe's lungs as if she'd sucker punched him in the stomach. Shaking his head as if he couldn't believe it, he took off his glasses and wiped a palm over his face. "Emma."

"I had no choice."

"You did. You could have left us both there."

"And starve to death in the darkness, I *know*. But I'm done. Done with it all. And if this gives me some control over my future, so be it." She reached over to the coffee table to pour herself another stiff drink. "I'm sick of it all. The Great Beast isn't the only person who wants to go home. If—"

"Emma."

"If it's telling me the truth and it wants to go home, all the better. You and I can go live with Poppa for a while until we find you another job at a college—"

"Emma!" When she stopped talking, he continued. "What about the rest of the city? What about the thousands of people who live here?"

She winced. "I can't lose you. I just can't. I love you, and I won't give it up. We can sound an alarm. Tell everyone to evacuate. I don't *care*. I'm not saying goodbye to you again."

"Other people will die."

"Don't bother lecturing me about being selfish. If you hate me now because of this, so be it." She shut her eyes. She sounded just like the things in his shadows that had overtaken him. Willing to murder thousands in her name. How was this any different? How was she any better?

She wasn't.

She just didn't know the people who were going to die this time. Last time it had been Patrick and Gigi who were on the chopping block. Now it was just a nameless number who would lose their lives when she set the Great Beast free.

But it was different in one way. One very important way.

"If I do this, it ends. The curse of Arnsmouth ends. No more Dark Societies. No more 'evil' magic used by power-mad lunatics. No more people caught in the middle of it, dying as sacrifices or being tortured by monsters. It ends. All of it ends." She didn't look up at him, instead watching the light reflect off the whiskey in her glass. "That's worth it."

"And if you're wrong, *everything* ends."

"Yeah."

There was a long moment of silence. When she looked up at him, he was gazing at the wall, his brow furrowed in confusion.

"My fault. I don't know how to change it back." She sipped her drink, glad for the whiskey's sharp burn. "I didn't exactly intend to change it in the first place." The walls shifted from eggplant to forest green. She snickered. "Oops."

"Emma Mather with the power of the Saint of the Key at her disposal." He grunted. "We're all doomed."

"Right now, all I can do is accidentally change the color of the walls! You went all…tentacle monster. You don't get to complain."

"I had everything under control until you shot me." He gave her the look that said he was trying to scold her but only half meant it.

She laughed and rubbed her temple with the heel of her hand. "Rafe, I…" She wasn't even sure what she was trying to say. "I'm sorry. I hope you can forgive me for all this."

"Do you really love me?" His voice was soft.

Blinking, she was confused before she remembered…oh. Right. He didn't remember. Shoulders slumping, she wondered if he felt the same about her. Or if that had just been the work of the corruption that infested him. "Maybe if you weren't so damned *serious* all the time, and…"

Who was she kidding? "I do. I think I loved you the moment I saw you. When I shot you, I thought I killed some part of myself. And when you were gone, I didn't know who I was anymore. No—I didn't know who I wanted to be. Because all the options weren't worth it. Every path forward was empty without you there."

Unable to look at him, she stared back down into her drink. "I love you, Rafe. You said it to me before, but…that was likely Them talking, not you, and that's okay. I don't—"

When his hand touched hers, she jolted. She hadn't heard him move. He was kneeling at her feet. Twining his fingers into hers, he leaned down and kissed her bruised and bandaged knuckles. "I loved you the moment you lifted my wallet from my pocket in my office."

Smiling, she tried not to start crying again. "Not when I undid your belt?"

"No, that's when I decided I needed to have you. Loving you came a few minutes later." He smirked.

Throwing her arms around his neck, she forgot about her drink and sent a good portion of the whiskey onto the rug. She didn't care. She kissed him with everything she had, whiskey be damned.

Arnsmouth be damned.

She wasn't ever going to let him go.

CHAPTER TWENTY-SEVEN

"Stop looking at me like that, it's a great plan!" Emma folded her arms across her chest in defiance. It wasn't just a great plan; it was a flawless plan.

Break into the Church of the Benevolent God with Rafe. Find the door down to the Tenebris. Break into that—she didn't expect that locks were going to be much of a problem for her anymore. She *was* the Saint of the Key, after all—sneak down to the giant mechanism, and then…

Uh…

Throw the key into it?

Demand it stop?

Ask it nicely to open?

"All right, it's a terrible plan," she admitted, her shoulders slumping. "But it's the only plan I have. The Beast didn't give me much to go on."

Rafe was pacing back and forth across his study, only stopping now and then to pet Hector, who was sitting on his desk, purring, tail swishing contentedly.

She could control reality.

But the cat still hated her.

She figured it was just a cosmic law at this point.

"Hopefully when you arrive there, you'll have a better sense for what the next step will be." Rafe had his hands clasped behind his back as he walked. "We'll need to pack the car and have it ready to go. I don't know how much time we will have before everything collapses."

But that wasn't the first part of her flawless plan.

The first part needed to start sooner than that. It was the part that made her weirdly the most nervous. Namely, because she didn't know if she could pull it off.

She needed to convince as much of Arnsmouth to evacuate the city as possible. And the only thing at her disposal to do it? Her newfound "power" as the Saint of the Key. She chewed her lip.

As if reading her mind, Rafe stopped his pacing. "Do you know what you're going to conjure yet?"

"I'm not conjuring anything. It isn't real." She was pouting. She didn't care. She was having a rough few…it'd almost been a year. *Shit.*

"If you wanted me to believe I was being stabbed to death right now, my heart would stop beating in my chest. Never underestimate what the power of the mind is capable of doing to the body." Yep. Professor Saltonstall was officially back.

It made her smile. "I missed you."

He went to say something that was probably going to be snippy before seeing the look on her face and thinking the better of it. "I'm glad to be back."

Pushing up from the chair, she walked to the window and looked outside. It was a beautiful July day. Leaning against the jamb, she watched people walk down the sidewalks, blissfully ignorant of what was going to happen. "So…what do you think? Blot out the sun?"

"Hm. No. People will assume it's an eclipse or something

they can just wait out."

"How about waves of killer monsters?"

"Do you want to traumatize them as well?"

That was a fair point. She let out a puff of breath. "All right…moon people."

"See previous comment about trauma."

With a grunt, she shut her eyes and rested her forehead against the glass. It was warm from the sun, feeling just the barest bit cold underneath her skin.

"Nothing frightens people as bad as an earthquake." She heard the voice of her father beside her, as real and as present as the moment he'd actually said that, which had been several years ago in the tropics. *"Couple that with some volcanic ash? You'll see people moving faster than rabbits running from hawks."*

She smiled. "Thanks, Poppa."

"Excuse me? I am not, nor shall I ever—"

She gestured her hand for him to shut up. He fell silent, leaving her to focus. Could she really trick the whole city? Was she that powerful? She clasped the little brass key around her neck and squeezed it.

She heard things that weren't real all the time.

Her brother had seen things that chased him to the end of his life.

Now it was time for everyone else to feel what it was like. The world rumbled beneath her, trembling in the force of the imaginary quake. She heard a crash and a thud from behind her, but she ignored it.

Volcanic eruption. Right off the coast. She had seen it from their boat in the islands, watching the molten rock that flowed like molasses roll over itself, cracking like bread, as it met the ocean water. The steam that had risen from where fire met water had been so intense it made it hard to see what was going on.

And now it would be there in Arnsmouth Harbor. *Let there be ash, and rock, and steam. Let the earth tremble.*

She heard screams from outside. When she finally opened her eyes, people were pointing up at the sky. Sure enough, a gray-brown cloud had formed over the city, blotting out the sun. Snow the color of fireplace soot began to fall from it, raining down on the city in thick chunks.

People began to run.

She smiled.

Hopefully that would save a few people, at least.

"Next time, a warning would be nice."

Turning around, she laughed. Rafe was sitting on the ground, rubbing his head. He had fallen over in her imaginary-yet-real-enough earthquake. He must have smacked his head on a table. Rushing over, she helped him up to his feet. "You poor thing."

"Yes, yes." He touched his fingers to his temple and pulled them away, checking for blood. Luckily, he seemed fine. He eyed the window and the falling ash. "A volcano?"

"In the harbor."

"Clever." He smirked. "Chaotic, but clever."

"Me? Chaotic? Never." She went up on her tiptoes, and he bent to meet her so she could kiss his temple where he smacked his head. "Go pack. I'll make us some lunch, and when we're ready, I'll call Gigi. But she's not an idiot. I'm sure she'll have taken the hint already."

"What about the Bishop?"

Emma frowned and glanced out the window. "I suspect he'll be waiting at the Church. Although I very much hope I'm wrong."

Though she suspected she wouldn't be.

Patrick could sense it the moment it happened. The moment there was a new Saint in the city of Arnsmouth.

And he had three guesses who it could be. Gigi was with him the night it happened, so that option was out. That left Robert, who had taken possession of the Candle. But the little urchin was nowhere to be found and was likely laying low until everything was well and truly over.

When the skies began to rain ash and the ground rumbled beneath his feet, yet *nothing* seemed to be broken? He had his answer.

Emma Mather.

The streets were flooded with people panicking to get out of the city. *Good girl. Whatever it is you're doing, you don't want casualties.* He did his best to encourage those he saw to leave town. He helped families lift their baggage onto the packed streetcars or into the back of automobiles. When the streets began to quiet down and the sun began to set, he returned to the sanctuary of the Church and waited.

The sun was a strange, terrible shade of murky orange-brown through the haze of the volcanic ash. It was ash that he knew wasn't real—that none of it was real. But he also knew it didn't matter. If he went and found the source of the explosion and sank his hand into the lava, he would feel the burning pain. He'd be so very convinced of the choking heat that his brain might even convince his body to die.

The Key was the most dangerous of the societies…by far.

And that was why they had *never* been allowed to exist. They hadn't "gone underground" or "disappeared." No…they were rooted out at every opportunity.

When the doors to the church opened, he was relieved to see it was Gigi. He smiled at the beautiful woman who walked in, wearing her finest fur coat and leather driving gloves.

"My automobile looks like a *mess* in this shit." She brushed flakes of ash from her coat. "I don't care if it's real or not. Emma and I are going to have a word." She picked a piece of the soot from her hair.

"So, you know?"

"Not hard to figure out. Come on, we're leaving." She waved her hand dismissively in the direction of the door that led to the offices and apartments for the clergy. "Go. Get your…two things that you own. Hurry up about it."

Frowning, he shook his head. "I can't."

"Are you kidding me? She's giving us a warning. It's time to do exactly as everyone else in this city who has a brain is doing—it's time to leave." Gigi stormed down the aisle of the church, glowering at him. "Get your things."

"I have to stop her. If she's planning on doing what I *think* she's doing—" He huffed a tired, disbelieving laugh. "Gigi, she's going to set it free."

Gigi froze. "What? How do you know?"

"That has always been the motivation of the Key. To open the Tenebris and set the Great Beast loose on the world. With it will go all of our world. Everyone *everywhere* will be sucked into its darkness. What's the point of running when it'll just swallow us whole?" Patrick cracked his neck from one side to the other, feeling the joints pop and snap as he did.

"Why would she do that?"

"I don't know."

"Because I made a trade."

The room went quiet. Gigi turned. There, standing in the doorway, was Emma. She was wearing a brown leather coat and pants, propriety be damned. And standing there beside her…was Professor Raphael Saltonstall.

Gigi responded best, as she always did. "Fuck." She laughed. "Look who washed ashore. Hello, professor. Welcome home. Are you singular or plural at the moment?"

"Gage." He dryly greeted the woman in response. "And singular. As far as I can tell."

That was a relief.

Emma had her hands tucked into her pockets. "You should both leave town. Please."

"I've been trying to tell him that, darling, but he's got it in his head you're here to end the world." Gigi placed a cigarette in her holder and lit it, taking a drag from the Bakelite end.

"I hope not." Emma's gaze tracked to Patrick and held it. "But we'll see."

"What *are* you trying to do, then?" Gigi eyed her fingernails idly.

"It said it wants to go home. That it just wants to be free so it can return to where it came from." Emma smiled sadly. "I understand how it feels."

"It was lying to you. It'll say anything it can to trick you into setting it loose." Patrick pushed off the railing he was sitting against and cracked his knuckles. "And you know I can't let you."

"I was afraid you'd say that." Emma sighed and walked into the church. "And I'm sorry."

"So am I."

She smiled.

Patrick's world fell away.

Emma watched Patrick scream and collapse to the ground. He thrashed, trying to find something to hold on to. Despite lying on the cold floor of the Church, she knew what he could see in his mind. He was falling into an endless abyss.

"All right." She tilted her head to the side and watched the man panic. It was only a few moments before he hyperventilated and passed out. That was definitely for the best. She didn't want to hurt him. "Having dark magic is kind of fun."

"Isn't it?" Gigi commented and took a drag from her cigarette.

Emma looked at the other woman. "I don't want to fight you."

"Fight you?" The jazz singer barked a laugh. "Darling, you could end me with a thought. I'm not even going to bother trying." Sauntering down the aisle of the church, she sat down next to the unconscious Bishop and crossed her legs. "I'm going to sit here and wait for his holiness to wake up."

Emma smiled. "I'm glad we're friends."

"Me, too, darling. Now go on." She flicked her hand in their direction. "End the world. Set it free. Whatever it is you're here to do." She paused. "And for what it's worth, strawberry—I would have made the same choice."

"Thank you." Reaching back to Rafe, she took the professor's hand and led him down the side aisle.

It wasn't hard to find the iron door. It was oddly out in the open—likely because it was very securely locked. She had tried to summon her own doorway to get to the Tenebris—and skip all this nonsense in between—but it seemed that wasn't in her purview. Sadly.

Stupid doors.

Standing at the door, she pondered it for a moment. The key she had around her neck was ridiculously too small for the large iron object. With a shrug, she grasped the handle and with a pause, turned it.

Part of her hoped it stayed locked.

Click.

But she knew better.

Pushing the door open, she was greeted by a set of old stone stairs that looked as though they were hewn from the granite of the earth where it was built. The familiar old crumbly bricks formed the walls.

"I hate this place," she murmured.

Rafe placed his hand on her shoulder and, leaning in, kissed her forehead. "You don't have to do this."

"And risk what'll happen if I don't? No. I won't lose you. I won't give you up again. I simply won't." She leaned back against him, feeling some relief as he circled his arms around her to hold her to his chest. She turned her head to rest it against his neck. "If this all goes wrong and it was lying to me…at least we'll be together."

"That is true." He kissed the top of her head again. "Come on. Before the Bishop wakes up."

Nodding, she braced herself, then laughed. "What do you say?" She grinned up at him cheekily. "Let's go end the world."

Rafe's heavy sigh only made her laugh harder.

Taking his hand, she led him down into the darkness.

Tick.

CHAPTER TWENTY-EIGHT

"You know what really gets my goat?"

"What?" Rafe smiled faintly at the woman walking ahead of him. By the hells, he loved her. And of course she would be the one to unravel the universe around them.

"I get amazing powers, and I get to have them for exactly one day before I lose them one way or another. How is that fair? You had at *least* a month being a squiggly-wriggly shadow demon before you jumped into the pit." She threw up her hands. "I get one lousy damnable day."

Chuckling, he shook his head. "For what it's worth, I'm rather glad you only get 'one lousy damnable day.' I'm rather terrified to see what Emma Mather would do with the ability to rewrite reality on a whim. Besides make snide commentary on my decorating choices, that is."

"I thought I liked the burgundy, for what it's worth. I didn't think I had a problem with it. But apparently I do." She laughed, glancing over her shoulder at him. "I think you have great taste in decor. A bit stuffy, a bit rigid, but it matches the owner."

"I'm surprised you didn't change anything while I was…" He hesitated. It was still strange to know that he had been dead for months. Stranger still to have no memories of being overtaken by his infestation. "Gone."

He was still corrupted. The shadows still writhed with the presence of the Many who lurked and waited for their chance to return. The ward on his back had been restored by the Great Beast, reverting his state of being to precisely what it was before the moment she put a bullet in him.

An odd choice on behalf of the Great Beast, but one he appreciated. *Perhaps it understood that Their designs were incompatible with its plot to be free. I don't think They would take the risk to release Their maker, if it meant potentially losing her.*

And he couldn't exactly argue with that line of thinking. He would do anything to protect her. Anything to keep her safe and have just a few more minutes with her by his side. It wasn't as though they really had the chance to share many quiet moments since all the madness had begun. It seemed they spent every second flung from one chaotic tragedy to the next.

What was one more?

"Do you think they're mad at me?" She gestured at a shadow on the wall where one of the creatures of his infestation was spreading out along the bricks, trying to reach a lightbulb that was keeping it at bay.

"I don't believe so."

"I did…kind of betray them." She winced and reached out as if to touch one, nervous that it might lash out at her. "I just couldn't let them go on a murder spree."

The tendril reached out to meet her. She stopped walking. They both watched as it gently curled around her fingers, then around her palm. It didn't pull, and it certainly didn't devour her flesh like they did to Rafe's other victims.

She smiled. "I missed you. And not just because the sex was fantastic." Chuckling, she spread her fingers a little wider and let the tendril weave up around her wrist and settle there. "I hope you understand."

"I think they do." It was still odd to see how his infestation treated her. But he had no doubt in his mind that all creatures, no matter how seemingly evil and cruel, were capable of love. He didn't used to believe it. But now he could see it in front of him, plain as day. Who was he to argue? "Come on. We shouldn't dawdle."

Frowning, she pulled her hand away. The shadow released her. "I just realized that if…if the Great Beast goes home, like it says it wants to…they'll be gone, too."

"I suppose so." It was a relief to him to think he might be free of the corruption that had hounded him since he first learned of the Dark Societies. But seeing the sorrow on her face, he opted to keep that to himself. Gathering her up in his arms, he held her close and kissed her temple. "They will go home as well. They will rejoin their maker. It's as it should be." *They are fungus eating the corpses of the world around them. They should not exist. The fact that They love you is an exception to a very dangerous rule.*

Once more, he kept his thoughts to himself. Especially when she kissed him with a fervor that said she wasn't trying to kiss *him,* she was trying to kiss *Them.* She was saying goodbye.

When she broke away, she wiped a tear from her cheek. "I'm always losing things." She turned her back to him and began to walk at a faster pace. "Let's get this over with."

He couldn't agree more.

Slipping his hand into his pocket, he checked to confirm his gun was still there. His little pickpocket could never be trusted. But there it was, right where he left it.

And all he could do was pray he wouldn't need it.

Patrick woke up with a groan. He remembered the ground opening up beneath him and swallowing him whole. He remembered screaming, and thrashing, and then nothing. He must have blacked out.

"That couple does love to run ragged on you, don't they?"

Gigi. He lifted his head, grunted, and put his head down. He needed another moment. "Seems so."

"You're two for two when it comes to Arnsmouth's new favorite duo." She huffed a laugh. "You poor thing."

"I'm fine." Sitting up, he rubbed a hand over his face. He felt like he was going to lose his lunch all over the slate floor, but it was already starting to pass. "We need to stop them."

"Do we?"

"What?" Grabbing hold of the end of one of the pews, he hefted himself to his feet. "You're joking. Of course, we do."

Gigi sighed. "Look at this city. Look at this pattern of death and misery. The Societies—"

"Can be *controlled*." He shook his head. "Contained."

"By what? Feeding us back into the thing that made us? Again, and again, forever until the end of time? No. Enough is enough." Gigi stood and walked toward the altar, looking up at the double-ended cross that stood proudly on the table. "Maybe Emma is right. Maybe it's time to throw out the bathwater, baby be damned."

"You can stay here, then. I'm going to go stop them before they *end the damn world*." Patrick moved to leave when he heard the click of the hammer of a revolver.

"No. You won't."

Slowly, he turned back to face the jazz singer. She had her

ivory-handled derringer pointed straight at him. He didn't quite know what to do with himself. "Would you?"

"Kill you? No. Put a bullet in your knee so you can't walk?" She smiled thinly. "Absolutely."

He knew better than to call her bluff. He had learned very quickly about the woman. Lifting his hands in surrender, he walked back into the center of the aisle and faced her. "Why are you doing this, Gigi?"

"Because…" Her haughty expression wavered. He watched as it faded, leaving something mournful in its wake. "Because I watched Emma lose the man she loved to that machine. And because I saw what it did to her in the wake of losing him."

"This is about her, then?"

"Of course not!" She laughed. "This is about me, darling."

Lowering his hands to his sides, he watched her curiously. "I don't understand."

"Men." She pinched the bridge of her nose. "Listen to me. What I'm trying to say is, I refuse to suffer the way she has. I won't let it happen."

"I'm…still confused."

"Because that is what's going to happen to you! Maybe when they finally get wise and replace you like they should have done *years* ago—

He chuckled.

"—or maybe when some monster does it for you." She ignored his laugh. Shaking her head, she kept the gun aloft, never wavering. "And I will not lose you."

"We're going to lose everything if she succeeds and ends the world, Gigi." He took a step toward her.

"Or maybe we won't. I don't think Emma would go through with this if she really believed it was the end of everything. And if it is?" She shrugged, resigned. "Then so be it. I'd rather not exist than exist without you."

He hesitated. He wasn't certain what to say. They had never spoken about, well, *them.* He was too nervous to bring it up, and she seemed more than content to just go about their merry way without spelling it out. "Gigi, I…"

"She's willing to sacrifice it all for the man she loves. And…" She swallowed thickly, uncertainty showing on her perfect features for the first time since he had known her. "And so am I. I love you, Patrick Caner, and I want nothing more than to spend the rest of our miserable lives together. And we can't do that with—with all this—" She gestured to the church around them. "Hanging over you. Over us. So, yes. I'm going to let Emma do this mad plan of hers. Maybe it does just want to go home. And then you can—you can quit all this, and we can leave here."

Smiling like a prisoner hoping for a reprieve yet certain it would be the noose, she continued. "I want to move west. To California. I think I could make it as a movie star. They're going to start doing them with sound and color, and I want to be there when they do. We could go together. Wouldn't that be lovely?"

"It would." His heart was broken in two. Two halves rattled around in his chest at her words. The half that loved her, that wanted to hop in her car and speed off to California with that fluffy Persian cat of hers. And the half that had a duty to perform. "Gigi, I—"

"Before you say anything—I have a confession to make, priest."

"Bishop."

"Shut up!"

He stayed silent.

Cringing, she looked away, and shame crossed her features. She fidgeted with the chain of her purse. Whatever she was about to say was clearly scaring her. "There is a reason I fell in with the Blade. There's a reason I hungered for the power it could bring me. I spent my life before coming to Arnsmouth in search of my answers as...I was wrong. I was different. I wasn't *me*. I was a shadow of my true self, and...I found myself often wondering if dying wouldn't be better than how I was living. I wished—oh, how I wished—that I could be seen as the true me."

He let her talk.

"I should have told you this sooner." Taking a deep breath, she finally worked up the courage to say whatever was terrifying her so very much. "I—I used to live my life as a man."

Patrick smiled. Just a little.

She furrowed her brow. Her expression of uncertainty cracked into one of anger. "You *knew?*"

He shrugged, his smile growing.

"You bastard!" Taking off her purse she threw it at him. He deflected it with his arm, and it fell uselessly to the floor. "I should shoot you just for that!"

"I would really rather you didn't." His smile faded. Gigi was shaking with the aftermath of the confession. He carefully took a step toward her, not wanting to risk her threat.

"Why—why didn't you say something? I spent—I spent this *whole time—*"

"I'm sorry. It honestly was none of my business. To be blunt, it never mattered to me. I fell in love with *you.* And besides, we all have our pasts to contend with." Reaching up, he pulled the white tab from the front of his collar. "I used to live my life as a priest." He dropped it to the ground at his feet.

Gigi ran toward him, and for a moment, he braced himself for violence. She threw her arms around his neck and embraced him. Before he could react, she was kissing him and crying at the same time. He wrapped his own arms around her and held her close.

When Gigi leaned back, he gently stroked her tears away. She sniffled and nudged his hand. "You'll muss my makeup."

Emma might end the world.

Or maybe she'd set them all free.

He kissed her back and decided he was all right finding out which it would be.

CHAPTER TWENTY-NINE

"All right, so...now what?"

Emma wasn't quite sure who she was asking. But there she was, standing above the whirling, enormous mechanism, and...had no idea what to do next. The Great Beast hadn't actually given her any real instructions.

Was she supposed to chuck the key into the Tenebris? That seemed like a very bad idea to try first, seeing as she might need it later.

Was she supposed to go find a tiny lock somewhere? She looked down at the glorified brass cabinet key and turned it over in her fingers.

She hated the thing beneath her. Not as much as she expected the Beast hated it, but she also had her reasons. She had watched Yuriel die. She had watched Rafe die. The idea of blowing it up did feel cathartic.

The question was just...*how?*

Peering over the railing at the spinning gears and cogs, she didn't see anything that gave her any clues. "What do you think?"

"Me?" Rafe said from beside her. "Why are you asking me?"

"Because you're the smart one." She smiled over at him.

He shook his head, clearly fighting a smile of his own. "Emma, are you certain about this?"

"Not in the slightest. But I'm not going back, if that's what you're asking." She turned to face him and, reaching out, took his hand.

He squeezed it. "I have no clue what you're meant to do next, I'm afraid. There's never been a Saint of the Key before. But I…Emma, are you sure this is a good idea?"

"Absolutely not. But we've been through this. I'm not losing you again. And I'm not letting this nonsense continue." Dropping his hand, she walked away from him. She had already walked around the room in a circle twice, looking for any clues along the walls. But there was nothing except the stone walls and the wired lights.

She walked it a third time, Rafe trailing behind her. When she still couldn't find anything, she walked back down the center path, hating how narrow it was and how the movement of the mechanism beneath her made her feel as though she was in a carnival funhouse. If she stared at the spinning gears and springs for too long, it made her dizzy.

Pacing around in circles just felt silly. And there was no way of knowing how long it would be before Patrick came down and dragged her away. Or threw her into the Tenebris.

Wait.

Oh, no.

She stopped in the center of the catwalk that stretched over the gears. Swearing, she put her hand over her face. "Damn it all—*fuck*. Fucking, fuck, *fuck*."

"What is it?"

"I think I know what I need to do. You said there's never been a Saint of the Key before?"

"Correct. I believe the Church hunted down all the practitioners before they had a chance to ascend."

"Well, I think I know why the Church never let it happen." Turning to face Rafe, she froze.

He had a gun pointed at her.

Her shoulders slumped. "Rafe?"

"We're leaving. Now. Turn around and walk." He pulled back the hammer. "Please."

It would be easy enough to make him believe the gun had turned to snakes. Or simply vanished. But that wasn't the point. The point was that he was willing to point a gun at her. And maybe willing to kill her. "And if I say no?"

"Then I will stop you. The Great Beast cannot go free, Emma. You aren't thinking clearly."

"Then stop me." She took a step toward him. "I'm going to hold up my end of the bargain. I'm going to stop this madness. Even if it means I die. Even if it means the city caves in. And if it's lying and destroys the world, so be it. We can't keep it locked up down there forever."

He held his ground, gun still pointed at her. "The risk is too great."

"Then do it. I've shot and killed you once." She smirked. "Seems only fair you get a turn."

Wincing, he put his finger on the trigger. "Emma...please." She saw his eyes shine with moisture. "We can leave here. We can sort this out."

"And then what? Patrick and I can't exist in Arnsmouth at the same time. There's only one seat in that train car. So, we throw him in? Kill him? Do you know what that would do to Gigi? No. I won't doom her to that." She took another step toward him.

"We can contain your power. Place a ward on you the same way that was done to me." He held firm as she approached, never lowering the gun from where it was pointed straight at her chest.

"I think I'm past that. And I think you know it." When she reached him, she put her hand over the top of the gun—not to take it away, but to press the muzzle to her chest directly over her heart.

Tears slipped free from his eyes and ran down his cheeks. "Don't make me choose."

"I had to. I had to pick between starving down there in the darkness or agreeing to set it free. I had to pick between you and my brother." Oh, great. She was crying again. Fantastic. She didn't even bother to wipe the tears away.

"Wh…what?" His eyes went wide.

"It gave me a choice to sweeten the deal. I could have one of you back. But only one." Pulling in a wavering breath, she slowly let it out again. "I can't live without you, Rafe. I can't. I refuse to."

Rafe said nothing in response. The only sound that filled the space was the terrible, incessant mechanical clicks and the wind generated by the spinning machine. It kept blowing strands of his dark hair in front of his eyes, but he seemed not to care.

"I lost you once." He was speaking so quietly now it was hard to hear him. "When I threw you into that mirror and took your memories away. My life was…I didn't realize how lonely I was until I had you there, filling the holes with your laughter and chasing away the emptiness with your smile. When you were gone, the silence was deafening. I knew then I loved you. I have tried so hard to protect you, Emma. And I have failed at every turn. And for that I am so very, very sorry. Please forgive me, if you can."

She shut her eyes, bracing herself for the bullet. "There's nothing to forgive. I love you. Go on."

"I wish there was another way."

"But we know there isn't."

Holding her breath, she waited for it. Waited for the bullet to pierce her heart and end her life. Waited for the agony she knew would come with it.

She heard the hammer of the revolver unclick.

Rafe lowered the gun.

When she looked up at him, he was unashamedly crying. After looking down at the revolver in his hand for a moment, he tossed it over the railing and into the Tenebris below. She didn't even hear it clank against the metal. Rafe shook his head weakly. "Why did I think I could kill you now, when I couldn't so many times before?"

Throwing her arms around him, she pressed her cheek to his chest. He wrapped his arms around her in return and simply held her. They must have stayed like that for a solid minute before she looked up at him. "I'm scared."

"Me, too." He smiled gently. Reaching up, he cradled her cheek in his palm. "I'm not sure what will happen next. But if there is one thing in this world I have faith in, it's your ability to charge into a situation ill-prepared and come out the other side intact."

"Mostly intact."

"Mostly." He leaned down to kiss her, holding the embrace for a long time.

When he broke away, she nodded and took a step back. "No time like the present." Puffing out a breath, she hopped up and down for a moment, trying to work up the nerve to jump.

She hated falling. She loved heights, but falling was the *worst.* Turning to face the gap in the railing, she couldn't help but laugh quietly to herself. This was how her misadventure had started—standing on a ledge, breaking into Elliot's apartment.

This time she was going to jump. And there was some strange relief in that. This was her choice.

But *fuck* if she wasn't terrified. She was shaking.

She almost yelped in shock as Rafe took her hand. Jolting, she looked up at him in confusion. "What're you doing?"

"I can't lose you either, Emma." He stepped up to the edge of the railing beside her. Lifting her hand to his lips, he kissed her knuckles. "I'm going with you."

Smiling, she hugged his arm. "On three?"

"Sure." He smiled back.

"All right. Here's to the end of the world." After a breath, she readied herself. This was it. This was—

Rafe wrapped his arms around her and jumped, dragging her with him.

She screamed as they fell.

"You asshole!"

The sun was shining.

Birds were chirping.

A butterfly lazily crossed overhead, delicate white wings against dotted white clouds.

And Emma had an enormous headache.

Turning her head, she found herself lying in the grass. Lying in the grass with a very heavy weight on her which was making it immensely hard to breathe. She shoved on it, and it grunted before rolling off her.

The weight had been Rafe. Who looked just as miserable as she felt. His hair was a mess, his glasses were crooked, and his clothes were disheveled. She knew she probably looked no better. Sitting up, she brushed herself off.

Furrowing her brow in confusion, she looked around.

She had no idea where they were. They were in a clearing on a hill. Judging by the grass, it had been recently mowed.

"What..." Rafe groaned.

"I don't know." She swiveled about, trying to suss out more information. A large building sat behind them. She recognized it—it belonged to the Gardners. They were at the Gardner estate, which put them just south of Arnsmouth. "I think we're alive?"

"If we aren't, death has given me a migraine." He sat up, took off his glasses, and worked at trying to straighten the earpieces and the bridge at the nose.

"We're at the Gardner estate. Why, I don't know. And—oh." Then she saw it. *"Oh."*

The Gardner estate sat high on a hill that overlooked Arnsmouth.

That *should* have overlooked Arnsmouth.

Standing, she wobbled on her feet but managed to stay upright. Tugging on the shoulder of his coat, she silently pointed.

Placing the glasses back on his face, he twisted and squinted to see what it was she was referencing. He was on his feet a moment later. Taking her hand, he walked closer to the end of the hill, as if that might explain more of what they were seeing.

Arnsmouth was gone.

Fire flickered and burned, and smoke rose from what could only be described as an enormous pit. The ocean was attempting to fill the gap, the water hitting the blaze and turning to steam, much like her fake volcano had done.

So, she hadn't been *entirely* making it up after all. Her timing had just been wrong.

"I hope people got out," she murmured.

Squeezing her hand, he stayed silent. "It left."

"It also saved our lives." Pointing to the driveway, she nudged him in the side with her elbow. "And look."

It was her automobile. Stuffed full of luggage with a cage in the front seat. A cage that contained a somehow-more-irritated-than-usual, and very alive, Hector. She couldn't hear the animal from where she was standing, but she could see the cat open her mouth and holler at them.

Rafe laughed. It was overwrought, and it was exhausted. "I hope the others escaped."

"Me, too. Your infestation—are they gone?"

"Yes. I can't hear them anymore. The Great Beast is gone."

"I hope it's happy now." Emma hugged Rafe's arm and rested her head against his shoulder, watching what was left of the city of Arnsmouth burn.

They stood there in silence for a long time, listening to the birds happily singing from their branches, oblivious to what had just transpired. When the sun began to set, it was finally time to go. Walking toward the car, she climbed into the driver's seat. Rafe put the cage with Hector on it on his lap, and scratched the animal's cheek through the bars, a tender smile on his face.

As the first rays of the sun began to dip to the horizon, she started the engine.

"Where to?" he asked.

Emma smiled. "Home."

EPILOGUE

"We got another postcard." Emma smiled as she propped it up on a table by the wall. "I don't think the Bishop has anything better to do now."

Rafe huffed a laugh from where he was sitting, a newspaper in his hands. "Don't let him fool you—he enjoys being a kept man. Husband to a movie star is a nice life."

"Gee, and you don't know *anything* about being a kept man." She laughed and sank down on the sofa next to him.

"I fully intend on getting another teaching position once we return from our trip." He wrapped an arm around her, kissing her temple.

"It isn't just a trip, it's a honeymoon." She nestled her head against his shoulder. "I'm surprised you wanted to spend so much time on a boat."

"I have a deep urge to see the world now that I know I'll be alive long enough to enjoy it." He flipped the page of the newspaper with a rustle. "They've finally started filling the pit."

It had been a year since the Tenebris collapsed and took Arnsmouth with it. Some of the buildings had survived, but most hadn't. She shut her eyes. She didn't like to think about all the people who hadn't made it out of Arnsmouth either because they chose to stay or simply because they couldn't leave.

What did that make her? Was she a murderer? Or had she saved the world? Or were lives spent the cost of saving more?

It wasn't just a numbers game. One life lost was enough to make it a tragedy. She snuggled into him, needing the comfort of his presence.

The nightmares were still there, plaguing her. Now and then she would be overcome with the sensation of falling and she would wake up screaming. But Rafe was always there to soothe her fears and hold her until everything subsided.

They had been married a few weeks prior but decided to postpone their honeymoon until the weather was better to take the steamship around the globe.

Emma was convinced that Rafe was only willing to spend a year on a boat with her was because he was sick of living in her father's house. While Rafe and Poppa got along swimmingly—the two men would often launch into deep debates over politics, religion, science, whatever suited them—he was a proud man who wished to be self-sufficient. She understood.

"I hope Hector doesn't get seasick." Emma smiled. "She does love it here."

"She does."

The cat had made the huge Mather estate her home quite quickly and without complaint. Pretty soon, she was the queen of the castle, taking over several surfaces in her Poppa's study and declaring to the staff that it was *her* kitchen now, and all the food in it was *hers*.

The cat still hated Emma.

She was going to blame it on the fact that she was a

woman, and maybe the cat was just angry at other females, when she found Hector and one of the maids cuddled up asleep on a bench in a back hallway.

It was then that Emma knew it was personal.

"She'll love hunting the mice onboard." Rafe turned the page again. "She is remarkably adaptable for a cat."

He couldn't leave the fluffy animal behind, and she understood. A year was a long time to be gone.

"I can't wait to see Japan again." Shutting her eyes, she pictured the beautiful country. "Sushi is amazing. I wouldn't have believed that rice and raw fish could be so damn tasty, but it really is."

"I'll take your word for it."

"You won't have to, soon." Shifting, she took the newspaper away from him, folded it, and set it aside. He watched her with a curious expression but didn't resist as she straddled his lap and leaned in to kiss him. "I'm so excited. It'll just be you and me."

"And the crew."

She rolled her eyes. "And the crew."

"And Hector."

With a defeated sigh, she dropped her head to his shoulder. "And Hector."

Chuckling, he ran a hand up her back. "I am ready to put all this behind us as well. I'm eager to see what comes next."

"What comes next is you and I are going to strip naked, and you're going to do terrible, twisted things to me, Professor Saltonstall." She grinned fiendishly at him.

"Well. Far be it from me to deny a lady." His hand wound into her hair and grasped it in his fist.

Emma gasped at the sting and let the sensation rush through her.

The Great Beast was gone.

It was free.

And it had kept its end of the bargain.

It had set them free in return.

The seas were calm on the open ocean. Snuggled up in their cabin, she rested her head against Rafe's chest. Hector was curled up in a ball by his feet, contentedly asleep. Rafe was quietly snoring. She was the only one left awake.

The shadows were thick in the room, the moonlight streaming in from the cabin window. The glass was caged off on the outside to protect the thick marine glass from foul weather. The result was a dappled pattern and crisscrossed lines of shadows that swayed as the ship rocked in the mild waves.

Luckily, Rafe did not suffer seasickness. Nor did Hector.

Who *still* wouldn't let Emma pet her.

Emma was tempted to give up, but damn it all if she was going to become a quitter now at this point in her life.

It was just as she was shutting her eyes and dozing off that she felt it.

Something wrapped around her ankle.

Something like a snake, muscular and thin.

Something that only lived within the shadows.

Emma smiled.

FIN

*Thank you for reading Tenebris: An Occult Romance
I do hope you enjoyed it.*

ABOUT THE AUTHOR

Kat has always been a storyteller.

With ten years in script-writing for performances on both the stage and for tourism, she has always been writing in one form or another. When she isn't penning down fiction, she works as Creative Director for a company that designs and builds large-scale interactive adventure games. There, she is the lead concept designer, handling everything from game and set design, to audio and lighting, to illustration and script writing.

Also on her list of skills are artistic direction, scenic painting and props, special effects, and electronics. A graduate of Boston University with a BFA in Theatre Design, she has a passion for unique, creative, and unconventional experiences.

Printed in Great Britain
by Amazon